PRAISE FOR ERIN NICHOLAS

"Sexy and fun!"
> —Susan Andersen, *New York Times* bestselling author of
> *Playing Dirty*, on *Anything You Want*

"Erin Nicholas always delivers swoonworthy heroes, heroines that you root for, laugh-out-loud moments, a colorful cast of family and friends, and a heartwarming happily ever after."
> —Melanie Shawn, *New York Times* bestselling author

"Erin Nicholas always delivers a good time guaranteed! I can't wait to read more."
> —Candis Terry, bestselling author of the Sweet, Texas series

"Heroines I love and heroes I still shamelessly want to steal from them. Erin Nicholas romances are fantasy fodder."
> —Violet Duke, *New York Times* bestselling author

"A brand-new Erin Nicholas book means I won't be sleeping until I'm finished. Guaranteed."
> —Cari Quinn, *USA Today* bestselling author

"Reading an Erin Nicholas book is the next best thing to falling in love."
> —Jennifer Bernard, *USA Today* bestselling author

"Nicholas is adept at creating two enthralling characters hampered by their pasts yet driven by passion, and she infuses her romance with electrifying sex that will have readers who enjoy the sexually explicit seeking out more from this author."
> —*Library Journal*, starred review of *Hotblooded*

"They say all good things come in threes, so it's safe to say that this is Nicholas's best addition to the Billionaire Bargains series. She has her details of the Big Easy down to a tee, and her latest super-hot novel will have you craving some ice cream and alligator fritters. This is a romance that will be etched in your mind for quite some time. The cuisine and all-too-dirty scenes are enough to satisfy, but the author doesn't stop there. This novel may also give you the inkling to visit the local sex store—incognito of course. It's up to you."

—*Romantic Times Book Reviews* on *All That Matters*,
TOP PICK, 4.5 stars

"This smashing debut to the new series dubbed Sapphire Falls is a cozy romance that will have readers believing that they'd stepped into the small Nebraska town and settled in for a while. This well thought out story contains likable characters who grow on you right away, and their tales will make you smile and want to devour the book in one sitting. Four stars."

—*Romantic Times Book Reviews* on *Getting Out of Hand*

"The follow-up to the debut of the hot new series Sapphire Falls will wow readers with its small-town charm and big romance. This story teaches us that everything does happen for a reason and true love can be found even where one least expects it. The characters are strong and animated. It's a complete joy and highly entertaining to watch the plot unfold. Paced perfectly, a few hidden surprises will keep bookworms up past their bedtime finishing this satisfying tale."

—*Romantic Times Book Reviews* on *Getting Worked Up*, 4 stars

"The Sapphire Falls series has quickly become a favorite amongst romance readers because of its small-town charm and big-time chemistry between the lovable characters. This installment is extra steamy and the storyline captures the comedic yet sweet tale of country boy who meets city girl. Travis and Lauren's banter is adorable!"

—*Romantic Times Book Reviews* on *Getting Dirty*

"If you are a contemporary romance fan and haven't tried Erin Nicholas, you are really missing out."

—*Romantic Times Book Reviews* on *Getting It All*

"The fourth installment in the Counting on Love series will sweep readers off their feet. It's the perfect friends-to-lovers story with a little humor and a lot of steam. Cody and Olivia make a fantastic couple, and readers will adore their journey. Get your hands on this one ASAP!"

—*Romantic Times Book Reviews* on *Going for Four*, 4 stars

"Nicholas's tendency to give her fans a break from the hot-and-heavy stuff by making them laugh every now and then is genius!"

—*Romantic Times Book Reviews* on *Best of Three*, 4.5 stars

GOING
DOWN
EASY

ALSO BY ERIN NICHOLAS

The Sapphire Falls Series

The Bradfords Series

The Anything & Everything Series

Anything You Want
Everything You've Got

The Counting On Love Series

Just Count on Me (prequel)
She's the One
It Takes Two
Best of Three
Going for Four
Up by Five

The Billionaire Bargains Series

No Matter What
What Matters Most
All That Matters

The Boys of Fall Series

Out of Bounds
Illegal Motion
Full Coverage

The Taking Chances Series

Twisted Up
Tangled Up
Turned Up

Opposites Attract

Completely Yours
Forever Mine
Totally His

Single Title

Hotblooded

Promise Harbor Wedding

Hitched

GOING DOWN EASY

Boys of the Big Easy: Book One

ERIN NICHOLAS

Montlake Romance

This is a work of fiction. Names, characters, organizations, places, events, and incidents are either products of the author's imagination or are used fictitiously.

Published by Montlake Romance, Seattle

www.apub.com

Amazon, the Amazon logo, and Montlake Romance are trademarks of Amazon.com, Inc., or its affiliates.

ISBN-13: 9781503900660
ISBN-10: 1503900665

Cover design by Eileen Carey

Printed in the United States of America

To my family, as always. You are the reason any of this matters. To my sister, who took the first research trip to New Orleans with me—thanks for your sacrifice. To Lauren, who championed this book from word one and makes me smile with every text, email, and phone call. And to Lindsey and Liz, who are always on my side . . . I couldn't do this without you!

Chapter One

It was still amazing to Gabe Trahan how well Addison Sloan's ass fit in his hands. It was as if it had been made specifically for him to cup and squeeze as he pressed her close while he kissed her. Or when he was dancing with her. Or when he was thrusting deep and hard.

His body stirred at the thought of doing just that as she pushed her fingers into his hair and arched against him as if he hadn't just given her two—count 'em, *two*—orgasms upstairs before she'd gotten dressed for work. But they were standing on the sidewalk in front of his tavern, and her cab was waiting. This was supposed to be a goodbye kiss, not a get-her-hot-and-ready kiss.

The problem was, not only did her ass fit his hands perfectly, but the rest of her fit against the rest of him pretty damned well, too, and it was extremely difficult to stop fitting against her once he started.

Addison pulled back a minute later, breathing fast, her pupils dilated. "I have to go."

Yeah, he knew that. It was the second Monday of the month. That meant she was headed across town to the architectural firm where she was consulting on a once-a-month basis, to do whatever she needed to do there, and then she'd head to the airport to fly back to New York, and it would be another month until he'd see her again.

He leaned in, putting his nose against her neck, inhaling her scent. It was his favorite thing about her. And considering he knew every inch of her intimately, that was saying something. This woman had a lot of really nice inches.

"I know," he said. "Just give me a minute."

She sighed, her fingers curling into his scalp. The sound was almost wistful. "Shit," she said softly. "This goodbye thing was supposed to get easier."

Yeah, he would have thought so, too. In fact, he would have expected that by the sixth weekend with her, he would have been over her. Especially considering they didn't really have a relationship. They had sex. And beignets. And jazz.

When she was in town, they stayed up all Saturday night having the hottest sex of his life. Sundays, they woke up late and spent the day in the French Quarter, eating and shopping and people watching. Then Sunday night, they burned up his sheets all over again. He loved showing her the classic New Orleans stuff—the café au laits and po'boys, the jazz bands on the street corners, the riverboats and the French market. She was addicted to it all. She couldn't seem to get enough. And seeing it all through her eyes was like rediscovering it for himself.

But they didn't talk about anything too personal, and they didn't communicate at all in between her trips to New Orleans. All he knew was that she was a restoration architect from New York who had been consulting with a local firm on a big project in the Garden District. She came to town once a month on Friday morning, showed up at Trahan's, the tavern Gabe owned and operated with his brother, Logan, on Saturday night, spent the rest of the weekend with him, and then went to the architecture firm again on Monday before heading back to New York that night.

When they were together, they talked about the food, music, and people around them at the moment. Occasionally they dipped into their interests and hobbies, their work, their friends to some extent, but nothing else. They kept it all in the moment, in the present, no talk of their pasts or their futures.

He had no idea if she had siblings, what her favorite color was, when her birthday was, or what kind of car she drove. But he knew that she loved sex against the wall, that she had a particular fascination with his abs, that jazz music made her horny, and that the sounds she made when he sucked on her nipples were the hottest things he'd ever heard.

And that was enough.

Or at least that should be enough.

She was a fling. A once-a-month diversion—that he thought about far too often in the time between her trips to New Orleans. A very fun way to spend thirty-six hours or so every once in a while.

She didn't even live in New Orleans. They barely knew one another. He had no desire to go to New York City.

And yet, it was definitely getting harder and harder to say goodbye to her.

Hell, after the first night she'd come to Trahan's with her friend and local architect Elena LeBlanc, and Addison had ended up in his bed for the weekend, he hadn't expected to see her again. But the next month, almost to the day, she'd been sitting on the stool at the end of the bar. And he'd been shocked by how happy he was to see her.

"Quit your job and come waitress at the bar," he told her now, pulling back and looking into her big brown eyes.

She laughed lightly. "You mean, quit my job and spend my days giving you blow jobs behind the bar while you serve drinks?"

It would have been playful and funny if he didn't suddenly want that with an intensity that freaked him out. "Hell yeah," he growled, lowering his head for another kiss.

It was, as always, long and hot and not nearly enough.

He started to back her up against the side of the building when her cell phone started ringing.

She pulled back and dragged in a deep breath. She stared up at him. "Damn, you're good at that."

"*We're* good at that." This was like nothing he'd ever felt before.

Addison continued to watch him as she dug her phone from her purse and lifted it to her ear. "Addison Sloan." She paused. "Yes, that's fine. I'll be there in twenty minutes." She disconnected and smiled at him. "I have to go."

He took a deep breath and stepped back, shoving a hand through his hair. "I know." Fuck, he should be *relieved* that she'd gotten the call and had to get in the cab. That was how he would have felt with any other woman. But no, he felt irrationally irritated that she was being called away.

He took another step back. Maybe if he couldn't smell her, he'd snap out of . . . whatever this was.

It was not okay that he wanted her to stay and that he wanted to see more of her. If she did live in New Orleans, he would have called this off a long time ago. It didn't matter what her favorite color was or when her birthday was. He knew the important things—she was a New York City workaholic who, obviously, traveled extensively for her job. She wasn't what he was looking for.

"So I'll . . . see you," she said, suddenly acting awkward.

Gabe tried with everything in him to seem nonchalant about that. No, dammit, to *be* nonchalant about it. "Yep, see ya." He never asked when. He never confirmed that she'd be back the next month. He always bit his tongue before asking any of that.

"Thanks for . . ." She glanced up at the window to the apartment above the bar. "Everything," she finished with a naughty smile that made him want to put her up against the wall of the building, taxi driver be damned.

"You're very welcome." He couldn't help the half smile that curled his lips. God, this woman was the best hot-good-time he'd ever had. "And thank *you*."

Her cheeks got a little pink, but she laughed and moved toward the cab. "My pleasure."

Yeah, it had been. Heat rocked through him as he watched her open the car door, slip inside, wave to him through the window, then pull away, headed for the offices of Monroe & LeBlanc, the best restoration architects in town.

Gabe took a big breath and worked on pulling himself together. He'd never been messed up over a woman, and he wasn't about to start now with one who could never be anything more than the best lay he'd ever had.

So what if her laugh made warmth spread through his chest? It also made his dick hard, and *that* was all that mattered. So what if watching her eat beignets made him want to pull her into his lap and hug her? It also made him want to hike up her skirt before pulling her into his lap so he could slide his hand up her inner thigh. And *that* was what he should focus on. So what if he really fucking wanted to know when her birthday was? He also wanted to know if she'd let him blindfold her in bed, and *that* was what he should be thinking about.

He yanked open the door to the tavern and stomped inside, pissed that he was upset that she had left. Of course she'd left. She fucking lived in *New York City*. He was her New Orleans fuck buddy. That was it. And it was really, really good. Why couldn't he just be happy with that?

"Good morning, Sunshine."

Gabe came up short when he realized that he wasn't alone in the bar.

"I assume Addison just left," Logan said from where he was perched at the bar, a cup of coffee to one side and paperwork spread out in front of him.

Gabe glared at his brother and headed around the corner of the bar and straight for the coffeepot. "What the hell are you doing here so early?" Gabe was the primary bookkeeper for the business. Not the big tax and employee payroll–type stuff. Their accountant, Reagan, took care of that. Gabe went over the weekend receipts and got the deposit ready for the bank on Monday mornings. He took care of inventory and ordering and paying the basic bills, while Logan was the one who dealt with repairs and maintenance on the building and appliances. They both handled issues with the employees, customers, and vendors.

Truth be told, it just depended on the day and the issue, which of them was best at it.

"We have that meeting at one," Logan told him. "I'm getting some of the stuff together that they want to see."

"Meeting?" Gabe asked, turning with his cup of coffee and taking a long pull of the strong, dark brew. One thing he could say for his little brother—he made good coffee.

"With the architects?" Logan said. "The restoration? Remember?"

Of course he remembered. Well, he remembered that they were meeting with architects about restoring their building at some point.

"That's today?"

"Yeah. In about three hours," Logan told him with an eye roll. "Did she fuck you stupid or what?"

Gabe frowned. "Watch it." Even though, yeah, it kind of felt that way. He couldn't seem to focus on anything but Addison this morning. Still, he hated hearing Logan put it like that.

But he should be grateful to his brother for pointing out what this thing with Addison *should be*. Fucking. A fling. Orgasm central. Hot, no-strings-attached-and-thank-the-good-Lord-for-it sex. Something that he'd be getting over any fucking day now.

Instead, he found himself wondering if he should send flowers over to the office where she was today. That would be okay. It wasn't like he was sending flowers to her home or something. That would be more personal. And he wouldn't write anything sweet or romantic on the card. These would be thanks-for-the-two-blow-jobs flowers. Or you-do-cowgirl-better-than-anyone-I've-ever-met flowers.

"Hey, you okay?" Logan asked.

Gabe realized he'd zoned out. Thinking about sending Addison flowers. And not your-ass-fits-perfectly-in-my-hands flowers. More like I-already-miss-you flowers.

He could *not* send her I-already-miss-you flowers. Damn, he needed to get his shit together.

"Yeah, I'm fine."

Logan gave him a yeah-right look. "Damn, I knew I should have waited on her and Elena that first night," he said.

Gabe felt his hand curl into a fist and had to work to relax it. It was ridiculous to be jealous over the idea of his brother being the one to serve Addison that first night. And the insinuation that it would be Logan kissing her goodbye on the front sidewalk on Monday mornings if he had made her that first bourbon sour.

But the idea of someone else flirting with her, touching her, kissing her, making her laugh, watching her eat beignets, wrapping his arms around her as they stopped to listen to a band on the corner of Royal and St. Ann . . . he definitely wanted to punch something.

If that wasn't a huge red flag, he didn't know what was. Dammit, he was a fucking mess.

"Shut the hell up," Gabe told his brother. "I forgot the meeting, but it's fine. What do we need to get together?"

Logan gave him a knowing grin but dropped the subject of Addison. At least for now. "I've got photos of the inside and outside from Grandma," Logan said, pushing an envelope across the bar. "I'm putting together a list of things that have been done over the years, the stuff that's original like the bar, the stair and balcony railings, the interior doors, the flooring in the back rooms. We also need to list the things that have been replaced and updated. The windows, the flooring out here, the exterior doors. That kind of stuff."

Gabe nodded as he leafed through the photos in the envelope.

The building that housed the tavern and the living quarters upstairs had been in the Trahan family for five generations. It was one of the first buildings built in the French Quarter after the fire of 1794 and, obviously, required a lot of routine maintenance. The basic structure was in good shape, but some of the unique characteristics of the Creole-style building needed a special touch to restore it to its original glory—something that was extremely important to Gabe and Logan's grandmother Adele. She was eighty-eight and had been nagging them to do the restoration for about three years. She'd gotten to the point where she was now claiming that she'd haunt the place if they didn't get it done before she died.

Gabe didn't want that. He knew Adele would be an irritating spirit, unlike the three fairly good-natured ghosts that already, supposedly, occupied the building. He wasn't sure he totally bought the stories, but they'd been passed down through the family for years, and he had heard some strange noises and had found things out of place for no reason. He'd never *seen* anything. And he was very okay with that. There was no reason to add a potential fourth haunting.

Now they finally had the funds to do a true restoration of the building, and they'd been courted by two of the best restoration firms in the city. They'd decided to go with Monroe & LeBlanc. Not just because Addison had been consulting with them on another project and had mentioned to Gabe, more than once, that the firm would do an amazing job on the tavern—though her opinion probably had far more weight than it should, everything considered—but because Gabe and Logan both sincerely liked and trusted Elena LeBlanc, one of the partners. She was a regular at Trahan's, and they considered her a friend. Plus, she'd brought Addison into the bar that first night, and, hell, no matter how much he wished he wasn't completely whipped, Gabe couldn't deny that he was grateful to Elena for the introduction.

"So can you make up that list?" Logan asked. "I've got this about done."

"A list of the things that have been replaced rather than repaired and restored over the years?" Gabe asked. "Sure. Reagan probably has a lot of it, right? We would have needed to report that stuff for taxes and stuff?"

Logan sat up a little straighter. "I hadn't thought of that. Yeah, she would. I'll get that from her."

Gabe lifted a brow. "You're going to do that list, too?"

Logan studied the page in front of him. "Well, like you said, she probably already has those records. It won't be hard to pull those out."

Gabe leaned back against the counter behind him and watched his brother try to pretend to be cool about talking to Reagan. "Right, so I can easily get that from her," he said.

"Don't you have receipts and stuff to do this morning?" Logan asked.

He did. But he would always take time to harass his little brother. "That can wait. Reagan might need a little time to pull everything together for us. I should call her right away."

Logan already had his phone out. "I've got it."

Gabe smirked and lifted his cup. Logan was a player. He loved flirting—and more—with the local girls and tourists alike who came into the tavern. He never spent a night alone unless he wanted to. He was cool and charming and could get a girl to giggle and blush faster than any guy Gabe knew. But when he was around Reagan, he stumbled over his words, fumbled paperwork, said stupidly inappropriate things, and generally acted like a doofus. Clearly, his little brother had a thing for the sweet accountant. But Logan wasn't making any headway. Logan couldn't seem to keep his foot out of his mouth, and if it were Gabe, he'd be hiding out whenever Reagan came around. But Logan seemed to think every time was going to be *the* time he managed to get his act together and charm her, so he kept trying. And Gabe couldn't deny that he enjoyed the show.

Cooper needs a sibling.

The thought seemed to come out of nowhere, but it was nothing new, really. Gabe and Logan were close, and while no one drove him crazier than Logan, there was also no one he'd rather have at his back. His son needed someone like that—someone who could tease him but who would also take care of him.

"Hey, don't forget you're picking Cooper up tonight from day care," Gabe said.

"Yep, got it. What are you doing again?"

"Helping a couple of guys from the group bring some new tables to the community center."

"The group" was the single-parents support group Gabe attended regularly. They'd decided to donate new tables to the community center that allowed them to meet weekly for free.

The group was like a second family, and Gabe had appreciated their support over the past three years he'd been attending. His mom and brother helped with Cooper, and he couldn't imagine doing it without them, but the group made up of other single parents had given him a true "village."

"Oh, will Dana be there?" Logan asked.

Gabe rolled his eyes. Logan had gone from excited over talking to Reagan to interested in what another woman was doing tonight. Typical.

"I keep telling you, she's not your type," Gabe said.

That was an understatement. The uptight single mom who'd lost her hero husband in Afghanistan was not the type to fool around with a playboy bartender who thought responsible babysitting meant no one bled. Of course, Logan only ever babysat Cooper, and Cooper's only chance at bleeding was getting a paper cut from one of the pages in his books. Still, Logan would give the organized supermom a heart attack if he were around her kids. Or she'd kill *him*. Either way, Logan needed to stay away from Dana. Which Logan knew in the back of his mind. But it didn't stop him from flirting at every family picnic. Dana's cool reception to that flirting hadn't slowed him down, either.

"No," Gabe said. "Just me, Caleb, and Austin."

Gabe loved hearing the female side of single parenting. Women just had a different take on things. But he couldn't deny that he felt a bond with the other guys who were also doing it alone.

"But you'll see her Thursday at the meeting, right?" Logan asked.

Gabe sighed. "Yeah."

"Tell her hi from me."

Logan gave Gabe a grin that he'd seen a million times directed at women across the bar. But Gabe didn't have breasts, and he did not find Logan charming.

"How about I just say, 'Logan, this is never going to happen,' right now and save us all some time?"

"She doesn't say it's *never* going to happen," Logan said. "She says, 'I don't think so.'"

"That's not the same thing?"

"Of course not."

He should just let it go, Gabe knew, but he couldn't help asking, "Why?"

"If someone asks if you'd like brussels sprouts for dinner, what would you say?"

"Hell no."

"Exactly."

Gabe shook his head. "I don't get it."

"When you don't want something, you know it. And it's easy to say no to it. When you're not sure, or when you *do* want something but you don't want to let on, you say things like 'I don't think so.'" Logan sat back with a grin. "Dana has never said no to me."

"Not even a variation?" Gabe asked, not sure Logan was right.

Logan's grin dropped. "If she had, I would have backed off."

Yeah, okay, that was fair. They'd seen enough women getting unwanted attention and guys who didn't know how to take a hint to respect that no meant no. "I'll tell her hi for you," Gabe said.

"Thanks." And the grin was back.

Gabe finished off his coffee and mentally reviewed how to rearrange his day for the meeting he'd blown off. If that was three hours from now, it would put them at about eleven and . . .

Suddenly it hit him. Addison would probably still be at the office at eleven. She always caught the last plane out of New Orleans on Mondays, working all day at the firm when she was there.

He would get to see her again before she left.

His heart thudded far harder than was warranted, even by the fact that she'd given him the best blow job in the history of blow jobs. A hard thud that probably meant he liked her for more than her blow jobs. A lot more.

He grinned, thinking about her surprise when she saw him walk into Monroe & LeBlanc. She was always the one to make the appearance at the tavern, on her own timeline and terms, so he was the one to turn, see her, and feel his heart thump in a very not-just-a-fling way. Now it would be her turn. Maybe her reaction to seeing him unexpectedly would tell them both more about how she felt.

Gabe's grin dropped away immediately. Did he want to know more about how she felt? What did he want her to feel, exactly? And why would it matter? She fricking lived in *New York*. Even if she were head over heels, it wouldn't matter. He was not in the market for a long-distance relationship.

Even if what he had going with Addison felt like he was already in one.

Okay, he hadn't been interested in going out with—or even fooling around with—any other women since meeting her. Okay, he thought about her way more often than he should. And okay, he really fucking wanted to send her flowers. But he did not want to be involved with a woman who lived more than a thousand miles away and was in town only once a month.

It could only be a fling, with the miles and time between them. They couldn't get more serious than that. Because with his business and his son, he couldn't make regular trips to New York, and he wouldn't introduce Cooper to a woman he'd see only every thirty days at most. Addison didn't even know he had a son. Because that part of Gabe's life wasn't a part of whatever he and Addison were doing. Hell, nothing about his life was really a part of whatever he and Addison were doing.

Besides, Cooper was only five. If he got attached to Addison but didn't have her in his life on a regular basis, it would be confusing.

And frankly, if Addison was only in town for a little more than forty-eight hours each time, Gabe wasn't sure how much of that time he wanted to share with anyone else. Even Cooper. Which probably made Gabe a bad father and an asshole. So it was better not to go there.

"Reagan didn't answer," Logan said a moment later. "So you might need to start putting together a list, after all."

Gabe nodded. That was good. He needed something to do. Something other than thinking about Addison and how she might react to seeing him at the architecture offices and how he wanted her to react to seeing him.

"Did you leave Reagan a message?" Gabe asked.

Logan ducked his head. "Yeah." He looked almost . . . embarrassed.

Gabe grinned. "What did you say?" He knew Logan had put his foot in his mouth.

"Doesn't matter."

Oh, yes, it did. But Gabe would just ask Reagan. She really didn't understand why Logan acted like a dipshit around her. She thought he was like that with all women. Which was hilarious, considering Logan was a well-known charmer and ladies' man.

"Okay, I'll get the list done," he said, pushing away from the counter and heading for the back office. He'd get right on it.

As soon as he sent Addison some flowers. Without analyzing why he was sending them. And he was only writing, *See you soon, Gabe* on the card. Nothing frilly, nothing romantic, and nothing about blow jobs.

◆ ◆ ◆

Gabe had sent her flowers.

Addison stood staring at the gigantic bouquet of white flowers sitting on the desk she was using for the day.

"These are magnolias, right?" she asked Elena. Elena was one of the partners at Monroe & LeBlanc and had been a classmate of Addison's in college. She'd been the one to call and ask for Addison's help on the project they had finished two weeks ago. The project that had been, unbeknownst to Addison, her application for a job with the prestigious restoration architectural firm. The job she'd started today.

"They are. The state flower of Louisiana." Elena stroked the petal of one of the gorgeous flowers. "Someone knows your weakness for all things New Orleans."

He definitely did. Addison hadn't even needed to read the card to know who the flowers were from. Gabe knew she was a sucker for anything that was traditionally associated with the city. Beignets, bourbon, masks, beads, gas lanterns, and balconies with looping wrought iron railings. For six months he'd been taking her out on the Sunday she was in town and letting her soak up the city. And now she'd gone from associating those things with New Orleans and the unique spirit of the city to associating them with him. And the hottest, most decadent, most satisfying-yet-never-get-enough sex of her life. She could simply hear a jazz trumpet and her panties got wet.

But why was he sending her flowers? That was new. So far, their routine was she showed up at the bar on Saturday night, they spent the weekend together, she left on Monday morning, and then thirty days later, they repeated it all over again. There was no contact in between times. No texts or calls—they didn't have each other's number. No letters or gifts—he didn't have her address. And definitely no flowers.

"See you soon, Gabe," Elena read from the card. She lifted her eyes, meeting Addison's. "Gabe? Who's Gabe?" Then her eyes widened. "Wait. These aren't from Gabe *Trahan*, are they?"

Oh, crap. Addison took a deep breath, thought briefly about lying, and then realized there was no real reason to not tell her friend the truth. "Yes."

Elena's eyes widened, almost as if she hadn't expected that answer. "Really? You've seen him since that first night?"

Addison rounded the desk and set the folder she was carrying on top of the nearest stack, straightening the pile of already straight files. "Yes," she said simply. The fewer details she offered, the better, probably.

"When?" Elena asked. "I had no idea you'd seen him again."

And then it hit Addison . . . Elena wasn't just her friend anymore. She was Addison's boss.. Was this going to reflect badly on her? Was a just-when-she-was-in-town affair something Elena would frown upon?

"I didn't think it was important to mention. We just . . . went out a couple of times." They had. They'd gone out to Preservation Hall for jazz. They'd gone to Café du Monde for coffee and beignets. They'd gone to the French Market. They'd gone to Gabe's bedroom. And his shower. And his kitchen table. And his balcony . . .

"You're *dating* Gabe Trahan?" Elena asked, planting her hands on her hips.

"No," Addison said quickly. "Not dating. We've had . . . drinks when I've been in town." And many, many orgasms. And laughs. And fun.

"Which time?" Elena asked.

"Which time what?"

"Which time that you were in town did you have drinks?"

Addison sighed. "Each time."

"You've seen him *every* time you've been in town since you met him?" Elena asked, clearly shocked.

"Yes. But," Addison added before Elena could go on, "it's nothing serious. It's been . . . a fling. Just a little fun. No big deal. And"—she took a deep breath—"this weekend was the last time. Now that I've moved here, I won't be seeing him anymore."

Saying it out loud made her heart clench even harder than it had when she'd driven away from him that morning.

Elena was frowning. "Really? You broke it off?"

Well, no. She hadn't said the words *I'm not going to see you again after this.* But it wasn't like she was ending a relationship. She was simply going to stop sleeping with the guy she was only sleeping with. She ignored the voice in her head that said, *It doesn't feel like you were only sleeping with him.*

"I ended it this weekend," she hedged. She'd ended it by saying goodbye to him. And meaning it this time.

Technically, she had only been sleeping with him. So she might have gotten a little addicted to the sex and the fun. So her heart might have gotten a little involved. Gabe Trahan was the kind of guy that hearts just went a little nuts over. He was funny and sexy and sweet and dirty and confident and charming and gorgeous. She wasn't dead or stupid. Of course she had a little thing for him that went beyond lust.

But—and this was a very important but—she didn't *want* anything more than sex from him. Well, okay, sex and beignets. And jazz. But just those things. Just those fun, harmless, no-big-deal things.

"I just . . ." Elena looked at the flowers again. "I had no idea."

Addison frowned. "Is it a problem?"

"Well, no. Not exactly. Probably," Elena said, still frowning at the flowers as if trying to figure something out.

"What do you mean 'not exactly' and 'probably'?" Addison asked, trepidation suddenly creeping up her spine. *Dammit.* She hadn't mentioned this to Elena because, honestly, it didn't matter.

Gabe was . . . okay, Gabe was amazing. He was the best time she'd ever had, and she knew that she was in danger of falling for him. Which was incredibly stupid. She didn't even really know him. She knew things about him just from being around him. He was funny and intelligent, he loved his bar and its patrons, he loved his city and was so patient about letting her go all touristy on him when they went out. He was kind to the homeless people who approached him for money, instead giving them his business card and telling them to go to his tavern and show the card for a meal. He joked with business owners throughout the French Quarter when he ran into them, and it was obvious he was well liked and respected. And damn, the things that guy could do with his mouth and hands and . . . other parts.

"Gabe and Logan Trahan are coming in for a meeting today," Elena said. "You knew that first night we went in for drinks that we were trying to convince them to hire us."

Addison nodded and crossed her arms over her middle. Okay, Gabe and Logan were coming into Monroe & LeBlanc. No big deal. Addison would just hide out while they were here. And every other time they were scheduled for a meeting..

"Well, they finally came around," Elena said. "They called for a meeting about two weeks ago."

"That's . . . great." It was. Trahan's Tavern was a gorgeous old French Quarter building that definitely needed the best restoration architects in the city. Monroe & LeBlanc were those architects.

Which Addison just might have mentioned to Gabe a time or two. Or five.

Before she'd known she'd be working here, of course.

"You didn't have anything to do with that, did you?" Elena asked point-blank.

"I did mention to Gabe that you are the best," Addison said. "And I absolutely love his building. It would be an amazing project."

Elena sighed. "Well, shit."

Addison chewed her bottom lip.

"So he might have hired us because he's sleeping with you?" Elena asked.

"What?" Addison shook her head quickly. "No, he doesn't even know I'm working here. I never told him. I mean, he knew I was consulting, but he doesn't know I've taken the job and moved here. Like I said, it was a fling. I kept it going longer than I'd intended and longer than I should have, but it's nothing serious, and it's over now." Again, her heart clenched in her chest. *Dammit.*

"You don't have any interest in the project, then?" Elena asked. "You didn't encourage him to hire us thinking you could work on the tavern?"

Addison stared at her. The building was amazing. It was exactly the kind of project that Addison would love to tackle. It was the quintessential French Quarter building in the Creole style, built in the early

1800s. Those buildings were one of the things she loved best about New Orleans, and the chance to work on them was one of the reasons she'd taken the job offer from Monroe & LeBlanc. But she would never sleep with someone to get a project.

"I don't know how to respond to that," she told Elena. "I would never do that."

Elena let out a breath. "Okay, good. I mean, I know. At least, I hope so. I just . . . had to ask."

"No, you didn't have to ask," Addison said. "But I really think it would be best if I wasn't here when Gabe and Logan come in. I'll take my lunch break during that meeting."

Elena looked pained. "I'm sorry, Addison. I didn't mean to insult you. This is just . . . unexpected."

"It's *nothing*," Addison said firmly. "Gabe Trahan and I are over."

And eventually her heart would probably stop clenching every time she thought or said those words.

Elena looked at the bouquet of magnolias. "Are you sure *he* knows that?"

Addison sighed. She had really hoped to get away with just never setting foot in Trahan's again, and that would be that. But okay, she was maybe going to have to be a grown-up about this. Especially if her firm was doing the restoration of his bar.

"I'll talk to him," she told Elena.

"You sure you can break it off?"

Addison shrugged. "*He* will."

"You sure?"

"Definitely."

"And why is that?"

"Because I have something that always sends men running in the opposite direction. A five-year-old daughter."

Chapter Two

Gabe wiped his hands on his jeans. He was nervous? Seriously? He'd seen every inch of the woman he was about to meet up with. He knew that she came fastest when he fucked her on all fours. He knew that she had a tattoo that turned him on instantly—it was a quote that ran under the curve of her left breast and read, "But it is lightning that does the work." He also knew that it came from one of her favorite quotes from Mark Twain—"Thunder is good. Thunder is impressive. But it is lightning that does the work." He knew that she never added sugar to anything, but that if you gave her honey, she'd drench whatever she had in it. And he also knew that her tongue, combined with honey, was the best thing he'd ever had on his cock. And he knew that she'd gotten the delivery of magnolias and that she was definitely feeling touched by them. He loved Addison's fascination with all things southern and, specifically, New Orleans.

So he was in a good place. He'd given her two orgasms, French-press coffee, a lemon scone, and a bouquet of magnolias today. If she wasn't happy to see him after all of that, then . . . he was screwed.

And now, sitting on the most uncomfortable chair he'd ever met, in the fancy waiting area of Monroe & LeBlanc, with the glass-topped coffee table covered in *Architectural Digest* and *New Orleans* magazines, he was nervous as hell.

"We should have worn ties," he muttered to Logan.

Logan looked up from the copy of *Architectural Digest* he was paging through. "What? Are you kidding?"

They were dressed, as they always were, in jeans and T-shirts. One of the things they both loved best about their jobs was the lack of a fancy dress code. Gabe owned ties. It was always good to have one in case of a wedding or a funeral. But he had never in his life worn a tie two days in a row. He couldn't imagine working in an office where he had to dress up every day.

Though he didn't hate the dress code at Monroe & LeBlanc. After all, they were the reason that Addison put on those pencil skirts that hugged her ass and showed off her legs and the silky blouses that buttoned up the front and just hinted at her cleavage. The cleavage that was one of his favorite things on earth.

He shifted on the looked-padded-but-wasn't-really chair and wiped his hands on his thighs again. *Fuck.* He really just needed to see her, to see that she was happy to see *him*, and . . . hell, say goodbye to her again, he supposed.

He didn't want to do that.

And that thought alone made him groan. Shit. How had this fling gotten so out of hand?

"Relax," Logan told him, turning another page. "They're the ones trying to impress us. They want our money. We could show up here in potato sacks and they'd still try to impress us."

Logan was right. Gabe's nerves were all about Addison. And he hated that. He was *nervous* about seeing the woman he'd, just that morning, put on her knees in front of him in the shower and said, "Suck my cock" to? *That* was ridiculous.

"Gabe. Logan."

They looked up to see Elena LeBlanc coming toward them. They both got to their feet. Elena shook their hands with a big smile.

"We're so happy you came in today," she told him. "We're very excited to talk about what we can do for Trahan's. You know how much we love your place."

Elena had started coming to the bar because of its architecture and history. She'd kept coming because of the drinks and Gabe and Logan. That was how about 80 percent of their business worked. People happened upon the bar because of its location in the French Quarter, home of some of the best food and drink in the country, nestled along a quieter street away from the craziness of Bourbon or the tourist traffic on Decatur. There were other shops and restaurants in their area—antique shops and art galleries—that brought people over from the busier streets. Then the historic, charming look of the tavern with the weathered stone exterior, the gas lanterns hanging overhead, and the wide-open French doors, brought them inside. And from there they were hooked. The drinks, food, and general vibe kept people coming back. Either Gabe or Logan—sometimes both— manned the bar every night, and they'd built a reputation of authentic New Orleans hospitality, fun, and charm. They'd made several Best of New Orleans lists over the years, and several area tour guides recommended the tavern to their crowds of visitors.

"We're excited to see your ideas," Logan told her. "You know that this project has been on our minds for a while."

"And your grandmother's," Elena said with a laugh.

Both men nodded. "And our grandmother's," Logan agreed.

"Well, come on back to the conference room," she said. "I'll be leading the meeting with a couple of our architects sitting in. We also have Mason Gary, one of our lead contractors, coming in. He'll be the one on-site with you. And Travis will stop in too." Travis Monroe was Elena's partner. He'd actually started the company about ten years before Elena had joined him straight out of school. Travis was well known in the Quarter, having done the restoration on several historic buildings. His love of the city and its unique architecture was well established.

Which meant that Gabe and Logan probably would have chosen Monroe & LeBlanc anyway. But yes, Addison's encouragement had mattered to Gabe. As stupid as that was. He had no idea if Addison was a good architect. All he really knew was that between her legs was his favorite place to be.

And he had to remember that. All he really knew about her was sexual and physical stuff. The other stuff, the softer, sweeter, I-really-like-her stuff was mostly in his head.

Except the thing where no other woman had ever fit up against him as well as she did. And how, even though she didn't like to cuddle, in her sleep, she always sandwiched one of his feet between hers. And how he only got grunts if he tried to talk to her before her first cup of coffee in the morning but that at night, after just one Pimm's cup, she was exceedingly chatty.

Those seemed like intimate things. Like more-than-a-fling things.

But then he also had to remember that even when she was chatty, it was never about anything too personal. She kept all that locked down tight.

And that was beginning to irritate him more and more.

"Gabe?"

He heard Elena saying his name and focused. They were now in the conference room—he didn't even remember the walk through the hallways—a huge room with glass all around. Three of the walls were windows looking out over New Orleans, the fourth was a glass wall between the conference room and the hallway outside.

"Sorry. Yeah?" he asked.

"Can I get you anything? Coffee? Water?"

Bourbon. He really wanted a bourbon. "Coffee would be great."

"Black?"

The only time he drank it any other way was with milk at Café du Monde with Addison . . . "Yes. Black. Definitely black. Very black."

Damn, he needed to get over the sweet brunette with the amazing mouth. The mouth that never told him anything personal, never asked *him* anything personal, never talked to him on the phone, never said anything like, "I'll miss you."

The sweet brunette who had just walked past the conference room.

Gabe lunged for the door as Addison passed the glass wall, her head bent over an open folder. Her long, dark hair was pulled back—because after he'd joined her in the shower, he'd been unable to help bending her over his bathroom vanity and taking her from behind while she watched in the mirror, and she hadn't had time to style it.

"Addison!"

She was halfway down the hall, but he saw her freeze, her back going ramrod straight. She didn't turn immediately, and Gabe frowned, stalking toward her.

"Addison," he repeated.

She turned then, a big smile on her face. But this smile was new. He knew her oh-my-God-I'm-happy-to-see-you smile. She gave it to him one Saturday a month when she took her place at the end of his bar after not seeing him for thirty days.

This was not that smile.

"Gabe." She didn't, however, seem surprised to see him.

He stopped in front of her, far too close for two people who were simple acquaintances running into each other in a public hallway. "Did you get the flowers?"

Her gaze softened momentarily. "I did. They're gorgeous."

"Good. I was hoping to run into you."

That did make her eyes flicker with surprise. "Really? You didn't mention that you were coming in here today."

"I forgot that Logan and I had a meeting scheduled with Elena. We decided to go with Monroe and LeBlanc for the restoration."

She nodded. "Elena told me this morning. After wondering who the flowers were from. And after wondering if you'd hired them because we were sleeping together."

He blinked at her. "Oh."

Addison lifted an eyebrow. "Yeah, oh."

"I . . ." He ran a hand through his hair. "I didn't think of that. I just wanted to send you something."

She tipped her head. "Why?"

"What do you mean, 'why'?"

"We've been doing . . . this . . . for a while now," she said. "Why are you suddenly sending me stuff today?"

"It just occurred to me." He lifted a shoulder. He'd wanted her thinking of him. And knowing he was thinking of her. It was as simple, and as complicated, as that. And he wasn't sure this was a good time to share that thought process with her. Then he said, "I was thinking of you and wanted you to know it," anyway.

She looked surprised, then pleased, then annoyed. All three emotions flashed across her face within a few seconds. Gabe was kind of impressed.

"That's really nice, but we're not really to the flower-sending stage, are we?" she asked.

And that annoyed *him*. "I didn't realize there was a specific flower-sending stage."

Addison took a deep breath. "I guess it just seems . . ."

"Nice?" he supplied when she trailed off. "Sweet? Thoughtful? Romantic?"

"Yes," she said firmly with a frown, looking around as if to make sure no one was listening. "Romantic."

Well, good. "Then you're welcome."

She scowled up at him. "I don't want romantic, Gabe. Or sweet or nice."

That was stupid. "You're actually annoyed that I sent them?"

She blew out a breath. "Yes."

Bullshit. She'd loved them. Magnolias were exactly the kind of thing to make her go all soft and sweet and giddy. Giddy was exactly how she looked and acted and, dammit, *felt* when they were out and about in the Quarter. He loved that look on her. It was what made him put up with things like the souvenir shops on Decatur and the line at Café du Monde and eating the gumbo at the place on St. Peter that Addison loved. He didn't eat gumbo anywhere but at his mother's house. Because she used his grandmother's recipe, and *no one* made gumbo like his grandma. They didn't even serve it at the bar because it would never live up to what he believed gumbo should be.

"So you'd rather I just stick to things like sucking bourbon off your tits or fingering you to orgasm on my balcony while you watch a parade?"

Her cheeks got pink, her eyes got wide, and she stepped close, lowering her voice. "Stop it."

"I'm just trying to figure out what's going on here." Except that he knew what was going on here. She only wanted sex from him. And he should have been fine with that. Truthfully, only about half his frustration was because of her. The other half was directed at himself. Because he wasn't fine with that. At all.

"Gabe!"

Suddenly a booming male voice from down the hall interrupted them.

Gabe dragged in a deep breath, not even realizing until then that he'd been breathing harder. He gave Addison a last look. She was also breathing faster, and her cheeks were still pink. Then he turned and gave Travis Monroe a smile. "Hey, Travis."

Travis took Gabe's hand in a firm shake. "Good to see you," he said, thumping Gabe on the back. He looked at Addison. "I see you've met our newest associate."

Gabe didn't look at Addison as he nodded. "Addison and I have been spending some time together since she's been here consulting."

"No kidding." Travis looked back and forth from one to the other. "Well, then, you're probably especially happy about her move."

"Her move?"

"We're thrilled to have her. Addison is a perfect fit in New Orleans. Don't know what she saw in the Big Apple anyway." He grinned at Addison. "Hey, we should have you sit in on the meeting with Gabe. You'd love his bar. The structure and history are right up your alley."

Gabe didn't know what the hell was going on, but instinctually he wanted to let the other man, and any other human being, for that matter, know that Addison had very much seen his bar. So to speak. "Addison's been at Trahan's a number of times," he told Travis. "In fact, she's the one who encouraged me to hire you guys. I couldn't ignore her recommendation."

Travis looked at Addison with surprise. "I didn't know that. Well, thanks, Ad. And Gabe, glad you listened to her."

Yeah, he really didn't like Travis calling her Ad. "I think Addison could talk me into just about anything," Gabe said.

Travis laughed. "Then she's definitely sitting in on the meeting."

"Oh, no," Addison said quickly, shooting Gabe a you're-in-huge-trouble look.

Well, good. He hoped he was. He didn't like her little comment about how she didn't want flowers and romance. He didn't like that she hadn't mentioned to Travis that she knew Gabe and his bar. And what the hell was this about a move? Had she *moved* to New Orleans? As in, was now living here? She was their newest associate? He supposed they could refer to consultants as associates, but that seemed odd. And he had every intention of delving into whatever the hell was going on.

"I know that Elena has a lot of great ideas for Gabe and Logan. This is my first day. I don't want to barge in."

"Don't be silly," Travis said. "It's Gabe's first day with us, too." He clapped Gabe on the shoulder. "And it sounds like you have a more . . . intimate knowledge . . . of Trahan's than Elena does."

Wow, okay, so Travis had definitely picked up on the fact that the time Gabe and Addison had spent together had been . . . well, exactly what it had been. Intimate.

"I think it's safe to say that Addison has a really good idea of what I need," Gabe said with a nod.

He heard her little gasp even as Travis laughed, and Gabe could admit that he had probably gone over the line with that. He didn't need to spell out that they'd had an affair. Travis didn't need to know that. But fuck. He hated that she clearly *didn't* want Travis to know. Because he was her boss? Or because she just didn't want people to know she'd hooked up with a bartender a few times when she was on a semivacation from her life in New York? He'd known from minute one that Addison was a classy woman who was used to wining and dining in places a hell of a lot nicer than Trahan's. But she'd seemed to love the bar. Hell, *she* was the one who kept coming to find *him*.

But yeah, he needed to rein in this desire to shout to the world that he'd had Addison Sloan in his bed. Probably. At least with her boss, or whatever Travis was to her. Well, if she was insulted, he'd send her apology flowers later. Maybe hibiscus this time. And since he wanted to be at the flower-sending stage, maybe he'd just fucking send her flowers every damned day whether she liked it or not.

"I would *love* to have Addison sit in on the meeting," Gabe said. "And after the meeting, I'd love to take her to lunch to celebrate her move and her new job and her being a part of this project."

Addison was already shaking her head. "I can't just jump into a project that someone else has been working on," she said. "Just because you and I are *friends* doesn't mean that I can just come in here and take over."

Friends? They were *friends?* Anger tightened his chest, but he made himself breathe.

"But there's nothing to take over," Gabe said. "This is the first meeting. The first meeting that's only happening because you told me it was a good idea," he added. "I'm sure Elena and Travis would agree that having good chemistry between client and *associate* is an important aspect of any project. And I don't think anyone can deny that you and I can really get stuff done."

If by "get stuff done" he meant mind-blowing, I'll-never-get-over-this orgasms in every position and room in the apartment. Which he did.

Even she couldn't deny that. And yeah, he was over the line again. And no, he didn't care. Again. He'd send her some sorry-I-outed-our-fling-to-your-boss pralines, too. He *knew* she liked those.

Gabe couldn't believe how knotted up he felt. *Damn.* He knew that his feelings for Addison had been growing, but now, being face-to-face with the idea that maybe hers had *not* made him feel uncharacteristically possessive and desperate and pissed. And he so rarely felt any of those things, and never where a woman was concerned, that he wasn't sure what to do.

"I really insist you sit in, Ad," Travis said. "Elena won't mind a bit."

Because Travis was furthering Gabe's own agenda, he didn't pull back and punch him for calling her Ad again. But his palm itched a little with the urge anyway.

Addison was clearly gritting her teeth as she smiled and said, "Fine."

"And lunch after," Gabe said. Hey, he'd already pushed his luck, might as well go for it all. She was, apparently, going to be pissed, and maybe even yell when he got her alone, but that was fine. He wasn't feeling particularly sunny and happy right now, either. And he'd never seen her pissed. That could be interesting.

And if she had moved to New Orleans and not bothered to mention it, she wasn't the only one who might be yelling.

Because, what the hell?

"I have a lot to do today," she told him, meeting his eyes directly, her chin lifting slightly. "It's my first day at a new job and all."

Okay, so *now* she was going to lay that out there. *Nice.* "You have to eat," he said. "And I'm sure Travis would consider this work rather than play. I mean, we'll go somewhere public so it can't get *too* fun."

Yep, there he was stomping right over that decency line again. He'd have to throw some beignets into the sorry-I-was-an-asshole gift basket he was going to owe her.

But frankly, seeing the sexy spark of fire in her eyes was worth it. Not to mention making his point that this was *not* only a friendship or a working relationship. This was . . . well, he wasn't exactly sure now. But by the time lunch was over, he was going to know.

"What do you mean that you intended to just not see me again?"

Addison hated the look on Gabe's face. This entire day had been a huge fucking mess. Despite the fact that she'd started it out with two orgasms at the hands—and mouth—of the man now sitting across from her. She was now sitting on the sidewalk of one of her favorite New Orleans restaurants over a lunch date she'd never intended to have, initiating the breakup conversation she'd never intended to have, which would end the relationship that she'd never intended to have.

Because, no matter how much she would love to tell herself, and Gabe, for that matter, that this *thing* between them had been nothing but sex, that simply wasn't true.

It was a relationship.

And she'd fallen for him.

And when she'd lived three weeks of the month in New York City, that had been okay. Or relatively okay. She'd missed him. She'd thought about him. But she couldn't go and see him, and while she could have called the bar, she didn't have his personal number, and she'd been able to resist the urge to stalk him at Trahan's. Most of all, she hadn't needed to tell him about Stella. Or really anything about her life. She'd been able to escape for a couple of days, basking in the Big Easy and Gabe. Like indulging in a decadent dessert once a month. It was amazing and delicious and didn't do any damage to her regular routine and diet.

But when she was living within two miles of him, it was never going to work. As crazy as it sounded, being closer to him geographically and able to see him more often would make a relationship harder. Or impossible. Considering she didn't want an everyday, all-the-time, blend-our-lives-together relationship.

She tucked her hair behind her ear and tried not to look directly into Gabe's eyes. His gorgeous blue eyes that reminded her of ice but could burn as hot as the blue of a candle flame and never failed to melt her resistance, and her panties, and her heart.

"Our routine was for me to just show up at Trahan's when I wanted to see you," she said, then immediately winced, because what was coming next was going to sound terrible. "So I thought the easiest way to break things off was to just stop showing up." *Because I didn't want to see you anymore.* She didn't have to say the rest of the words. They seemingly hung there in the air between them anyway.

Gabe's jaw tightened, and his fingers flexed around the glass mug of iced tea he was holding, but he nodded. "Got it."

She breathed. Maybe he did. "I just didn't think we needed to have a big, deep conversation about it, since things were . . ."

"Not big or deep," he supplied when she wasn't sure where to go with the rest of that sentence.

She wanted to protest that. Because saying this thing between them *wasn't* big and deep seemed to imply it had all been superficial and unimportant. And it really hadn't been. But it was better not to admit that. It was better to walk away thinking that it was a temporary fling and nothing more.

Gabe's tone and posture were casual. He sat back in the scarred wooden chair, one ankle propped on the opposite knee, his right arm draped over the back of the chair, his big left hand cradling the glass mug. But even if she'd only technically spent about twelve days total with him, she could tell that he was feeling anything but casual. Which, stupidly, made her stomach swoop a little. They couldn't keep going, but she had to admit that it was nice to think that letting go wasn't *easy*.

She lifted a shoulder. "Right," she lied. Maybe it wasn't supposed to have been big or deep, but it had felt like it was. Or could be. Or would be.

"I didn't realize that your moving to New Orleans was an option," he said, his voice low and his drawl coming out as he lengthened the words.

Damn, that drawl. His wasn't nearly as pronounced as many she heard in the city. Even his brother Logan's was more obvious. But when Gabe was relaxed, it came out. And when he had his mouth against her ear and was saying things like "Come for me, baby," or "Damn, girl, you do things to me," it was rich and thick.

And it also apparently showed up when he was pissed.

She fidgeted in her seat, partly uncomfortable and partly turned on. "It wasn't. Or I didn't think it was."

"Until you had the right reason."

She nodded.

"The job with Elena and Travis was the right reason?"

She nodded again. "Working with the buildings and houses in New Orleans is an amazing opportunity," she said. "I don't just know and love the architecture, but the history, too."

"And what if I'd asked you to move down here?" he asked point-blank.

Okay, so they weren't going to meander around things. That was probably good. She shook her head. "No, I wouldn't have moved down here for you." There. That might sound harsh, but it was true.

Those blue-flame eyes flickered, but he held his casual posture. "What about some other guy? If you'd met someone else that first night?"

She was already shaking her head by the time he'd finished the question. "No. Not for a relationship. Definitely not." And yes, she put a little extra emphasis on those last two words. "The job would be the only reason. And only *this* job," she said. "I want to do restoration work on buildings I love and appreciate. For people in a city that also loves and appreciates them. I really think *this* job in *this* city is the only thing that could have gotten me out of New York."

Gabe ran his thumb up and down the side of his mug, tracing a line through the condensation. And her traitorous body, which seemed wanton only for this man, responded to that stroking motion by that digit as if he were running it over her skin. Or her nipple. Or her clit. *All* those parts tingled just watching it.

"Obviously this morning when I was coming in your mouth in the shower and then fucking you over the sink in the bathroom, you knew you were moving here—*had* moved here," he said.

His tone, and that drawl, was low and slow, as if they were discussing how her Cajun chicken salad was. But those words . . . and that look in his eyes when she met his gaze . . . Her whole body went hot and soft just sitting across the table from him.

She knew, of course, that Gabe was a dirty talker in the bedroom. She knew that he liked to lean in and say all kinds of naughty, delicious things to her when they were standing in line for beignets or listening in on part of a ghost tour or watching a street magician perform at Jackson Square. But that was when they were flirty and having fun and would be going back to his apartment that night. *This*—and the things he'd said to her in the hallway at the firm—was nothing like that. These were sexy and direct and dirty and, clearly, designed to get a reaction from her and give him some kind of advantage. Even if it was just to shock her.

"Obviously," she managed to say in response to his comment. She even, somehow, managed to inject a little sarcasm in there.

"How about last month when you were letting me get you off with the vibrator we bought on Bourbon before making you ride my cock?" He paused, letting those words swirl around them. "Did you know then that you were going to move down here?"

"I found out that Monday," she said, her mouth dry and her panties wet as that memory replayed in vivid color and graphic detail.

"And did you figure then that you were going to end things with us?"

She nodded.

Suddenly he shifted on his chair, leaning onto the table, his eyes flashing. "Then why in the hell did you show up in my bar two nights ago?"

Addison swallowed, her heart beating hard against her chest wall. "I should have stayed away," she admitted softly. "I know that. I knew it as I was walking up the sidewalk and through the door. I knew it the second you looked over and saw me."

"But you didn't fucking stay away," he practically growled.

She shook her head. "I couldn't."

Gabe swore and shoved a hand through his hair. "Goddammit, Addison."

"I know."

"This is . . . bullshit." He pinned her with his gaze again. "You can't stay away. I don't want you to stay away. What the hell is going on?"

"There's just . . . It's complicated," she said. "It's not as easy as my just moving here and us continuing to go out on the weekends."

"Why not?" he demanded. "You want more than that? Let's talk about that."

She shook her head. "You're . . . amazing. But no, I definitely don't want more than that."

He blew out a breath, seeming almost relieved. Had he offered more accidentally?

"Then let's keep doing what we're doing," he said. He leaned in again. "I've never wanted a woman like I want you, Ad. Let's just keep it going. It's good. It's really, really good."

Her heart softened, and she felt herself leaning in, too, and almost nodding. But no. She couldn't fucking nod yes to that. They couldn't keep it going. She wasn't in New Orleans alone. She couldn't spend every weekend, or even one weekend a month, with him the way she had been. Her parents weren't here to watch Stella. And dammit, *she* had to be with Stella on the weekends, showing her daughter around the city that was her new home, introducing her to beignets and exploring the museums, not off screwing some hot bartender in the French Quarter. And seeing the city, eating beignets, and exploring the museums with him.

Dammit.

She took a deep breath. "Okay, fine, there's something I have to tell you."

"There's someone else." He said it flatly. No drawl. No huskiness. No hint of humor. None of the things she usually loved in his voice.

"No—" But then she thought about it. That was definitely one way to put it. "Well, okay, yes."

He blew out a breath. "Dammit, Addison."

"But it's not what you think," she told him. She paused and added, "It's maybe worse."

"Worse than you fucking me behind some other guy's back?" he asked.

It was insulting that he'd think that of her. But then again, he didn't really know her, did he? So she simply shrugged. "Yeah, kind of."

"What's worse than that?"

"The someone else is a girl. And is five. And is my daughter."

Gabe stared at her. Addison just sat quietly, letting all of that sink in. She watched him processing it.

Then she watched as his mouth—easily one of her top three favorite body parts of his—spread into a huge grin.

A *grin*.

Oh yeah, she really loved it when he grinned. Sometimes it was sexy—like after he'd said something naughty and was watching her reaction. Sometimes it was mischievous—like when he'd thought of something they hadn't done yet, in the bedroom and otherwise, and he was about to show her. Sometimes it was flat-out happy—like when he was joking with his brother or other patrons at the bar. And sometimes it was big and bright and made her feel like the most special woman in the world—like the one he gave her when he would first turn and see her sitting at the bar on a Saturday night.

This one was like none of those. This one was like she'd just given him the greatest gift anyone had ever given him. It was a little like the Saturday-night grins but even more.

"You have a kid?" he asked.

She nodded. "Stella."

"Well, holy shit, Addison."

"I know. I—"

"That's fucking *amazing*."

Wait, *what*?

Chapter Three

"It's amazing?" she repeated.

Gabe reached across the table and grabbed her hand. His palm was slightly rough, and his hand engulfed hers, making her feel small and delicate and . . . warm. Very warm. It reminded her of the way he wrapped himself around her in bed. He always wanted to hold her after sex, and his huge body around hers always made her feel protected and safe and loved. And when that L word hit her brain, she always pulled away. She wasn't a cuddler. She didn't need to be held and protected and taken care of. She took care of herself and her stuff. Like Stella.

And now she wanted to pull away, too. It was strange. She typically did hold hands with him. Gabe was a very physically demonstrative guy. He always seemed to want to be touching her—running his hand over her hair, putting his arms around her from behind and pulling her up against his body, resting his hand on the back of her neck. And she let all of that go. Because she actually really loved it. The feeling that he just couldn't help but touch her and the way it said to the rest of the world, "She's mine." But she only let it happen in public. It seemed safer that way. Like when the rest of the world was bustling around them, she couldn't get totally lost in him. But in private . . . when it was just the two of them, the touching was sexual. And then she pulled away. They didn't spoon, she didn't sit in his lap, they didn't cuddle on the couch.

Now he squeezed her hand, his eyes bright and happy. Those blue eyes that made her a little stupid.

"It is completely amazing," he told her with a nod. "There's something I haven't told you, either."

Her stomach knotted at that. *Oh, boy.* Here they went. Personal stuff..

"Gabe, I—"

"I have a son. Cooper. He's five, too."

Addison heard the words. They weren't complicated words. Not overly long or hard to pronounce. And he'd put them together in simple, short sentences. But for several long seconds, she couldn't make them make sense.

But when she did, she felt her eyes widen and her heart thump, and she definitely pulled her hand back.

"What?"

He nodded again. "I'm a dad."

Well, holy-complicate-everything. She frowned. "But you . . ." Okay, she'd been about to say, "You never said anything about having a kid," and realized that was maybe the stupidest thing she could have come up with. She had been the one to first decide that they shouldn't get too personal in their conversations. He'd gone along with it readily, she noted, but yeah, that had been her idea. And she hadn't said boo about Stella. "You don't even have juice boxes in your fridge," she finally said weakly.

Keeping Stella from Gabe was pretty easy, considering she was thirteen hundred miles away in New York, and Gabe really saw very little of Addison's personal life. But she'd been in his apartment. At his place of work. Hanging out with his brother.

There were no photos up anywhere. Of course, it was a bar. And she'd only been in the office of Trahan's once. And it had been such a mess of paperwork and boxes that there was no way she would have seen a photo. But the apartment was another story. There were no toys, no kids' books—or really many books of any kind, come to think of it—and there wasn't even a place where a kid might sleep.

"He lives with his mom," she concluded out loud a moment later. And hell, that meant there was an ex. Another woman in Gabe's life.

Frankly, in her opinion, there was nothing awesome about any of this.

"No, he lives with me," Gabe said. "Well, with my mom and me."

"Your mom?" She frowned. "You live with your *mom*?"

He looked a little sheepish. "Yeah. Because of Coop," he added quickly.

"But the apartment."

"Logan lives there. But it belongs to the bar. I use it when I'm working late or over the weekend."

Or when I need a place to take a woman for sex. He didn't say it, but Addison could have sworn she heard the words out loud. "I see." She sat back and crossed her arms.

"So this really is amazing," he went on. "We're both parents. That was the one thing that was keeping me from thinking this could really turn into something. Well, that and your living in New York."

He gave her a little grin, and Addison honestly wished he'd quit doing that. She loved his grins. But now, in this context, they were making things even more difficult.

"Now neither of those things is an issue," he went on when she said nothing. "And I'm sure that Stella was why you didn't think we should keep seeing each other. And I get it. It's a big deal to bring someone into your kid's life. But there's nothing to worry about. I love kids. I love being a dad. I've always wanted more kids."

Addison actually felt her mouth drop open. Gabe was an enthusiastic guy. It took about five minutes in Trahan's with him behind the bar to figure that out. He laughed big, he told big stories, and he had big sex. Big, amazing, blow-her-mind, enthusiastic sex. It shouldn't surprise her, really, that he'd jump from a weekend fling to "I've always wanted more kids." But it did. Because who said that? Who looked at the woman he barely knew and who had *just* told him about her daughter and said, "I've always wanted more kids"?

"Wow, so I guess we should just get married and all move into your mom's place and start having family movie nights," Addison said. "We should start trying for more kids right away. Maybe we'll get lucky and have twins."

Gabe lifted a brow. "It's weird, but you sound a little sarcastic when you say that," he said. Sarcastically.

She lifted her eyebrows back at him. "You think?"

"What's the problem?" he asked.

"Seriously? You mean besides the fact that I'm trying to break things off and you just essentially proposed?"

He sat back in his chair, again assuming that casual, nonchalant posture, but with the tight jaw and flashing blue eyes that said "I'm not amused."

"We don't have to get married right away. We can have a long engagement if you want. But don't think for a second that the idea of twins scares me off."

Holy crap. She now knew something about Gabe Trahan that she hadn't realized before this moment. He was crazy.

"Okay, so on that note, I need to be getting back to work. And getting *off* your project. And maybe hiring a bodyguard," she said, scooting her chair back.

"Addison."

Her heart was pounding, and she was trying to decide if she was freaked out or just completely flabbergasted, and yet, him saying her name, just her name, stopped her. Well, it was him saying her name in that low, commanding tone.

She sighed and looked up at him, pressing her lips together.

"Don't leave."

"I . . ." She swallowed, then lifted her chin and met his eyes. "I'm not interested in any of that. I'm sorry."

She wasn't really sorry. It was perfectly fine for her to not want to get married and have more kids with him. But she was sorry that this was going to be the end of Gabe and her. It was just one more way that being a mom screwed with things. She loved Stella. Her daughter was a bright, shining star full of energy and happiness and love, and she made Addison look at the world in new ways and had shown her a kind of love that Addison had never imagined before. Nine times out of ten, Addison would rather be with Stella than anyone else.

But there was that one time out of ten when Addison missed being an adult with full control over her routine and her time. Put bluntly, Stella got in the way of some things. Like moving to London. Getting a full night's sleep if there was even the tiniest rumble of thunder. Having a kitchen table that didn't have swipes of marker and gouges from scissors. Spending the weekend with nothing but wine and Netflix. Having a hot fling with a New Orleans bartender.

But heaven forbid Addison actually express any of that. It was the biggest parental sin to actually admit that having a kid was downright exhausting and not always fun. She'd learned that the hard way. She didn't have many friends who were parents—that was probably part of the problem. Women who weren't moms but wanted to be couldn't imagine the emotions that bounced back and forth between incredible love and extreme frustration. Almost constantly. And the few women she did know who were mothers were those supermoms who had reproduced multiple times, did it all, and loved every second of it.

She really needed some new friends.

Where were all the parents who would lay down their lives for their children but who also cherished a trip to the damned grocery store alone just so they could have some time to themselves? She couldn't be the only mom who had skipped out of work early so she could make the grocery-store trip alone while her kid was still in day care. And who grabbed her favorite box of cookies off the shelf and ate them as she shopped so she wouldn't have to share. And had stopped just short of grabbing a bottle of wine and uncorking it in aisle four.

She needed to find *those* moms to hang out with.

Wasn't it possible to love your kid with all your heart and still sometimes resent that every meal decision had to include vegetables that a five-year-old would eat without argument, that every page in her day planner included something involving a doctor's appointment, day care, or a play date, and that every weekend had to include educational and mentally stimulating activities?

"Okay, it's too soon to talk about marriage and twins," Gabe said. "Fine. Let's talk about having dinner tomorrow night. We can introduce Stella and Cooper."

Oh my God. Her stomach dropped like she'd gone over the top of a roller coaster. She started shaking her head. "No. Definitely not. *Absolutely* not."

Gabe frowned. "I'll cook."

Yeah, because the idea of cooking was what was sending her into a panic.

Though, yeah, the idea of cooking for two more people, one of whom was another five-year-old who, with her luck, would hate all three of the vegetables that Stella would actually touch, did actually make her feel like she could break out in hives at any moment. "I don't want to have dinner with you and Cooper," she said. "I don't want to meet Cooper. I don't want you to meet Stella."

Clearly, being up front, straightforward, and even blunt was how she was going to handle this. Because she *really* needed Gabe to get this. And because the dread over dating a man who had a kid was very real and was short-circuiting her ability to be calm and reasonable.

Gabe was clenching his jaw again. The only time she'd really seem him do that before today was when he was struggling to maintain control when she had him in her mouth or was the one on top setting the pace. She loved that look on his face. Until now.

Now it was clear he was similarly struggling with control, but she didn't really want to see him lose his cool in this case.

"Want to explain to me how come you keep showing up in my bar and spreading your legs for me, but you don't want to meet my son or introduce me to your daughter?" he asked in a tight, low voice.

Did she? No, not really. And if she'd only showed up and spread her legs for him once, she wouldn't. But she *had* kept going back to the bar. She'd had the power to end this a long time ago, and she hadn't. So she supposed she owed him an explanation.

And that explanation might be exactly what she needed to get this let's-live-happily-ever-after idea out of his head. Usually just the idea of Stella was enough for most guys to call it quits. But if Gabe was a devoted father who wanted to be a husband and family man, then her attitude about the whole thing would probably be enough to turn him right off.

"Okay, look, when we first got together, it was a surprise to me. I don't do hookups. But the chemistry was off the charts and I was high on New Orleans and you were safe. You lived far away, and it didn't seem like your first one-night thing with a girl who happened into your bar," she told him.

She knew—then and now—that she was stereotyping the charming, southern French Quarter–bartender thing, but that was honestly part of the reason she'd stuck around when he'd asked her to, and gone upstairs with him after last call. That and his abs. And ass. And those freaking blue eyes that made her want to take her clothes off and watch them dilate with want.

Then she'd refused to think about the fact that it really might be a regular weekend thing for him. She'd also tried very hard to keep from wondering about who he might be taking up those same stairs with him on the weekends she wasn't in town. She'd told herself it didn't matter.

"I didn't intend to go back to Trahan's after that first weekend," she told him honestly. That was why it wasn't supposed to matter who else saw the upstairs rooms of Trahan's.

"But you couldn't stay away," he said, reiterating her earlier admission.

She nodded. "Yeah." Clearly, he liked that idea and wasn't about to let her forget it. "And every time was supposed to be the last time. But it was . . . a break. A vacation. A chance to just be a woman who only had to think about what *she* wanted and not worry about things like bedtimes and four food groups and swearing and drinking and if the people I was spending time with would be good or bad influences on my daughter." She took a breath. "It was too tempting to keep doing all of it when I was here. The food, the music, the sex," she said, because there was no sense in pretending that hadn't been a huge part of it. "When I was here, Stella was taken care of, and I could just be me." She leaned in. "And that's something you need to know—I love her. Dearly. But I also love time without her. A lot." She watched him for his reaction to that.

"All parents feel that way sometimes," Gabe said. "I get that. And I'm not saying that the kids need to come along on every date or anything."

"I don't want her to come along on any dates," Addison said stubbornly. "And I definitely don't want Cooper to come along on any dates."

Gabe frowned at her. "Why the hell not?"

"Because I have one too many five-year-olds as it is," she said, feeling her frustration growing. "Look, I know that sounds terrible, but the thing is, Gabe, Stella is way more than I had intended to have at this point in my life. Or maybe ever. Being a mom is hard, and frankly, I have no desire to double that. I don't want another kid."

There, she'd said it. She knew it sounded bad, but she couldn't care about that. She needed Gabe to not want to get Cooper and her together. So if she needed to be a little bitchy about this whole thing, that was for the best. She was sure Cooper was a great kid, but . . . No, actually, she had no idea if Cooper was a great kid. He might be a hellion. But even if he was the sweetest child in the history of the world, it didn't matter. He was a kid. And kids needed things. A lot of things.

She was raising Stella to be very independent, and thankfully her daughter was blessed with a naturally autonomous spirit. She'd been potty trained by one, was dressing herself by age three, and now, at age five, she was able to bathe with only supervision, get her own snacks, and read her favorite simple books. She'd be in kindergarten in the fall, and Addison was excited about the new challenges and stimulation for her always-on-the-go girl, but she also knew that the school routine would add more to *her* calendar. There would be certain times Stella *had* to be certain places. There would be fund-raising bake sales. There would be parent-teacher meetings and PTO meetings and God knew what other meetings. And Addison would be at them all. Because that's what a good mom did. But she certainly didn't want to be going to two sets of parent-teacher meetings and doctors' appointments and recitals and . . . She stopped and took a breath as her heart rate quickened with even the *idea* of the added stress.

And really, getting involved with Gabe would be tripling the people who needed her, not just doubling. Gabe would need things, too. And while he was, obviously, a capable, successful adult, it wasn't like she could just never consider his schedule or what *he* wanted for dinner.

She wasn't selfish. Well, okay, maybe she was a little selfish. But dammit, being a mom was hard. She'd had plans that had been sidetracked by becoming a mom. She was so glad to have had Stella. She'd learned a lot about herself. Good and bad. And she'd never considered ending the pregnancy or putting the baby up for adoption. She'd made the choice to have sex with the most irresponsible man on the planet, and now being a single mom to Stella was the consequence of that. Addison believed in dealing with the consequences of her choices. So she was now a mom. And she was good at it. She worked at it. She took it seriously. But she hadn't *chosen* it.

She'd never pictured her life with a child at any point prior to the at-home pregnancy test turning out positive. So she kind of thought she could be forgiven for not always knowing exactly what she was doing and for not always being thrilled with the way Stella impacted her decisions and routines.

Gabe was staring at her, and Addison braced herself for him to say, "I don't want a woman with that attitude anywhere near my kid." That was what she wanted him to say. But once he said the words, it would be the official end between them, and dammit, there was a chunk of her heart that didn't want that.

Just like there was a chunk of her heart that wished she never had to make broccoli again in her life. But that chunk was always overridden by the chunk of her brain that said she had to because it was what a responsible mother would do.

"Doing it all alone must be hard," Gabe finally said.

She frowned slightly. "Well, yeah. As you know."

"I was fishing there for just how alone you are," he admitted, sitting forward in his chair again. "As in, how involved is Stella's dad."

"Stella's dad is becoming a rock star in LA," Addison said, unable to keep the derision out of her tone. "Needless to say, Stella was a surprise to both of us. He wanted to be cut loose, and after about the fifth horrible decision, I was more than happy to make that happen. He signed over all parental rights, and we haven't heard from him in two years. Not even on the radio," she said with an eye roll.

Gabe nodded. "Good to hear."

"That I have horrible taste in men?" she asked. "Shouldn't that *concern* you?"

One corner of his mouth curled slightly, the first sign of anything resembling humor since they'd taken their seats. "You seem like the type to learn from your mistakes."

She nodded. "Definitely. Hence the whole no-more-babies thing."

"Right." Something flickered in his eyes. "Thankfully, you haven't figured out that babies come from sex. Because then I *would* be concerned. And have a pretty bad case of blue balls."

She lifted a brow. "I have a very good IUD and always buy my own condoms. And I always put them on myself so I know it's all done right. In case you haven't noticed."

For a second, he looked surprised. Then he looked impressed. "Damn. You do, don't you?" Then he tipped his head. "Should I be offended that you don't think I know how to put a condom on correctly?"

She couldn't help it. She laughed. "I'll also take it as a compliment that you were so into everything that you didn't even really notice."

"Well, you get your hands near my cock and I'm pretty much unable to think at all," he said, his voice suddenly husky.

And just like that, heat arrowed through her. She swallowed hard. "Anyway," she said, pushing all images of Gabe's cock from her mind. Kind of. "Stella's dad isn't a consideration in anything. I'm doing it all on my own. Just the way I like it. Yes, it's hard. But I'd rather it be hard than frustrating as hell when I'm dealing with someone else's opinions on how I should raise my kid or cleaning up the messes they cause with their decisions."

Gabe rubbed a hand over the back of his neck, looking frustrated but also a little resigned.

"You must understand," she said. "You're doing everything with Cooper on your own, right?"

Okay, yeah, she was fishing about Cooper's mom, too. Totally.

"No," he said, shaking his head. "I can't imagine that."

"Oh." Addison chewed the inside of her cheek. How much did she ask here? Did she have a right to ask anything? She was trying to break up with the guy. A guy who she didn't even *really* have a relationship with. Did it matter, at all, what his situation was with Cooper's mom?

But she suddenly wanted to know everything. Had they been married? How often did he see her? Had she broken things off with him or the other way around? How did he feel about her now?

"I don't know what I'd do without my mom. And Logan. And my friends. I have a lot of help. It really does take a village," Gabe said. "Being a dad *is* hard. I hear you. I don't think I could do it on my own."

Okay, red flag. He wasn't the fully independent, I've-got-my-life-under-control guy she'd thought—or hoped—he was. Was he looking for a woman because he wanted someone to make things easier on him?

"Your mom and Logan?" Addison repeated. "Where's Cooper's mom?" There. Might as well get right to the point.

"Gone," Gabe said.

Addison gave him an eye roll. There was no way he actually thought that was a good enough answer. "Left or dead?" she asked.

"Left, then died."

She blinked at him. Oh. "Sorry."

He shrugged. "She left when he was about one. She had never planned on having kids and didn't appreciate how much a baby changed her life." His look was pointed.

Yeah, yeah, just like her. But Addison hadn't left. She'd done the opposite of leave. She took care of *everything* in Stella's life.

"She took off," Gabe said. "And then was killed in a car accident about a year later."

"Wow. That's rough." Addison wasn't sure how to read his expression. Was he sad about that? Angry? Indifferent?

"You can ask," he said after a moment.

"Ask what?"

"If I was in love with her. If she broke my heart. If I miss her."

She didn't love that he was reading her emotions that easily. "Okay. Were you in love with her, did she break your heart, and do you miss her?"

"I was not in love with her. We were dating when she got pregnant but had only been together about three months. If she hadn't gotten pregnant, I doubt it would have lasted much longer, actually. She broke my heart only in the sense that my son will never know his mom. And no," he said with a sigh, "that probably makes me an asshole, but I wouldn't say I really miss her. But I do miss having a partner in raising my son."

Addison realized that feeling relieved that he hadn't been in love and didn't miss the other woman was ridiculous. "You have your mom and Logan, I thought."

He just looked at her for a moment. "And you're kind of judging me, right?"

"For what?"

"For having my mom help raise my son."

She shook her head. "Of course not. Everyone needs to do what they need to do. I'm the opposite—I don't want anyone else involved. I think I can make the best decisions for Stella, and so I don't make it a group project. But you have to do what you have to do."

"So you don't think I *can* raise Cooper by myself?" Gabe asked.

Addison raised her eyebrows. Wow, he'd been quick to jump to that. "I don't think I really know you well enough to say that one way or another. And it doesn't matter what I think."

Again, he just watched her for a few ticks before saying, "What if I told you that it does matter what you think?"

Okay, that was a really good reason to get the hell out of here now. She didn't want his opinion on how she was parenting, and he shouldn't want hers. That went way beyond the weekend-hookup thing they'd had going. She reached down and grabbed her purse from the sidewalk at her feet. "I would say that *you* don't know *me* well enough to care what I think about your relationship with your son," she told him. "And if I didn't know we were at the flower-sending stage, I definitely don't think we're at the stage where we give each other opinions about our personal choices."

He shifted forward and wrapped a big hand around her wrist. "Addison, don't go."

"I have to."

"And I'm not going to see you at Trahan's again, am I?"

She shook her head, feeling tears pricking the backs of her eyes. *Wow.* She didn't miss Stella's dad even after having a true relationship with him and raising a daughter—at least for a couple of years— together. But she'd been with Gabe for only a few hours, really, and she knew she was going to feel his absence from her life acutely. She pulled her hand away. "I'm sorry I kept coming by. I shouldn't have done that."

He gave her a long, intense stare and said, "Okay, I get it. But please, no matter what else, don't be sorry for that."

She sucked in a little breath. Then gave him a nod. Then, on impulse, she bent and kissed his cheek before straightening and walking away without looking back.

Gabe watched Cooper scoop mashed potatoes into his mouth and wondered if Addison made Stella mashed potatoes. And how did the little girl feel about fried chicken? Did Addison know how to make fried chicken? Did Stella eat green beans? He knew a lot of kids were picky about vegetables. Unlike Cooper. Cooper ate anything and everything.

"Wow, who pissed in your gravy?" Logan asked Gabe, kicking the chair out next to him at their mother's dining room table and settling into it with his own plate of chicken, potatoes, and beans.

Gabe tried to relax his expression. He didn't realize he'd been broadcasting the irritation he was feeling with all thoughts of Addison today. But it had been a week since she'd told him she wanted to end things, and he couldn't get her out of his mind. Damn the woman. She'd always teased his thoughts when they were apart, but now . . . she was a *mom.* She had a little girl Cooper's age. Her ex was completely out of the picture. And he'd thought she'd been damned near perfect *before* finding all of that out.

"Language, bro," Gabe said to Logan, for all the good it would do.

Logan laughed and looked across the table at his nephew. "Hey, Coop?"

Cooper looked up, his eyes the same coffee brown as his uncle's rather than the light-blue of his dad's. "What?"

"Don't say *pissed*, okay? It's not nice."

"Okay," Cooper told him.

Logan grinned at Gabe. "There. All fixed."

Gabe sighed. "You can't just watch your language around him?"

Logan bit into his chicken. "Apparently not," he said around the mouthful.

"Hey, Coop?" Gabe asked.

"Yeah?"

"Just don't do anything Uncle Logan does, okay?"

Cooper looked at Logan. "Don't do *anything* you do?" he asked.

"I guess," Logan said as if he wasn't sure what Gabe was talking about.

"What stuff do you do besides bad words?" Cooper wanted to know.

"Oh, well, there's a long list," Logan said.

"Logan," Gabe said warningly.

"No, I got this," Logan said, setting down his chicken and wiping his hands on his napkin as he addressed Cooper. "I make my bed every morning, I eat lots of fruit, I exercise, I get all my work done, and I'm always helpful to Grandma. So I guess your dad wants you to *stop* doing all those things, okay?"

Cooper frowned. "Really?"

Gabe ran a hand through his hair. Were all five-year-olds this literal? "No," Gabe inserted. "Not really."

"Uncle Logan doesn't do those things really?" Cooper asked.

Gabe sighed. "Well, yes, he does do those things."

"But you said I should not do anything he does."

Gabe nodded. "I know. I was being funny."

Cooper blinked at him. "I don't get it."

Logan laughed and dug into his potatoes. "He doesn't want you to do the *bad* things I do," he said. "I was just pointing out that I do lots of good things, too."

"What bad things do you do?" Cooper wanted to know.

"I drink beer and say bad words and kiss lots of girls," Logan told him. He took a forkful of beans.

"Kissing girls is bad?" Cooper asked.

Logan shot Gabe a grin. "Well . . ."

"How come people get married if kissing girls is bad?" Cooper wanted to know, setting his fork down.

Great. Not only a sticky conversation, but now dinner was going to take forever.

Gabe barely resisted punching his brother in the arm. "Kissing girls is not bad," Gabe said. And in spite of the fact that he'd kissed literally hundreds of girls in his life, the only one to flash through his mind at that moment was Addison. He gritted his teeth, then worked to unlock his jaw. "Kissing girls is actually really nice."

"*Really* nice," Logan felt the need to add.

Gabe kicked him under the table. "But you should only kiss girls when you care about them. Uncle Logan sometimes kisses girls just for fun."

"But kissing *is* fun?" Cooper asked.

Gabe always tried very hard to be totally honest and open with his son. He wanted Cooper to ask him questions and expect honest answers. But he was five. And no way in hell was Gabe giving Cooper any kind of sex ed with Logan sitting right there.

"Kissing girls is very fun," Gabe said honestly.

"So I *can* do that? And make my bed and exercise and do my work?" Cooper asked.

"Yes," Gabe said. "You can definitely make your bed and exercise and do all your work."

"But what about kissing?" Logan pressed with a shit-eating grin. "Can he do that?"

"Of course," Gabe said. He leveled a look at Cooper. "When you're older." The last thing he needed was a call from day care that his son had suddenly turned into a ladies' man.

"How much older?" Logan asked. "Like, how old were *you* when you first kissed a girl?" He took a bite of potatoes and chewed nonchalantly as he watched Gabe.

Gabe narrowed his eyes. Logan knew very well that Gabe had first kissed a girl when he was ten. Her name had been Jenny and she'd initiated it and *she'd* been the one to tell everyone about it afterward. Including her older brother, who had given Gabe his first black eye and his first lesson in you-don't-mess-with-your-friends'-little-sisters.

Honestly, these were the moments when Gabe would agree with Addison—raising a kid would be easier alone in many ways.

"*What* is going on in here?"

Gabe looked up as his mother came into the room from the kitchen with a basket of rolls in hand. And he amended his thought to "Raising a kid would be easier without his *brother* helping." Because honest to God, he had no idea what he'd do without his mother helping with Cooper. He loved his son with everything in him. He'd do absolutely anything to ensure Cooper's health and happiness. And he'd realized very early on that making Cooper's life steady and safe and happy meant moving back in with his mother and ignoring the stigma around that and dealing with the ways that was inconvenient and trying at times.

"Gabe's just telling Cooper how fun kissing girls can be," Logan said with a tattletale tone.

"We're talking about kissing?" Caroline Trahan asked as she set the rolls down and gave Gabe a questioning look.

"Logan started it," Gabe returned.

Caroline rolled her eyes and looked at her grandson. "What were they saying?"

"That I should make my bed, do my work, exercise, and kiss girls," Cooper reported. "Oh, and *not* drink beer or say bad words."

Gabe opened his mouth, then realized that Cooper had actually summed it up pretty well.

Caroline shook her head and took her seat. "Well, I guess that's not a bad list."

"It's okay with you if I kiss girls?" Cooper asked, picking his fork up again.

"Of course," Caroline said easily, reaching for the bowl of green beans. "When you're older, and if they want you to, and if you really care about them."

Cooper chewed a bit for a moment, then asked his uncle, "Do the girls you kiss want you to?"

Logan kept a straight face and nodded solemnly. "Yes. Yes, they do."

"And do you care about them?"

Gabe coughed, and Logan gave him the finger by running his middle digit up and down the side of his face away from their mother's line of sight.

"I like them all *very* much," Logan said.

"And you're old," Cooper informed him. "So it's okay if you kiss them. You shouldn't put that on the list with drinking beer and saying bad words."

Logan nodded, again without cracking a smile. "You know what? You're absolutely right, Coop. Kissing girls should totally go on the other list. The one with my bed and exercise."

Gabe kicked him again. There was no way Cooper would get Logan's insinuation, but Logan deserved the kick anyway.

"And have you noticed how happy your dad's been lately?" Logan asked, shifting away from the reach of Gabe's foot. "I think it's because he's making his bed and exercising more."

Gabe sighed. Cooper wouldn't notice the tone that made "making his bed and exercising" sound like something else altogether, but Caroline did. She shot Gabe a look.

"I don't think I realized there were changes in your bed and exercise routine," she said, casually taking a bite of chicken.

Gabe rolled his eyes. "Really, Mom?"

She shrugged. "Just that I know you . . . make your bed pretty often, but your brother doesn't usually feel the need to comment on it."

Logan snorted and finished off his potatoes.

Cooper frowned. "Dad doesn't make his bed."

Logan laughed outright at that and reached for more chicken. "Oh, sometimes he does, buddy. Trust me. He . . . tucks things in really tight."

And this time *his mother* snorted.

For God's sake. Gabe punched Logan in the arm. "How about we talk about something else?"

Thankfully, his mother came to his rescue. "Yes, Cooper, tell your dad about the alligators."

Gabe looked at his son. "Alligators?"

Cooper's eyes had gotten round. "Did you know that Louisiana has the largest population of alligators in America?"

"Nope, didn't know that. I did know we have a lot."

"The *most*," Cooper told him, again setting his fork down.

Why the child couldn't multitask was beyond Gabe.

"And they lay eggs!" Cooper told him. "Like birds!"

"That I did know," Gabe said. "How many eggs do they lay at a time?"

"So many," Cooper told him enthusiastically. "They can lay fifty at a time!"

"Wow, that is a lot," Gabe mused. He loved when Cooper got into something. He didn't multitask with his interests, either. When he was into something, it was 110 percent all about that one thing and nothing else. And Gabe always learned a lot. The interest might only last for a few weeks before Cooper would move on to his new obsession—though in the case of *Star Wars* and fire trucks, it had been for a few months each—but when he was interested in something, that was all he talked about, read about, looked up on the computer, and wanted to play with. It looked like Gabe might need to find some toy alligators soon.

"And they breathe like birds, too," Cooper told him. "It's super weird." But the way he said it and the expression on his face said that it was completely fascinating.

"We were talking all about alligators today," Caroline told Gabe. She gave him a little smile that said they had literally talked about them *all* day, and she was ready for someone else to listen to alligator trivia for a while. "So, I was thinking maybe Cooper would like to go on one of those swamp boat tours. They take boats out on the bayou, and you can see alligators right where they live."

Cooper's eyes got wide, and he looked from his grandmother to Gabe slowly, as if he wasn't sure he'd heard this information correctly. "They do that?" he asked Gabe.

Cooper had many interests—though, one at a time, of course—and he really did immerse himself fully in whatever the current one was, but he wasn't an outside kid. That was the best way Gabe could explain it. Cooper loved reading about things and watching online videos and collecting toys and playing with them. But he didn't have a lot of interest in the *real* versions. When he'd been into construction equipment—bulldozers and cement trucks and cranes—he read books and did coloring pages and played with miniature versions and watched a DVD called *Diggers and Dump Trucks* over and over and over. But when Gabe had taken him to a building site so he could see the equipment in action, he'd been scared and had wanted nothing to do with it all. Gabe had been disappointed. He'd arranged with the foreman to show Cooper around and had even gotten him a little hard hat. The same thing had happened with fire trucks. Gabe had taken him down to one of the local stations, and the guys had been happy to show Coop around, let him sit in the trucks, and give him a plastic firefighter hat. Cooper had buried his face in Gabe's leg and hadn't even touched one of the trucks.

Cooper was just a quiet, bookworm type of kid. He loved to learn new things, but he didn't really want to *do* new things.

So Gabe had to ask him, "Are you sure you want to do that, buddy?"

Cooper looked at his grandmother, who gave him a little nod. Then he looked at Gabe and nodded. "Yeah, I want to."

Gabe glanced at his mother, but Caroline was concentrating on her beans.

"You want to ride on a boat and go out and see real alligators?" Gabe reiterated. He was all for it. It sounded like a good time to him. He'd been on an airboat on the bayou before, and it was great. And he'd love to see Cooper getting more active with things he was into.

But suddenly Cooper was looking like he was having second thoughts. "The muscles that open an alligator's mouth are really weak," he said. "A human can hold an alligator's mouth shut. But they are *super* strong closing. Like if they close on something and don't want to let go, no way can a human can't get their jaw open."

Gabe just said, "Wow, really?" knowing that Cooper was processing everything.

Cooper nodded. "They don't usually attack humans, but they *can*. If they feel scared or have to protect their territory."

"Cooper," Gabe said. When his son looked at him, he went on. "I would *never* let anything happen to you. If we went on a boat ride, you would be totally safe."

Cooper nodded. But his mental wheels were clearly still turning.

"I think it would be really fun," Caroline said. "There are a few companies. We'd have to pick one."

Suddenly, Logan jumped with an *oomph*. Then he nodded and said, "I think it sounds really cool, and I know a guy who does those kinds of tours."

Apparently, Caroline had kicked Logan under the table on the other side. Gabe smirked, then lifted his glass of tea to hide his smile. He was going to have some bruised shins tomorrow.

"You do?" Cooper asked Logan.

"I do. His name is Sawyer. He's a great guy."

Cooper's brow furrowed, and he frowned at his plate. Then he looked at Gabe. "You think I should go?"

Gabe didn't know where Cooper's cautious side came from. It wasn't from him or Logan, that was for sure. They'd climbed trees, played ball, gotten dirty, had grass stains—hell, bloodstains—on their clothes regularly, and had even broken a couple of bones each. And Cooper's mom had been wild and fun and carefree. Gabe had first been attracted to her because she'd pulled up outside the bar on a Harley.

But Cooper didn't want to dig in the dirt or go swimming or climb up on, well, anything at all. He would jump and spin around with lightsabers or swords, depending on if he was into *Star Wars* or pirates at the time, but for months he'd resisted even getting on the tricycle Gabe had gotten him when he was three. Now he would ride his bike with Gabe in the evenings, but only when Gabe insisted, and even then he sometimes had to give a health-and-wellness lecture before Cooper would grudgingly head outside.

"Buddy," Gabe said sincerely, "you don't have to do it if you don't want to. I think it would be cool, and I'd be happy to take you, but I don't want you to be scared."

Cooper twirled his fork in his potatoes, clearly pondering. Finally, he nodded. "I'll think about it."

Gabe shot his mother a glance. She was frowning as she chewed. "Yeah, you think about it," Gabe told Cooper. "Let me know, okay? We can look up some information online later. I'll bet the companies have photos of what the tours are like. Then you can get an idea."

Cooper nodded, his frown easing a little. "Okay."

A few minutes later, Cooper had eaten all his beans and chicken and asked to be excused. Gabe knew he'd head straight for the computer and start looking at swamp-boat tour companies. Gabe gave permission and then scooted his chair back and started gathering dishes from the table.

"Gabe," Caroline said, halting him as Cooper disappeared into the living room.

He paused with a plate in each hand. "Yeah?"

"I really think the swamp-boat tour would be good for him."

Gabe frowned. "Okay. We're going to look into it."

"But he's going to see photos of people outside on boats, with life preservers on, touching alligators, and he's going to change his mind," Caroline said.

"You looked up companies already?" Gabe asked.

"I did. I wanted to know more about it before I suggested it."

Gabe appreciated that. "And the photos include the life preservers, huh?"

"They do."

That would freak Cooper out for sure. He wasn't someone who looked at stuff like that and thought, *Oh, good, they're all about safety.* He'd probably see that as, *Well, it looks like there's a pretty good chance we're going to end up on the bottom of the bayou.*

"And they touch the alligators?" Gabe asked.

Caroline nodded. "Baby ones. The photos show someone holding it and then kids petting it."

"Great," Gabe muttered. He was sure that most kids would find that exhilarating. Cooper would stare at it and try to figure out how much of his hand the baby alligator could take off in one chomp. "So I guess that's out."

"No," Caroline said firmly. "That's not what I'm saying. I'm saying that you should *definitely* take him. He needs to get out there and quit worrying about stuff so much."

"You don't think I wish he'd do that?" Gabe asked. "Don't you know how much I wish he'd get out there and get his hands dirty and try new things?"

"Then you need to encourage it," Caroline said.

Gabe sighed. "I can't make him do things that scare him."

"Yes, you can. You acknowledge that there are sometimes risks, but that you'll keep him safe and that the people who run the swamp tours know what they're doing. He's never going to get over this worry and being so damned careful about everything if *you*, the man he looks up to the most in the world, don't start pushing him."

Gabe's frown deepened. "My job is to keep him safe and make him feel secure and taken care of."

"Your job is to teach him," Caroline argued. "And yes, teaching him that he can depend on you and that you'll take care of him is important, but so is teaching him that taking risks can be worth it and what to do when things do go wrong. Because they will, and if he's never *done* anything, he won't know how to handle it."

"He's five!" Logan suddenly exclaimed. "Why would you make him do something that you know is going to freak him out? There are plenty of things that freak him out that we're *not* expecting."

Caroline and Gabe both looked at Logan with matching surprised expressions.

"You don't think he needs to be encouraged to be more . . . outgoing?" Caroline asked.

"I think we need to let Coop be Coop," Logan said.

Gabe again had the niggling thought about parenting alone versus with a team. Sure, there were things that would be easier on his own.

But what if he was wrong? Did Addison ever wonder about that? When she was making all the decisions, did she ever doubt herself? But now, looking from his mother, whom he loved and respected immensely, to his brother, who was actually saying what Gabe was thinking, he didn't know how helpful this really was. Who did he listen to?

This was why he was grateful for the support group. They were all in the same boat. He'd bring it up Thursday for sure.

And again, he thought about Addison. She didn't have a support system like he did. She didn't think she needed or wanted one. But how could she not? He really didn't get that.

Caroline sat back in her chair. "I don't know what to do with him," she said.

Gabe focused on his mother and felt his chest tighten. "What do you mean you don't know what to do with him?" he asked. Dammit, he didn't like that. Caroline was supposed to know exactly what to do. Gabe was counting on her to know.

She shook her head. "I just mean that he's nothing like either of you. You were rambunctious and probably heard 'Slow down,' 'Quiet, boys,' and 'Be careful' from me more than any other words when you were growing up."

Logan nodded. "That and 'If you end up dead, don't blame me.'"

Caroline swatted his arm, but she was smiling. "Cooper's just so different from you boys."

"So he's different," Logan said. "It's because he's smarter than we were. He knows being bitten by an alligator would suck and breaking a bone would suck and getting stitches would suck before they happen. Because he's thought about it all ahead of time. His brain works at a million miles an hour. Most kids don't think about consequences. So they go and do stupid shit and learn the hard way not to skateboard down steep hills," he said, pointing to a scar on his forehead that had come from hitting the side mirror of a pickup while skateboarding down a steep hill. "And not to jump out of trees without a soft spot to land," he said, rubbing his shin where he'd broken a bone jumping out of a tree onto hard dirt.

"Or that goading your brother and underestimating his pitching arm can have bad consequences," Gabe added, pointing at Logan's nose. That Gabe himself had broken when Logan had called him a pussy and Gabe had thrown an orange at him.

"I'll bet Cooper already knows that being hit in the face with an orange would fucking hurt," Logan said, rubbing his nose.

Caroline rolled her eyes, but she was grinning. "So you're chalking Cooper's being careful up to his being smart, not because Gabe babies him?"

"I don't baby him," Gabe said, scowling at his family members.

Caroline laughed, and Logan said, "Oh, you totally baby him."

"You just said we should let Coop be Coop," Gabe pointed out.

"Yeah, we should," Logan said. "But that's not why you baby him. If you were just letting him do his thing because it was his thing, that's fine. But you do it because *you* don't want to deal with him being scared or upset or hurt or sick."

"*What?*" Gabe demanded, setting the plates back down on the table.

Logan seemed totally unfazed. "You're the fun guy. The cuddly guy. The guy who wants to play and make him laugh and who loves to listen to him go on and on about whatever he's into now. You *hate* when there's anything negative going on."

"Well, yeah," Gabe said, putting his hands on his hips. "It's bad for me to want my kid to be happy and healthy?"

"Of course not," Logan said with a frown. "But you're phobic of anything but sunshine and rainbows. Mom deals with most of the hard stuff."

Gabe stared at his brother. Then looked at his mom. She didn't rush to deny it, but she did say, "Logan," as if warning him to stop.

"Okay, so I need to take my kid on a swamp-boat tour to help him face his fears about alligators—which, by the way, is probably a really healthy fear—to prove that I can handle the negative stuff, too?" Gabe asked.

"Being scared of the real world is not a healthy fear," Logan said.

"He's not—" But Gabe broke off. He didn't know that Cooper was exactly afraid of the real world, but he wasn't that interested in it, either. Which was fine. That was just Cooper. Probably. Wasn't it? "Whatever. I'll talk to him about the fucking alligators."

He grabbed the plates again and stomped into the kitchen.

And, unbidden: *What would Addison do?* flashed through his mind.

Fuck. That was the last thing he needed . . . to be thinking about the woman who wanted nothing to do with Cooper. And nothing to do with Gabe because of Cooper.

Shit. He had to quit thinking about her. He shouldn't care what she would do. She'd broken things off. She'd made her feelings very clear. He didn't have to like it, but it was her prerogative to not want to date a guy with a kid. And for all he knew, she was the world's worst mother anyway. But that didn't sit right the second he thought it. Because of the way she ate beignets.

Yeah, that sounded stupid even in his head. But it was true. He was basing his opinion of her parenting on how she ate beignets.

She always pulled out wet wipes and cleaned the table before she sat. She covered her lap with a napkin so that she didn't get powdered sugar on her pants. She pulled her hair back and secured it with a clip she always had in her purse so that she could lean in over the table and not get her hair in her food. But once she had those beignets in front of her, she went for it. She cleaned up afterward, but she didn't let a little powdered sugar get in the way of her enjoyment. And damn, watching her lick powdered sugar from her fingers was one of the hottest things he'd ever seen.

It was how she ate crawfish, too. And how she enjoyed the city. And how she had sex.

She was completely prepared, but she didn't shy away. She twisted and sucked crawfish, just like a native. But she always put the plastic bib on first. She used lots of sunscreen and kept her purse close so it couldn't be pickpocketed, but that didn't keep her from roaming all over New Orleans. She took it upon herself to be in charge of the condoms during sex, along with a second form of birth control, but once she rolled that baby on, she went for it.

Yeah, that was Addison Sloan. She was smart and prepared and in charge . . . but she didn't let it stop her from having a good time.

That had to be how she parented, too. Carefully permissive. She'd let Stella run free . . . as long as Addison could see her and get to her if there was a problem.

Gabe could definitely take a couple of lessons from her. Lessons in how to make his son feel secure while still exploring and trying new things.

He should call her.

Gabe scrubbed a hand over his face. He couldn't call her. For one, it would sound pathetic. "Hey, Addison, I know you don't want to date me or even fuck me anymore, but maybe you could help me be a better dad." Yeah, that would go over well. It would also sound like an excuse to see her. Which it would be. In part. Though he really would love to know how she'd handle Cooper and the alligators . . .

But no. What he needed to do was get the hell over her. Forget about her. Move on.

So, of course, he pulled out his phone and ordered a gift basket to be delivered to her office with a special invitation on the card.

Chapter Four

She would do anything for a great praline.

She wasn't proud of it. It wasn't something she wanted just anyone to know, because it could be used against her. But it was true. A fresh praline from the Magnolia Praline Company was the way to her heart.

Addison bit into one and moaned. And read the card again. "Welcome to New Orleans! Join us for our weekly meeting of the Single-Parents Support Group. This week's meeting will be on Thursday at seven p.m. at the community center on Beacon Street."

A single-parents support group? She'd never been a part of a support group before. But then again, the words *support* and *group* weren't really a part of her vocabulary. She didn't do things by committee. She didn't ask for opinions from girlfriends about her clothes, she didn't ask for input on her designs at work, and she certainly didn't ask for advice about parenting. She'd let someone else have a say in Stella's life once before. And he'd fucked everything up. So she was done with that.

She didn't even ask her parents for help.

Her parents—her father, in particular—had taught Addison and her sister from a young age all about taking care of their own business and dealing with the consequences of their actions. Addison had experienced it herself in small lessons. Like the time she'd had to write an apology note to their neighbor for picking some of her flowers. Or the time she'd had to sit and wait for an hour outside of her school because she'd been messing around with her friends and had missed her ride home. Being the CEO of the company, her father could have, of course, left immediately, but he'd waited until five o'clock to pick her up because then it could be a learning experience.

Her sister, Angela, on the other hand, had been a slower learner. Or more stubborn about learning. She'd been arrested twice—once for shoplifting and once for underage drinking—and had spent the night in jail both times before their father bailed her out. Angela had failed her freshman year of college and lost her scholarship, and their father had informed her that she would need to get a job and an apartment and would have to figure out a way to either get her degree or support herself, because she'd messed up her chance at doing it all for free.

So when Addison had gotten pregnant, she'd known that, while her parents would be there to help babysit and would come to Stella's birthday parties and would even start a college fund for her daughter, it was up to Addison to support her child and be the primary caregiver.

And that was exactly what had happened. They'd helped out with babysitting, even helped take care of her when she was sick and Addison needed to work. They'd helped pay for the swanky preschool that her father had felt was important. But not only had Addison never even considered moving in with them, they never would have offered.

Addison frowned. Where had that thought come from?

But she knew. It was Gabe. The man she couldn't stop thinking about even a week after their lunch. It didn't help that everything about the town she now lived in reminded her of him. From the balconies on the buildings she was working on to the magnolia trees all over town, everything made her think of Gabe.

But Gabe had a son. And lived with his mom, who helped raise that son. And Gabe thought that he and Addison would make the perfect couple because they were both single parents of five-year-olds.

Who had a really great time together.

And who had chemistry unlike anything she'd ever experienced before.

Yeah, yeah, okay, so on paper that sounded perfect. *Dammit.* She reached for another praline. They did have a great time together and had amazing chemistry. Minus the two kids, she'd be all over him probably.

But there was no taking the kids out of the equation. So that was that.

Still, she couldn't help wondering what Gabe's son was like. Was he a big blue-eyed charmer like his dad? He almost had to be. He didn't have a mom who might lend another perspective and balance some of that I'm-a-hell-of-a-good-time vibe that Gabe exuded. Then again, he did have his grandmother. It sounded like Gabe's mom was a constant, steady presence. And then *again*, Logan was also involved. Lord, if the kid's two main male influences were Gabe and Logan Trahan, the five-year-old probably already had girls lined up around the block.

Addison sighed and looked down at the invitation from the support group. Maybe she should check it out. She needed to make new friends. Or, at least, talk to other people with kids once in a while. Other people with kids besides Gabe Trahan. Because the less she thought about him and wondered about him—and his had-to-be-adorable son—the better.

"Hey, Addison, can I run something past you?"

Addison turned, swallowing her bite of praline before answering Elena. "Of course."

Elena took a deep breath. "Do I smell pralines?"

Addison shifted to show the basket. "Yep."

"Oh my God." Elena took the praline Addison held out. "Are these from Gabe, too?"

Ugh, even hearing his name made her chest hurt. "No. They're from a single-parents support group." She held up the invitation.

"No kidding." Elena took a bite of the maple candy and chewed. "You going to go?"

"Not sure. Maybe?"

"I could watch Stella for you."

Addison forced a smile. "Oh, that's okay. I have someone."

"I haven't seen her since you moved down here. I'd really love to have a pizza and movie night, Ad," Elena said.

Addison bit her bottom lip. She and Elena had been close in college, but when Elena had moved to Louisiana, they'd drifted apart a bit. Elena came back to New York to visit her family regularly, and they always made time for lunch and to catch up, but they weren't a part of each other's daily lives. Elena had met Stella a few times. But she'd never babysat. Addison would never have asked her. Well, even if they were a part of each other's daily lives.

"Then the three of us will have to set a date for a movie night," Addison said with a smile. "We'd love to have you over. But you're not babysitting for me. You're a friend. I'd never take advantage of that."

"It's not taking advantage if I offer," Elena told her.

"But it's . . . awkward," Addison said, unable to come up with a better word. "Don't worry, I have a lady." She moved to the other side of the desk. "What did you want to show me?"

"You have a lady?" Elena repeated, ignoring Addison's question.

"I do. She watches Stella after school."

"A stranger."

"Well, yes, but I went through a referral service. She has references and a background check and I'm paying her."

"So she has to do everything exactly your way," Elena said.

And that made Addison pause. And think. She met her friend's knowing gaze. And swallowed hard. Then she nodded. "Yeah."

"I would do everything exactly how you wanted me to," Elena told her.

"It's just complicated when it gets personal," Addison said. "I'm . . . picky. And I don't want . . ."

"To be disappointed," Elena filled in when Addison trailed off.

Addison sighed. "Yeah."

"I'm not your ex."

Addison shook her head. "I know. But I *wanted* help in the beginning. I was so overwhelmed. And who would be better than her *father*? If anyone was as dedicated as I was, it should have been him."

"Of course it should have," Elena agreed. "But he was an asshole. That doesn't mean everyone else who ever has anything to do with Stella will be."

"But it kind of means I have crappy asshole radar, doesn't it?" Addison said with a small smile. She'd admit it—she'd been burned by wanting to involve someone else in Stella's life, someone who should have loved her completely and who hadn't held up his end of the bargain. It was so much easier to just do it herself. Or to get help from people she could fire if things didn't go her way.

Elena laughed. "Well, we've all got at least one asshole who snuck past our security systems at some point." Then she gave Addison an affectionate, if slightly worried, smile. "You have to give someone else a chance at some point."

"Do I?" Addison asked. She wasn't convinced she did.

Elena sighed. "Okay, fine. But my offer stands. Anytime."

Addison relaxed slightly with that. "Okay. Thanks. And it's me, not you. You know that, right?"

"I definitely know that," Elena said with a nod.

Addison actually laughed at that. "Okay, so what did you come in here to show me?" Addison asked, hoping to steer the conversation away from the topic of how no one was good enough for her daughter. Probably even Addison.

Elena reached for another praline, but she held up the long cylindrical tube she'd brought in.

"I have a few plans for Trahan's Tavern, but I'm not sure about the front windows."

Even the mention of Gabe's last name sent a shiver of awareness through Addison. "Sure, I'm happy to take a look."

Elena unrolled the plans, and they spent the next few minutes discussing options for the front of the tavern as well as the ceiling and the inner doorways. Addison loved all the plans. Sure, she would have loved to be directly involved, but that was complicated. And Elena really was doing a beautiful job.

"When does the work start?" Addison asked as Elena returned the plans to the canister.

"Two weeks," Elena said with a smile. "We'll be working mostly in the morning so that we can avoid their busy times. We won't need to shut the tavern down entirely for a few weeks, and then we hope to be able to get it all done in a few days."

"That's great. I'm sure Gabe and Logan appreciate that."

Elena tipped her head. "He hasn't said anything about the work?"

Addison forced a smile. "Gabe and I haven't spoken since the day he was here for the initial meeting."

"Ah." Elena looked sympathetic. "I hope I didn't have anything to do with that."

"No. It was time to end things. It's easier that way."

Elena nodded. "How about we grab dinner? And maybe a couple of drinks? I'm a good listener."

Addison appreciated the gesture. "I'm sorry, I can't. I need to pick up Stella."

"Oh, right. It's so weird that you have a kid and I didn't even know," Elena said.

Addison nodded. "It does change my schedule up a bit."

"I can imagine." Elena didn't make it sound like a good thing.

"But I promise I'll always be available for client meetings and such."

"I know," Elena told her. "Just not for fun, right?" She gave Addison a smile.

Addison tried to return it but couldn't quite. "Just a different kind of fun."

"Right." Elena clearly didn't believe her.

Yeah, Addison probably needed some single-parent friends.

So, three days later, Addison was sitting with a cup of coffee in a circle of chairs with an eclectic but warm group of people who were happy to have her. Even though none of them knew who would have sent her a welcome basket of pralines.

That was odd, but Addison figured there must be a few people missing tonight. So far she'd met only nine members. There was Roxanne, a thirty-five-year-old divorcée with three kids, and Bea, a sixty-year-old who was raising her two grandsons, since her daughter had embezzled money from her employer and was now in prison for the next five years. There were also the two young girls—Lexi, who was seventeen with a three-month-old at home, and Ashley, the nineteen-year-old who had a little boy who was six months. The other two women were clearly very good friends, as they sat together, talking quietly. Dana and Lindsey were both twenty-seven, and each had two kids. Lindsey's husband was deployed to the Middle East with the army, and Dana's husband, Chad, had been with the same unit and had been killed in Iraq a year ago. And then there were the three men of the group. Caleb was thirty and was raising his sister's daughter after she and her husband had been killed in a car accident. Austin was twenty-five and had an ex-wife and partial custody of his twin girls. And Corey was forty and had lost his wife to cancer, leaving him alone with four kids.

Addison didn't know who had sent the gift basket and invitation, but she was grateful to whoever it was. She already felt optimistic about meeting these people and hearing their stories. Surely in this group there was *one* other person who wasn't supermom or -dad and didn't have it all figured out. Hell, they were in a support group, right? That had to mean they had some doubts.

When it was her turn, Addison took a breath and gave the group a smile. "Well, I've never really been a part of a group like this. I just moved here with my daughter, Stella, and we don't know many people locally. We're just getting settled, and I got the invitation to the group and thought it would be a great way to meet some new people."

Just then the door to the community center opened.

And everything suddenly made sense.

Gabe Trahan came striding into the room, big and gorgeous and acting as if he owned the place. Every member of the group greeted him enthusiastically, making it clear that this was hardly his first meeting.

And when his eyes met hers, Addison felt a flutter of butterflies in her stomach. He looked so good. And she'd missed him. God, that was stupid. She'd gone three weeks at a time without seeing him for the past six months. It had been only a little more than a week since their lunch. But she hadn't planned on seeing him again at all. That had to be why this separation had felt different.

She didn't let on how affected she was, though. She gave him a you've-got-to-be-kidding-me look. He simply grinned. Which only intensified the swooping in her stomach.

And she realized that she should have been expecting this. Gabe Trahan was not the type of guy to give up on something easily. Knowing him only a short time had already showed her that. He came off as laid-back and just out for a good time, but there was an intensity below the surface. A drive that showed in his bar . . . and the bedroom. Even in how he ate beignets. He insisted that standing in line and people watching was a part of the experience at Café du Monde, and he'd soaked it up each time. Even though he'd had hundreds of them in the past, he'd dived in as if every one was the first beignet he'd ever tasted, and he asserted that if you didn't leave with powdered sugar dusting your clothes, you hadn't done it right. He was all about getting the whole experience out of something—every last ounce of pleasure.

Why she'd thought he might let go of the idea of happily ever after between them just because she'd asked him to, she had no idea.

"Hey, everyone," Gabe greeted, scraping a chair back out of the circle and dropping into it. "Sorry I'm late."

"We have a new member," Bea told him brightly. "Addison, this is Gabe."

Addison lifted a brow at Gabe. Were they going to let everyone in on the fact that they knew each other and that he was the reason she was here?

"Hey, Addison, welcome," Gabe said. "What's your story?"

She narrowed her eyes. Okay, so no. "Got knocked up by an idiot six years ago, and now my life is peanut butter and crayons and wondering where I put my brain and if it's too early to drink. You know, the usual."

There was a beat of silence, and then Gabe grinned and the rest of the group started laughing.

"I like you," Roxanne told her.

Addison smiled, too. But the thing was . . . it was all true. And a thought occurred to her. Gabe had gotten her here. And now that she'd met everyone else, she kind of wanted to stay. But she couldn't go soft with him. She couldn't let him talk her into thinking that their being together was a good idea. She couldn't let him get too close. So she needed to show him exactly what she was like as a mother so he didn't get this fairy-tale idea going strong.

"Well, I have to be honest," she said to the group, meeting Gabe's eyes in particular, "at least with other parents who might understand. I didn't sign up for this Mom thing. I hadn't really given motherhood a thought. I was only twenty-four when I got pregnant. I had a lot of plans and dreams, and none of them included cleaning up another person's poop. I looked at moms with kids throwing tantrums at Target and pretty much thought, *Well, that's your own fault.* I had never actually thought about how I tie shoes, and certainly never thought about how to teach that skill to someone else. And I definitely never realized how damned frustrating it could be watching another human *unable* to make loops out of shoestrings. And I swear, if I never hear the words *goodnight moon* again in my life, I'll be very, very happy."

Several of the eyes in the group were wide and round. But Roxanne and Bea and Austin were all nodding.

"So I guess I need to know," Addison said, looking around the circle but again landing on Gabe, "is this the kind of group where I can say that stuff, or is it the kind of group where we only talk about how amazing our kids are and how great we're doing?"

No one said anything for a second. Then Caleb said, "I hate *The Very Hungry Caterpillar*." Everyone looked over at him, and he shrugged. "I know that's probably a huge insult to all children's literature or something, but I hid the book last week for a few days because I just couldn't read it again."

"I would really love for someone to explain to me why you can put cheese on a burger and it's fine, but if you put hamburger in macaroni and cheese, suddenly the world is ending," Austin spoke up.

"I didn't even feed my kids dinner for two days last week," Roxanne said, sitting back with her arms crossed. She looked around the circle. "Oh, come on, they're fourteen, twelve, and ten. There was food in the house. I just didn't make it. They had to eat sandwiches and canned soup. Big deal. But they were being horrible brats about the food I was making, so I decided to make them think about what I do for them a little bit."

"But they're our kids," Dana interjected. "We're *supposed* to do stuff for them, right? And yes, they take us for granted, but that's just kind of the way it is, isn't it?"

Roxanne nodded. "Sure. I mean, of course we're supposed to do stuff for them. But I think it's perfectly fine to teach them to be *thankful* for it. I don't need praise and glory all the time, but I also don't need to get shit from them when I've been working all day and then rush home to make dinner for them." She shrugged. "And mine are older than yours. I don't know if you can expect a four-year-old to totally understand, but a fourteen-year-old? Oh yeah, he can learn to be a little appreciative."

"I agree," Bea said. "We have to teach them to consider other people's feelings, and that should include ours."

"I don't know," Lindsey said from beside Dana. "We're their *parents*. I mean, even if they don't say *please* and *thank you*, we still have to take care of them." She looked over at Addison. "But I *did* sign up for this, so maybe that's why it's different."

Oh boy, so Addison hadn't made a friend in Lindsey. She opened her mouth, but Roxanne got there first.

The other woman sat forward in her chair. "Well, I signed up for it, too. In fact, it took us more than a year to get pregnant with our third. But that doesn't mean that I have to like my kids every second of every day or that I never think they're brats. I love them, completely. And I'll protect them from everything—including turning into little assholes."

Addison felt her eyes widen, and she realized that everyone else in the group seemed equally surprised. Okay, so maybe this group wasn't about blatant honesty and they did focus more on the positive and encouraging. And maybe she'd just broken it.

But a moment later, Caleb said, "I cut Shay's hair the other day because I can't, no matter what I do, figure out how to do a good braid or ponytail. And every time I try, she gets mad because it looks terrible, and she cries for an hour. After I cut it, she cried for six hours. But I'm not even sorry."

Roxanne gave him a grin, and even Lindsey laughed lightly at that.

Lexi, one of the teens, said, "I'll teach you how to braid."

Caleb gave her a half smile. "You braiding her hair when you babysat was what started the whole thing."

Lexi laughed. "Sorry. Tell you what, you have me babysit this weekend, and I'll convince her that her short hair is super cute and awesome."

Caleb's smile stretched, and he nodded. "Deal."

Something squeezed in Addison's chest, and because she couldn't seem to help it, she looked across the circle at Gabe. Who was watching her. With a smile. He gave her a single nod that somehow she knew meant "Everything's okay." How she knew that's what it meant, she couldn't say, and how he knew that she'd been worried that things were not okay, she didn't know, but she strongly felt that momentary connection with him.

"Okay, so in summary," Roxanne said, allowing Addison to tear her eyes from Gabe and focus on the other woman, "all kids can be jerks sometimes, and we love them anyway, and we have to keep feeding them and brushing their hair, but we don't have to always put up with their shit. And we don't have to be sorry when we don't."

"Amen," Bea said.

"Amen," Austin agreed with a smile.

Lindsey and Dana didn't add their agreement, but they also didn't argue.

"Okay, what else?" Corey asked the group. "Anyone have anything they want to talk about?"

Gabe shifted forward on his chair, resting his forearms on his thighs. "I do."

Everyone immediately focused on him, and Addison almost rolled her eyes. It was very obvious that everyone here loved Gabe.

"Great. What's going on?" Corey asked.

"Well, as you know, there's this woman I've been seeing."

What? Addison felt her stomach flip. He was going to talk about *her?* Right now? In front of her? And "as you know" indicated he'd already talked about her with this group. Oh boy. She bit her bottom lip and vowed to just stay quiet and not react to whatever was about to come. But this was low. Really low.

"The woman from New York?" Corey asked.

They even knew where she was from? Addison tried to remember if she'd mentioned where she'd moved from when she'd introduced herself.

"Yep," Gabe confirmed.

"You always light up when you talk about her," Bea said with a smile. "I know you really like her. Are things going well?"

If Gabe had scripted this and given these people exactly the right words to say to hit Addison directly in the chest, those would have been them. He'd not only talked about her but *lit up* when he did? They could tell he really liked her? Sure, that was going to be easy to ignore. Clearly, Addison needed to stop coming to this group immediately.

Gabe nodded. "I do really like her."

He hadn't looked directly at her yet, and Addison was grateful for that. "And now she's moved here."

"Oh, honey, that's great," Bea said enthusiastically. "I'm so happy for you."

Gabe gave her a smile that was sincerely affectionate, and Addison had to swallow hard. He was such a great guy. *Dammit.*

"Well, it's kind of a problem, actually," Gabe told her.

"Come on, don't be that guy," Austin said. "Just let it get serious. Give it a try. What's the worst that can happen?"

Caleb and Corey both nodded their agreement.

"Well, thanks for automatically assuming *I'm* the one who's commitment phobic," Gabe said drily.

Addison frowned. *She* wasn't commitment phobic, if that's what he was insinuating. Which, of course, he was. She was just having-another-kid phobic. Okay, so maybe that was a little commitment phobic.

Caleb gave a short laugh. "Dude, you *are* commitment phobic. That's not an assumption."

Addition looked at Caleb. Okay, *that* was interesting. Not only that Gabe didn't commit easily but that it was a well-known fact. Because the guy at lunch talking about getting their kids together and kind of joking about long engagements sure as hell hadn't seemed allergic to getting serious. Quite the opposite.

"Yeah, okay, maybe I have been. But not now. Not with her."

Her heart fluttering, Addison looked back at Gabe to find him staring right at her.

"Well, good for you," Roxanne said. "So what's the problem?"

"Her," he said, still looking at Addison. "She's intimidated by the fact that I have a kid."

"She's not *intimidated*," Addison blurted out. Then realized that she'd just made a potentially huge mistake. She glanced around. "I mean, are you sure that's what she's feeling? Is that what she *said*?" Because it was definitely not what she'd said. "You're assuming she's scared of the idea of a kid, but maybe that's not really it." She would not label her feelings as scared, exactly. *Exhausted*, *stressed*, and *overwhelmed* were much better descriptors.

"Okay, maybe that's not the right word," Gabe conceded. "But she broke things off when she found out about Cooper."

"Oh man," Roxanne said sympathetically.

"Wow. That sucks," Austin agreed.

"Well, honey, Cooper is a part of your life, and if she feels that way, you're better off," Bea said gently.

Addison nodded. Yeah, he was better off without her. But damn, her chest suddenly felt tight.

"Maybe," Gabe said with a slow nod. "I mean, I get that's how it seems. But I can't stop thinking about her."

His eyes were on Addison's again, and she was having trouble swallowing.

"I want to be with her. And I just want her to give Cooper a chance."

"Maybe you're taking it too personally," Addison said, again before thinking about the fact that she should just stop talking.

Gabe sat up straight, his expression one of disbelief. "I'm taking it too *personally* that the woman I've been dating—"

"You've seen her once a month for six months. That's like, what, twelve days?" Addison interrupted. "You consider that dating?"

Everyone else stayed quiet. Addison didn't look around to see their expressions—because she couldn't stop looking at Gabe. And, interestingly, at the moment she didn't care what everyone else thought of this.

"We've spent a lot of time in bed," Gabe said, his gaze intense. "*A lot* of time. But we've also gone out and had fun and laughed and talked. If it had only been sex, I might have agreed with you. But it was more than that."

He emphasized the word *more*, and Addison felt the butterflies take another swoop around her stomach. She cleared her throat. "But if she didn't even know about Cooper until recently, how much did you *really* talk? How much do you really know about her?"

"You *just* told her about Cooper?" Caleb asked.

But Gabe ignored him. He answered Addison instead. "I was thinking about that, actually," he said. "About how we didn't share a lot of personal details. But the thing is—I do know her."

He said it with confidence, and Addison had to admit she was curious about how he thought he knew her.

"She's super organized," Gabe went on. "She always has wet wipes and lip balm and pens and Band-Aids and stuff in her purse. But she also loves to be surprised. When I tell her I thought of a new place to take her and won't give her any details until we get there, she gets this look in her eyes that makes me want to give her surprises every day forever. It's like she has to be so on top of things and organized all the time that when she has the chance to let someone else come up with a plan, she's all in."

Addison felt the air *whoosh* out of her lungs, and she stared at him. Because that was exactly how she felt when she was with him.

"But she loves to surprise me, too," he went on. "Sometimes it's with sexy lingerie or edible body lotion."

His eyes heated, and Addison could feel it even across the few feet that separated them. Her body responded to it, too. As always. In spite of the group of people gathered around them.

"But sometimes it's with food from New York that she knows I've never had, or an I LOVE NY shirt just because it made her laugh to think of me wearing it, or it's by getting up and singing karaoke in a bar we happen to be passing."

Addison knew she shouldn't be staring at him. If anyone in the group was even the least bit insightful, they would be able to figure out that there was something going on with Gabe and her. But she couldn't look away.

"And I think she likes doing all of that because she doesn't feel like she can be spontaneous in her regular life. She has to be on and prepared and in charge all the time. But with me, she can let down a little bit, and she's discovered how fun it can be to make another person smile just for the sake of making them smile. Because you care about them. Because, yeah, the edible body lotion might just seem like it's about sex, but it happened to be my favorite flavor. Which she discovered by spending time with me outside of the bedroom. And the karaoke might just seem like a fun thing to do on a whim, but she chose my favorite song, which she knew because I told her in passing when we heard it on the radio. But she remembered. And it was almost like she wanted me to think of her when I hear it now."

Gabe finally stopped and took a deep breath.

"So I guess what I'm saying is that I think she cares about me and what's going on with us more than she's admitting, even to herself, and yeah, I think I know her. I know that she has a very put-together side that keeps things running in her life, but that she likes to let go of it a little from time to time and that she feels like she can do that with me. And I wish she'd trust me that just because Cooper might not be something she was expecting, it could turn out to be like one of those surprise dates I take her on—fun and sweet and something that would bring us closer together."

Addison had absolutely no idea what to say to all of that. None. She couldn't even make her mouth open. But her thoughts were spinning, and her heart was pounding, and she . . . wanted to hug him.

"Well, holy crap." Dana finally broke the silence.

"Right?" Lindsey asked her. She looked at Gabe. "So you need to tell *her* that."

"Definitely," Ashley agreed before Gabe could say anything.

"And you need to send her a recording of you singing that song," Roxanne told him.

"And some of that edible body lotion," Bea added. "For sure."

"Yeah, where do you get that?" Austin asked. "Asking for a friend."

They all laughed.

"Not sure, but I'll ask her," Gabe said, again looking directly at Addison.

The group continued to pepper Gabe with ideas about how to set about getting the woman back.

Getting *her* back.

Addison sucked in a deep breath.

Holy crap, indeed.

◆ ◆ ◆

One of the women standing by the coffeepot had a penchant for peach-flavored edible body lotion, looked amazing in purple thongs, and had a spot on her right ankle that, when sucked on, resulted in the most delicious moaning sound he'd ever heard.

And she was now avoiding eye contact with him, pretending they'd just met and that she really had nothing to say to him.

The group was taking their usual fifteen-minute break in the middle of the two-hour meeting, and Addison was chatting with Roxanne as if she hadn't had his cock in her mouth just a week and four days ago.

After he finished a brief conversation with Corey, Gabe headed straight for her. He knew that she saw him coming in her peripheral vision, because her spine stiffened and the smile she was giving Roxanne wobbled. Just for a microsecond. But he saw it.

He hadn't intended to talk about her to the group tonight. Certainly not with her sitting right there. He hadn't even known she'd show up for sure.

But she had. And the second he'd seen her, his heart had slammed against his rib cage, and he'd lost his cool. Again. Not on the outside but definitely on the inside. No woman, no *person*, had ever shaken him like this one.

And there was no way she was going to stand there and drink coffee as if they were strangers and she didn't care about the things he'd just spilled.

Roxanne moved off as Gabe approached. He had no idea if that was coincidental or if Roxanne sensed he wanted a moment with Addison, but he was grateful either way. He moved in behind her and reached around her for a cup, brushing his body against hers.

"Pink thong or pink panties?" he asked, for her ears only.

She spun quickly to face him. *"What?"*

"You always match your underwear with your skirts."

She stared up at him.

"You wore a tiny cherry-red thong with your red skirt, and a black thong with your black skirt, and blue bikini panties with your blue skirt. Today your skirt is pink. I'm just wondering if it's a thong or panties."

She seemed to be searching his eyes. "You remember what skirts and underwear I've worn every time I've been here?"

"I remember a lot of things, Ad," he said gruffly.

"Granny panties," she finally said. "White. Cotton. That's what I'm wearing today."

He could tell she was lying. "Doesn't matter. Still want to rip them off you."

Her cheeks flushed. "We're going to talk about this kind of stuff *here?*"

"Yep. Anywhere, anytime I get a chance to remind you about how things are between us."

"So one more reason not to come back to another meeting," she said, crossing her arms while holding her coffee cup in one hand. It was a defensive stance. One she'd never used with him prior to finding out about Cooper. Because she'd never felt defensive or like she had to protect herself.

Gabe's gut tightened, but he worked on staying calm. He reached past her for a packet of sugar, just for an excuse to brush against her again. "You're not going to quit coming," he said as he dumped the sugar into his cup and stirred.

"Oh?"

He took a sip and shook his head, watching her the whole time. "You've been doing this all on your own for so long, but now you've gotten a glimpse at what it can be like to have people to share it with. You'll come back."

He really hoped that she would, anyway. Yes, he wanted to see her, and this seemed one of the few ways to make that happen right now. But he really did think she could use the group. The people here were an interesting mix of backgrounds and ages and situations, but they were bonded by the crazy parenting ride they were all on, and it was rare that anyone missed a meeting.

"I don't know," she said. "Seems like the group spends an awful lot of time talking about *you* and your personal issues."

He felt his mouth curl. "Not always. But yeah, this woman has me really knotted up."

"And I thought this was a *parenting* group. Do you often use this group to talk about your women?" she asked with a frown.

"It's a *single* parenting group. Dating and meeting people and having relationships is a big part of being single, right? So yeah, we talk about all of that from time to time. Especially when it's something directly impacting the kids. Like this woman not wanting to meet Cooper."

Addison lifted her chin. "She sounds like a heartless bitch. You should just forget about her."

Gabe shook his head. "Wish it were that easy. But you should see the way she eats beignets."

Her eyes widened, and she seemed to swallow hard. "Beignets? You're basing your impression of her character on how she eats beignets?"

He nodded. "I know it sounds weird, but I think there's something to my theory."

She pulled in a breath and shook her head. "Yeah, that does sound weird." She started to move around him, presumably to end their conversation, but Gabe caught her elbow.

"Are you more mad that I got you here with pralines—and knew that would work—or that I talked about how I feel about you to the group and made you feel a bunch of things you don't want to face?"

She sighed and looked up at him. "Do you still have a son?"

He gave her an eye roll and a nod.

"Then it doesn't matter how I feel." She pulled her arm free and headed back for her chair.

Gabe watched her go, his heart squeezing with every step she took away from him.

"Ah, so the woman you're in love with is Addison."

Gabe looked over at Bea, who had come up on his side without him noticing. He sighed. "That obvious?"

She laughed. "Um, yes."

"I don't know if I'm in love. But yes, Addison is the woman I've been—was—seeing."

"Well, you *are* in love," Bea informed him.

Gabe didn't argue. It wasn't like the notion hadn't occurred to him. But since he'd never been in love before, and the woman in question wanted nothing to do with any of it anyway, he'd been ignoring it, for the most part.

"And she's a mom," Bea added. "I can see why you're frustrated with her not wanting to meet Cooper."

Gabe nodded. "Any advice?"

Bea glanced in Addison's direction. "Keep after her," she said. "You might have to make her face whatever she's afraid of."

Gabe thought about that. Then he said to Bea, "Cooper is fascinated with alligators. I'm debating about taking him on a swamp-boat tour. He wants to, but he's also nervous about the idea. It's like he wants to know *about* alligators—the cool stuff, the interesting stuff, the fun stuff—but he wants nothing to do with the real-life, possibly dangerous stuff. My mom thinks I should just make him go. Logan thinks I should just leave him alone. What do you think?"

Bea gave him a smile. "Tell you what, ask the group. I'll give you my answer in front of everyone."

Gabe frowned but nodded. "Okay."

Bea went back to her chair, and Gabe rejoined the circle as well, and for the second hour, everyone brought up a parenting challenge they were facing. They covered everything from teething for Ashley to rules for borrowing the car for one of Bea's grandsons. Frustratingly, Addison didn't share much about Stella. Just that she was excited about her new house and room, but that she was missing New York as well. Gabe found himself dying to know more. He wanted to ask all about Stella: What was her favorite color? Did she like sports or music or books or all of the above? What was their morning routine like? But that was all way too much. Not only would it completely scare Addison off, but it would raise eyebrows around the circle. And Caleb and Austin, at least, wouldn't hesitate to corner him later with a *What the hell, man?* But speaking of being scared, Gabe really wanted to hear Bea's advice to him about Cooper and the alligators. As he had when he'd first asked her, he sensed that there was something applicable to Addison in there somewhere.

So, when they got to Gabe, he told them about Cooper's new interest and his hesitation about the swamp boats. He told them his mom's and brother's feelings on the subject and asked what they all thought.

The group was pretty well split on the whole push-him-to-try-something-new versus the you-shouldn't-make-him-do-it-if-he-doesn't-want-to thing. And Addison didn't give an opinion at all.

"But I think he does want to do it," Gabe said, catching Addison's eye. Just like he really thought Addison *wanted* to have a relationship. But the reality of it was unknown and a little scary. "So at what point do I trust that I know him and want what's best for him and will keep anything horrible from happening and push him to let me prove it?"

Yep, there was definitely a secondary meaning to his words. He knew her. He wanted what was best for her. And he definitely wanted to prove to her that he wouldn't let anything horrible happen.

And he thought maybe Addison picked up on all that.

"Well, I have a thought," Bea finally said. "Nearly every situation in life has a positive side and a negative side. Staying home and just reading about alligators will keep his shoes dry and clean and all his fingers intact, but he'll also never know what it's like to touch an alligator. And until he actually touches one, he won't know if he likes it or not."

Gabe looked at Addison. Yeah, not getting involved with him and Cooper would keep her heart intact and her life clean, but there was a lot she was going to miss, too.

Finally, Addison spoke. "You don't think that a person, even a little boy, can know that he *doesn't* want to do something without doing it first and having a bad experience? We can't just sometimes *know* that something doesn't fit us?"

Bea gave her a soft smile. "I think that the chance of doing something you don't think you want to do and having it turn out wonderful is worth taking. And I think even a few amazing moments that touch our hearts can overpower any fear."

Addison had an almost melancholy look on her face. "Being afraid is a protective instinct. It keeps us safe."

"Sometimes," Bea agreed. "But while a fire can burn you, it's also the best way to make toasted marshmallows. And you have to get pretty close to the flames to get the sweetness."

Addison's face relaxed, and she laughed lightly. And Gabe's gut clenched with want.

And he suddenly realized that even if she didn't like touching the metaphorical alligator in the end, he was going to make sure she at least gave it a try.

Chapter Five

"Hey, Stell Bell?" Addison asked two nights later.

"Yeah, Mommy?"

Stella was on her stomach on the living room floor, drawing with her markers, while Addison sat on the couch reading about—much to her chagrin—alligators.

"Did you know that alligators breathe like birds?"

Her nose scrunched in confusion, Stella looked up. "What does that mean?"

"They don't breathe like other animals—air in and out from the same tubes—they breathe like birds. The air goes in one way and out another," Addison told her. That was pretty interesting, she thought. "Kind of neat, right?"

Stella gave her a funny look. "I guess."

Okay, so maybe she'd picked the wrong fact. Though she couldn't help but wonder what Cooper would think of the breathing thing. "They lay eggs like birds, too," she told Stella. "But they can lay thirty to fifty at a time."

"Okay, Mommy," Stella said, and went back to her drawing.

All right, so alligators weren't really Stella's thing. But . . . "We should go on a swamp-boat tour," Addison said nonchalantly.

"What's a swamp boat?" Stella asked, looking up.

Yeah, there was something about the word *swamp* that elicited all sorts of images. Maybe it wasn't the sexiest thing, but there was something intriguing about the bayou for Addison. And Stella was all about things that went fast. Like boats. "Come here, I'll show you," she said, holding up her phone.

Stella scrambled up beside her, and Addison shifted to make room. So rarely did Stella sit on her lap or up against her, Addison actually stopped for a moment before wrapping her arm around her daughter. Stella just wasn't a cuddler, and Addison didn't want to scare her off. Looking into the big blue eyes that Stella had inherited from her father—but that made Addison think of another man altogether with a thump in her heart that startled her—Addison wondered if she'd turned her daughter off cuddling. Addison had never been big on physical displays of affection, but she hated the idea that maybe she'd somehow given Stella the idea that she didn't want to hug and cuddle her. But Stella snuggled in close, and Addison took a breath. She was overreacting. After spending time with the single-parents group, she'd realized that there were all kinds of styles, and they were all good when they came from a place of love. Hers just wasn't the warm, fuzzy style. Her parents hadn't been warm and fuzzy, either. Addison saw herself as more of a teacher and a guide. She taught Stella good choices by talking and doing and by example. She comforted Stella when she was hurt or scared or sick, but Addison also tried to explain why something hurt or what was going on in Stella's body when she was sick. That way she'd know that it would eventually go away and that it was normal. And when Stella was scared—as she was of storms—they talked about what made a storm and why thunder was loud and how to be safe, with the hopes that taking some of the mystery out of things would make them easier to handle.

It didn't always work, but Addison felt it was harder to be scared of something that you understood completely.

And that thought sent her mind spinning to Gabe.

Again.

The entire reason she was looking up facts about alligators was because he'd said Cooper was newly obsessed with them. That had gotten her curious. What was so fascinating about alligators anyway? And if he knew all about them, didn't that help with the fear factor?

But she couldn't deny that when he'd been talking about how Cooper was interested in the *idea* of alligators but nervous about meeting one in person, Addison couldn't help but think that Gabe could have been talking about *her* and relationships.

The idea of a relationship with Gabe was definitely fascinating, but facing the real thing was more than nerve-racking.

So she thought maybe approaching the relationship the way she approached scary things with Stella might be smart. Learn all she could, then break it down into smaller, more easily understandable parts and make it less intimidating. But learning about Gabe definitely meant learning about Cooper. And the only thing she really knew about Cooper was his alligator fascination.

So she was reading about gators. As if knowing how alligators breathed and laid eggs would make being with Gabe less intimidating.

Her stomach flipped at the idea of really being with Gabe, and she wondered if she was just crazy. Everything she'd told Gabe was true— she did not want any more kids, and she didn't want a co-parent, not to mention a husband, and she didn't want Stella getting attached to someone who wasn't going to be around long. She'd always thought she might date again when Stella was older, maybe a teenager, and could understand that the relationships were just about companionship and fun and wouldn't start automatically thinking about dads and brothers and sisters. But maybe at her age now, it would be easier.

Five-year-olds didn't overanalyze everything. Just because Addison and Gabe might spend some time together, it didn't mean Stella would automatically assume Gabe was moving in or anything. Stella didn't really remember her dad being around. She had vague memories of some of the things they'd done together—the zoo, a Christmas with a stuffed teddy bear bigger than Stella, things like that—but she didn't really remember *him*. And she'd never asked about not having a dad or if she would ever have one. She'd also never mentioned wanting siblings. Addison had always been surprised by that, considering Stella went to day care and saw other kids with families. But she'd also been relieved and not about to bring it up if Stella wasn't asking.

So yeah, maybe Addison could meet the illustrious Cooper and satisfy that curiosity. And she could let Gabe meet Stella, since he seemed to think that was very important. And then they could just . . . kiss some more. Because she *really* freaking missed the kissing. It was strange, actually. She missed all of it—the sex, the laughter, the beignets. But if she had to pick one thing to do again, even if it was just once, it would be the kissing.

As her thoughts wandered, she and Stella paged through photos and information about airboats and swamp tours. They got to a page for the Boys of the Bayou tour company, and Stella was sold. The company took groups of all sizes out onto the bayou to see alligators and all the other wildlife and plants that made it a unique and captivating place. They had daytime tours, a sunset tour, a booze cruise, and even special packages for bachelor and bachelorette parties. And, most important to Stella, they had photos of people holding baby alligators, and tour guides feeding adult alligators in the swamp itself.

Stella might not care how they breathed, but she was all about holding a baby gator and watching one eat a huge chunk of raw chicken in person.

"Can we go? Please? Please?" Stella asked, getting up on her knees and facing Addison with a look that Addison was sure meant "I'm going to die if I don't meet an alligator."

Stella was gorgeous. Her big blue eyes like her dad's, her dark hair like Addison's, the curls that came from who knew where in the family tree, and the sweet smile all combined into a beautiful picture. But it was the light that seemed to come from within her, the enthusiasm for life, and the fearless spirit, that really made her dazzling.

On impulse, Addison hugged her close. "I think we can," she said. "It sounds like fun." She had to admit this was not her kind of thing. She didn't camp and hike and boat. She liked to walk outdoors if the ground under her was paved and she could stop every so often and shop. Or eat. Or both. But for Stella, she'd do anything.

"You're the best mom ever!" Stella declared, giving her a big kiss on the cheek before vaulting off the couch and running back over to her art supplies. "I'm going to draw airboats and alligators!"

Addison grinned. She did love Stella's exuberance and try-anything attitude. There were so many things Addison had done that she never would have otherwise because of Stella's enthusiasm and Addison's desire to give her daughter wonderful experiences. They'd run through the sprinklers in the park just because the sprinklers had been on and it sounded fun. Another day, they'd found a lost puppy and had taken it to a shelter, then ended up volunteering at the shelter once a month, playing with the animals. Once, walking by a fire station, Stella had asked if she could sit in one of the trucks. Addison had gone in and asked, and five minutes later, Stella was on a tour of the station, had a plastic firefighter hat, and had, indeed, sat in a fire truck. And Addison had sat in that fire truck as well. And enjoyed every second.

And Stella was only five. Addison was equally excited and dreading the things Stella would talk her into in the years to come.

And, as she watched Stella color in a not-too-bad-for-a-five-year-old alligator, despite her best effort *not* to, Addison wondered if Cooper liked to draw and if he had a puppy and if he'd ever sat in a fire truck.

◆ ◆ ◆

"Stella was terrible about going to bed and staying there," Addison said.

It was her third meeting with the group, and she'd quickly gotten comfortable talking and sharing. No one judged, and everyone had struggles with parenting. It was two hours that Addison very much looked forward to already. She'd booked a babysitter—much to Elena's chagrin—for Thursday nights for the next two months. And it was only 50 percent about getting to see Gabe. Okay, 60 percent. It was hard seeing him and not wishing they could go to Café du Monde . . . or back to the apartment over the bar. But she did love the moments when he'd come up behind her and say something sexy that no one else could hear, and the looks he gave her from where he always sat directly across the circle from her.

"So I came up with a system," she went on. "I put a clear glass jar in her room by her bed. After I'd tucked her in and we had bedtime stories done and drinks of water and everything else done, I'd put five pennies in the jar. Every time she came out of her room, she had to bring me a penny. At the end of the week, she could spend the pennies she had left on candy and gum and stickers and little toys at the pharmacy on the corner. So, the fewer times she got out of bed, the more money she had at the end of the week."

Caleb gave her a huge grin. "That is a fantastic idea. I really think Shay would go for that."

Addison smiled back. "No problem."

"I have a couple of other things maybe I could ask you about sometime," Caleb added.

"Sure."

"No." The single word from Gabe was delivered low and firm. Everyone swiveled to look at him, but his eyes were locked on Caleb.

"No?" Roxanne asked. "What's no?"

"Caleb knows," Gabe said.

Caleb nodded with a grin. "I sure do."

Addison rolled her eyes. Everyone knew. Gabe was telling Caleb to back off. And Addison knew that should annoy her. She should probably flirt back with Caleb a little just to irritate Gabe and show him that he wasn't in charge here. But it didn't annoy her. It made her feel warm. No, that wasn't true at all. It made her feel *hot*. She loved the idea that Gabe might be possessive of her, and *that* was the single most ridiculous, not-liberated, unfair thing she could have come up with. It wasn't fair for her to like him having feelings for her that she kept telling him he needed to not have.

"Okay, so does anyone else have any bedtime tips?" Bea asked, clearly trying to move things off Gabe's little power play.

"Well, I know everyone frowns on it, but about three nights out of seven, I give in and let the girls fall asleep in my bed," Austin said.

Dana shook her head. "I don't think that's a bad thing. As my mom said, they're not going to go to college unable to sleep in their own bed. If it makes them feel secure and sleep better, I think it's okay."

"How many here let their kids sleep in their beds sometimes?" Bea asked.

About half of the hands went up, including Gabe's. He gave Addison a questioning look, and she shook her head. She would sometimes lie down in Stella's bed with her, but Stella didn't sleep with Addison.

They'd been doing that a lot—sharing looks with one another that communicated little bits of information and details about their kids and parenting. And, she had to admit, she was soaking it up. She told herself that it was about learning things in an effort to make the idea of Cooper less intimidating. Or so she told herself.

Truthfully, it was more that she was very curious about Gabe as a father.

He was downright sexy as a bartender. Seeing him moving behind the bar that was clearly a second home, joking with his brother, laughing with his regulars, charming the newcomers had, she realized in retrospect, told her a lot about him. He was clearly an extrovert who loved his family and took pride in his work.

He was also incredible as a lover. He was hot and sweet at the same time, always making sure that she was totally into whatever they were doing, very verbal about how she made him feel, and full of words and looks and touches that made her feel like the most adored woman on the planet.

Interestingly, he was the same way with her outside the bedroom. He always had a hand on her. Whether he was holding her hand, resting a hand on her lower back, or putting an arm around her shoulders, he made her feel safe and cherished. And when he listened to her talk and made her laugh and told her she was beautiful, it was with full sincerity and even affection.

And she hadn't realized any of that until she hadn't had it anymore.

And it definitely made her want to see him as a dad. Because she was sure that the attentive, affectionate, fun-loving, protective, proud, and sweet Gabe was strong when he was with Cooper. And she was equally sure that she would find all of that incredibly appealing . . . and irresistible.

She was so screwed.

Gabe hadn't even pushed the idea of getting together or introducing the kids again. He hadn't asked her out. He hadn't invited her to his place for a quickie. He hadn't sent her flowers or pralines.

And yet she wanted to meet his son.

She even wanted him to meet Stella. Because what mother wouldn't want her daughter to get to know a man who could make her feel cherished and protected, who would make her laugh and pay attention to her favorite things?

Gabe was, no doubt, an amazing father, and as crazy as it was, *that* was what was tempting her about him.

Well, that and everything else she knew about him. And the kissing. *God*, she missed the kissing.

The group took a break ten minutes later, and it was Addison who approached Gabe this time.

"Does Caleb know that Lexi has a crush on him?" Addison asked as she joined him at the cookie table.

Gabe looked down at her with a grin. She wasn't sure if it was because of her question or because she'd initiated the one-on-one conversation, but she loved it anyway.

"He does. Well, we've told him. He's in denial about it."

"Yikes," Addison said. "It's pretty obvious. And he's what, thirteen years older than her?"

Gabe nodded, biting into a sugar cookie. "She babysits for him, so he tries to just ignore all of that and hope it's going to go away."

"And she's only seventeen."

Gabe nodded as he chewed. "Yeah. It's a little uncomfortable, for sure. He is really careful around her. But she's also amazing with Shay and is someone he knows and trusts. It's so hard to choose people to take care of your kids. Plus, Caleb likes to think he's helping her out by paying her, but also by feeding her when she's there and giving her hand-me-downs for her baby, Jack. Some of the clothes work, but also toys and car seats and stuff like that."

"I thought Lexi lives with her mom? Does she help out?"

"She does, but she's a single mom, too. Young. I think she had Lex when she was only eighteen. So she's working and stuff. Obviously, any help they can get is good, right?"

Addison nodded, feeling her heart warm. These people were something. She already found herself eager for the meeting each week and to find out how things were going at Bea's new part-time job and what was going on with the woman Corey was seeing and to hear how Austin's girls' first dance recital went. She was getting invested. *Damn Gabe Trahan.*

And yeah, Gabe Trahan was definitely a part of the appeal here. It was just such a great excuse to see him without making it about anything more.

Except that she wanted to make it into something more.

Fuck.

"So you *are* aware that Caleb is a dad?" Gabe asked, propping a hip against the table and facing her fully. "I mean, he's raising his niece, but he, for all intents and purposes, has a kid."

Addison bit off a piece of cookie and gave him a no-shit look. "Yes, I am aware of that."

"So this whole thing about dating him . . . that doesn't really make sense, right? Because you're not interested in guys with kids."

She lifted a brow. Yeah, dammit, she liked this possessive Gabe. That was complicated. "I'm not dating him."

"You're flirting with him."

"I'm giving him advice in the context of a single-parent support group."

"And smiling at him."

"I'm not supposed to smile at anyone here?"

"No, that's ridiculous," Gabe said.

Addison rolled her eyes.

"Just don't smile at Caleb or Austin." Gabe paused. "Or Corey. Just in case."

"Just in case of what?"

"He breaks up with Melissa. Or realizes that you're hotter and sassier than Melissa."

Addison couldn't help but be amused. "You've met Melissa?"

"No."

"Then how do you know how we compare?"

He braced his hand on the table and leaned closer. "Because you're hotter and sassier than all other women."

She laughed. "Well, that is absolutely not true."

"To me it is."

So cheesy. Yet that made her go a little soft in spite of herself. She'd missed him, and he hadn't been pressing her to give a relationship a chance, which was what she'd thought she'd wanted. But when he'd honored her wishes, she'd started wishing he'd push, just a little. She and Gabe had been hotter than hell together. They'd said all kinds of dirty, fun, naughty things to each other. But they hadn't really been sweet and romantic. Not verbally, anyway. His buying her a rose from a street vendor had been sweet and romantic. She supposed bringing him the I Love NY shirt had been sweet. And hell, just the way he touched her and looked at her had been sweet and romantic, she now realized.

"Then maybe I should stop smiling at *you*," she said softly.

He reached up and tucked a strand of hair behind her ear. "No. Anything but that."

Lord, Gabe had melted her panties with a look, he'd made her feel like the sexiest woman in the world with a look, he'd told her *I'd like to bend you over this table right now* with just a look. But the look in his eyes now . . . that one was downright dangerous. Because it was filled with affection and possessiveness and a desire that seemed so much more than sexual.

"Okay, everybody! Let's talk about the family get-together this month!" Bea called, saving Addison from responding to all of that *stuff* from Gabe.

Which was great, because she was pretty sure her response would be something along the lines of *Take me now and never let me go.* Those last four words being the problem, of course.

She swallowed and turned away, somehow making her way back to her chair.

"We were thinking that this time it might be fun to have a family game night," Bea said. "We can choose a variety of games and have multiple tables going. Some of the games will work great for a mix of age groups, or we can pair some of the older kids with the younger, or we can do teams. But I think there's a way to make it fun for everyone."

Addison leaned over to Caleb. "What's going on?"

"Once a month our meeting involves the kids, too," he explained. "We all get together and have a potluck and get a chance to know the kids we all talk about all the time."

Oh . . . crap.

Or maybe it was good. She would now have the chance to meet Cooper, but without admitting to Gabe that she *wanted* to meet Cooper. Because that might be too much to confess right now. Before she actually met the kid. Or figured out if she was just horny and into all things Gabe or if she really did want to meet Cooper.

What if the moment she saw him, she was reminded that one child was more than enough and that she wasn't sure she was always doing a bang-up job with the one she had? Should she be letting Stella sleep in her bed once in a while? Should she have a chore chart? Was Addison cuddly enough? Was Stella independent because that was Stella . . . or had Addison pushed her daughter away inadvertently?

She glanced over at Gabe, who was frowning at the way she was leaning toward Caleb. In spite of her swirling emotions, she rolled her eyes at him. He simply lifted a brow.

That single arched brow made her nipples tingle. *Wow.* So she was officially horny and into all things Gabe. That was good to know.

So why had she been reading about alligators?

She looked around the rest of the group. This wasn't just a chance to meet Cooper. This was All The Kids. Did she want to bring Stella and introduce her to everyone? Did she really need to know their kids?

But the answer was clear immediately: yes. She did want to get to know the kids they'd all talked about over the last three weeks. And her daughter was amazing. She'd love coming and meeting new friends and playing games.

And, of course, that meant Stella would meet Cooper. And Addison would meet Cooper. And Gabe would meet Stella. And somehow that felt really . . . dangerous. And complicated. And tempting.

Yes, tempting.

"You and Stella will be here, right?" Bea asked Addison.

She realized that everyone else had already committed while she'd been lost in thought, again wondering what Gabe's son looked like and what made him laugh and if he ate broccoli and if he was up a million times at night before he finally fell asleep.

"I, um . . ." She looked at Gabe. Like a freaking paper clip to a magnet. "I'm not sure."

"Oh, you have to," Roxanne said. "We so want to meet her."

Everyone else chimed in with their agreement. Even Lindsey said, "These get-togethers are really a lot of fun."

Addison finally nodded. "Yeah, okay, we'll be there."

The enthusiasm from the group warmed her. Until she saw Gabe's very pleased look.

Well, hell.. What had she done?

◆ ◆ ◆

Addison was killing him.

He'd been good. He'd been laid-back. He'd decided to just let the support-group meetings be the time he saw her. For now. But it was killing him slowly.

Every time he walked into the community center, he homed in on her like he was a missile. And it took everything in him to keep from stalking over to her, throwing her over his shoulder, and finding the nearest firm surface.

He missed her to his bones. He'd never felt like that about a woman before, and yeah, it was killing him.

"Hey, Corey, I don't mind staying late tonight and helping clean up," Gabe heard Addison say. "I have the sitter for a couple more hours. You head on home."

"I appreciate it, Addison," Corey told her. "Thanks."

"No problem. Happy to help."

"See ya, Gabe!" Corey lifted his hand.

"Have a good one," Gabe called to the other man.

Gabe continued to stack chairs as Addison crossed to the refreshment table and started putting the cookies into a plastic container.

Caleb, Corey, and he always stayed after and put the community center back together. Austin, Dana, and Lindsey showed up early to arrange the chairs and start the coffee. Roxanne, Bea, and Ashley took turns bringing the cookies. Only Lexi, the youngest member and the one with the fewest resources and two jobs to juggle, didn't have a specific task. From time to time she did, however, bring in leftover brownies from the restaurant where she worked, and she often lingered after meetings, helping clean up. But everyone knew that was because Caleb was there.

Tonight, however, Caleb had ducked out right away. Gabe had thought that strange, but now that Addison had dismissed Corey, too, Gabe thought perhaps she'd had something to do with getting rid of her new BFF.

Gabe picked up the stack of chairs, returning them to the storage closet. He knew that his jealousy over Caleb's flirting with Addison was ridiculous. For one, he knew his friend had a hard time reeling in the flirting. It was just Caleb. He'd been a huge playboy before the courts had given him custody of Shay just a year ago, and he sometimes fell back into old habits, forgetting that he now came with a diaper bag and a collection of stuffed cats—Shay's favorite thing in the whole world. For another, Caleb knew about Gabe's feelings for Addison and was just giving him a hard time.

Still, seeing another man grinning at her, making her laugh, and complimenting her made Gabe feel uncharacteristically possessive. And, after giving Caleb a firm *no* in front of everyone, he realized that he didn't care who knew it.

The door bumped shut behind Corey, leaving Gabe and Addison alone. Neither said anything as they continued to clean up the room.

But finally the chairs were all put away, the cookies were stored, and there was nothing to keep them there.

Except wanting to stay.

He stopped in the middle of the room, about ten feet from where she stood by the table. She slowly turned to face him. Gabe tucked his hands in his back pockets and told himself to take it easy. Maybe she'd just felt the need to pitch in for the group. Maybe it had nothing to do with him.

But he knew better.

"Did you decide what you're going to do about Cooper and the swamp-boat tour?" she asked.

Okay, he hadn't been expecting that. He shook his head. "Not for sure."

"He's still into the alligators, though?"

She was asking about his kid. Gabe wasn't sure why, but that made his chest feel warm. "He is. When Coop gets into something, he's all in. At least for a while."

She nodded but said nothing.

"Does Stella do that? Go all in on stuff?" he asked. He wanted to know about her daughter. He did. He didn't care if it was pushy. She could choose not to tell him. But he wasn't going to pretend he wasn't curious about—or completely captivated by—what Addison's daughter was like.

Addison took a deep breath. "She's into art and books," she told him. "But she always has been. She draws and paints and colors and loves clay." Addison smiled. "She wants to take a pottery class."

Gabe felt his mouth ease into a smile. "That sounds cool."

"She's young for it," Addison said. Then frowned slightly. "I think. I don't really know. I need to call around and see, I guess."

"So not just a hunk of clay at home, then, huh?"

"She's a doer," Addison said. "She knows they use pottery wheels and kilns. She would start with clay and stuff at home, but she'd eventually want to really *do* it. Literally get her hands dirty with it. I indulge things like that—classes and such—because . . . ," Addison trailed off, and Gabe had to resist the urge to take a step closer.

"Because why?"

"Because I was never like that," she said. "I was pretty content to read and imagine and pretend about things." She seemed to be thinking over what she'd just said and what she was about to. "My dad was a big proponent of learning from your mistakes and dealing with the consequences, and after seeing my sister go without her bike for an entire summer because she crashed it doing some obstacle-course thing and then had to save up her allowance to fix it, and seeing her miss a family trip to the zoo because she'd eaten an entire bag of candy that morning and gotten really sick, and seeing him give her cat away to a guy he worked with because my sister went camping with some friends and didn't arrange for anyone to take care of the cat, I guess I got . . . careful." She frowned. "Really careful."

Gabe felt his gut tighten with a mix of emotions. Addison was sharing something really personal about her past with him. She'd never done that before. And it was something kind of heartbreaking. Especially when he saw that look of realization, sadness, and worry on her face.

"He sounds like a hard-ass," Gabe said. He didn't want to insult her father, and probably wouldn't get any brownie points with her for doing so, but damn.

She shrugged. "Yeah, I guess. Though, in fairness to him, he made all of this really clear to us. The expectations were carefully outlined. I think he would have helped her with her bike if she hadn't been screwing around. And the zoo thing—he would have postponed the trip if she'd been actually sick, but since it was self-inflicted, he wanted to show her that choices have consequences."

"I'm sure being sick all day was a pretty bad consequence that taught her something," Gabe said with a frown. Yes, his mother and brother sometimes thought he was too permissive with Cooper, but damn, they were talking about *kids* here. Even adults screwed up some-times. Kids certainly did. They needed some slack, didn't they?

Addison nodded. "I know it sounds harsh. But, like, the cat thing . . . all she had to do was ask one of us to take care of it. In fact, I *did* take care of it while she was gone. But that wasn't the point. She hadn't asked me to. She didn't take that responsibility. And my dad had made it clear that if she was going to have a pet, she was going to have to take care of it."

Gabe took a breath. "Yeah, I get it. The cat needed her to be respon-sible. It just seems . . . overly hard on a kid."

Addison's frown deepened. "Sometimes I worry that I'm too hard on Stella."

Okay, *that* surprised him. Addison seemed totally confident in everything she did with her daughter.

"Really?"

Addison nodded. "I push her to be independent, to think through her choices, to learn from her mistakes. But then . . ."

She trailed off, and Gabe held his breath, hoping she'd go on but not wanting to push.

"I definitely indulge her interests," Addison said.

Gabe blew out his breath.

"When she wants to try something new, I probably even go over-board a little. Because I'm almost envious of her sometimes," Addison went on. "She's completely fearless. She wants to try everything and do everything and, while pottery isn't exactly dangerous, I want her to know that it's okay to get in there and try things even if they don't work out." She looked up at Gabe. "But I think it's good to teach con-sequences, too."

He nodded. "Of course. But she's five. And . . . I think a lot of times consequences kind of teach themselves. You touch something hot and it burns you. You stay up too late, you're tired the next day. You eat too much candy, you feel sick."

Addison just looked at him for a long moment, a bunch of emotions in her eyes all at once. "Alligators very rarely attack people, but it does happen."

Gabe blinked at her. "Okay."

"I'm just saying that Cooper's not *wrong* to be a little fearful of that."

"True." Gabe just watched her. He didn't know what was going on exactly, but he could be patient. Probably.

"Did you know that alligators will sometimes balance sticks and twigs on their heads in an attempt to lure birds that are building nests?"

Gabe wanted to smile. Or hug her. He didn't know where this was going, but yeah, he was going to wait it out. "I didn't."

"That's kind of amazing, right?" she asked.

He'd never given alligators this much thought in his life. "I guess it is."

"And there's a guy who told a story about trying to capture an alligator that was on a golf course. He kept trying to catch it with a snare, but the alligator would run from him. But he didn't run away from other people nearby. The guy finally realized the alligator recognized his shirt. When he took off the shirt, the alligator quit running from him, and he was able to capture it and rerelease it elsewhere."

Okay, that was mildly interesting. But even more so was the fact that Addison even knew about it.

"And female alligators are really protective of their babies," she said.

"Ad?" Gabe said huskily.

She wet her lips, seeming almost nervous. "Yeah?"

"You've been reading about alligators?"

She nodded.

"Why?"

"I, um . . . after you said Cooper was so interested in them, I was wondering what was so fascinating."

She'd been reading about alligators because of Cooper.

Gabe couldn't have named the emotion that rocked through him with that exactly, but it made him want to cheer and fist-pump and strip her down and push her up against the wall. He took a step forward. "And you've found some things."

She nodded again. "Yeah. And the thing is—those things don't mean I absolutely want to see an alligator in the wild, or touch one, but I can't deny that I'm a little curious in spite of the teeth and the scales and the whole could-kill-me-if-they-wanted-to thing."

He took another step forward, his heart suddenly pounding. They weren't talking about swamp boats and alligators now. "You're interested in spite of the scary stuff," he said.

"The scary stuff is still there, though," she said, her eyes widening as he took yet another step, narrowing the space between them.

"But it might be worth a trip out onto the bayou," Gabe said, taking the final step that put him right in front of her.

She swallowed. Then, thank *God*, nodded. "Yeah, it might be worth a trip just to see how it turns out in person."

She was willing to try. With him. Holy hell, he hadn't realized how much he needed to hear her say that. He reached up, put a hand on the back of her neck, and pulled her forward. She came willingly, flattening her hands on his chest but definitely not pushing him away. She looked up at him.

"You wanna get on my swamp boat for a tour, Ad?" he asked, his voice gruff.

One corner of her mouth lifted. "I do. In spite of myself."

Yes. Yes, yes, yes. "Thank you," he said.

The sincerity and intensity in his tone made her eyes widen. "Really?"

"Fuck yes," he said solemnly. "I promise I'll take care of you."

She blew out a breath. "I'm not very good about not being careful," she said, almost as if she was warning him. "I think about all of the what-ifs ahead of time. And sometimes I talk myself out of stuff entirely."

"I've actually got a lot of experience with someone who's overly careful about everything," he told her, breathing in deeply of her scent and the feel of her against him again. He felt a strange sense of relief and want ripple through him at the same time.

"And you indulge him," she said softly.

"I do. Because I always want the people who trust me to know that I'll take care of them and that I'll do whatever I can to keep them safe and that with me they can be who they are without fear."

She pressed her lips together.

"And I think you're going to be fine," he told her. "Because *you* indulge a risk taker and let her spread her wings and tell her that even if things don't work out, everything will be okay."

Addison pulled in a breath. "Pottery can be fixed. Pencil lines can be erased and redrawn. Not everything is that easy to fix when it doesn't work out."

"You're right," he said. He leaned in and put his forehead against hers. "But remember, when you're scared, I'm perfectly fine with you climbing into bed with me."

She gave a little laugh, the puff of air against his lips tightening everything in him instantly.

He gave a little groan. "I've missed you so damned much."

Her fingers curled into his shirt, as if she were holding on. "Me too," she admitted.

That was all he needed to hear. His lips crashed down on hers, his hand holding her head, the other cupping that ass that still fit absolutely perfectly in his palm.

Chapter Six

Addison rose on tiptoe to get closer, opening her mouth for him and moaning when his tongue slid along hers in a firm, sensual stroke.

They kissed for several long, hot minutes, just pressing close and tasting one another. But it didn't take long for the rest of Gabe's body to start demanding more of hers. He walked her backward a few steps to the table and lifted her to sit on the edge.

"Hey, we put our cookies here," she said with a mischievous smile as he stepped between her knees.

"Then this is exactly where you belong," he told her, running his hands up under the edge of her shirt to the smooth, hot skin of her back. "Sweetest thing I've ever put in my mouth."

She half laughed, half groaned at that. "You can't . . . put me in your mouth right here."

"Oh, watch me," he growled, lifting her shirt and taking in the sight of her breasts, encased in pale-peach silk. He ran a thumb over her nipple, watching it bead behind the cup of her bra. Then he lowered his head and sucked on the hard tip through the silk.

Her hand went to the back of his head, her fingers gripping his hair as she gasped his name.

He tugged the front of the cup down with a finger, exposing her flesh and swirling his tongue around her nipple. She wiggled against him.

"Gabe, we can't do this here."

"We can," he assured her. "We're going to. I'm starving for you, Ad."

Her breath caught, but she tried again. "Anyone could walk in."

"No one's due here again until tomorrow, and Corey locked the door behind him."

"How do you know?"

"He and Dana are the only ones who have keys."

There was a second's pause, then Addison breathed out. "Thank God." She reached between them and stripped off her shirt, then unhooked her bra and tossed them both to the floor behind him. Then she brought his head back down.

Gabe gave a gruff chuckle but instantly went back to teasing the most perfect breasts he'd ever seen. Soon she was reaching for his fly and had him unzipped and his aching cock in hand. Feeling her fingers wrap around him and squeeze and stroke nearly sent him to his knees.

"Holy hell, Ad," he said, his voice gravelly.

"Need you," she said simply.

"All you needed to say." He leaned back, unbuttoned her pants and, when she lifted her hips, whisked them off, along with the silk panties that, of course, matched the color of her pants. He took a moment to take in the sight of her. He felt like it had been three years rather than three weeks since he'd last seen her, touched her, lost himself in her.

He ran a hand up the inside of her thigh, glorying in the silky heat of her skin. "Spread for me, Ad."

His heart turned over in his chest when she parted her knees, bracing her hands on the table behind her, and leaned back slightly. He cupped the heat at the apex of her thighs and then slid a finger along the silky seam.

"You are so fucking gorgeous." He slid a finger in slowly, feeling the tight, wet heat that made him desperate to have it around his cock.

He wanted to push his pants down and thrust. That was almost all that would register in his mind. But it felt different this time. He'd missed her, he was aching for her, he wanted every damned inch of her against and around every inch of him. But there was more driving him tonight. He pumped his finger deep, relishing her groan and the way her body tightened around him. This didn't just feel hot. And it didn't feel playful and fun. This felt . . . primal. He wanted to take her. He wanted to possess her. He wanted to wreck her so that she couldn't walk away, so that she couldn't stop thinking of him, so that she would never find anything else to satisfy her.

And that was so unlike him that he froze for a moment. He wasn't that guy. He wasn't the Neanderthal type. But as Addison shifted on the table and said, "Please, Gabe," he thought that maybe he was, actually. It was just that he'd never wanted someone like this before.

He removed his finger so he could reach into his pocket for a condom and ripped it open. Then he paused and met her eyes. "My condom." It wasn't a question. It was a statement. This time they were going to use his condom.

It was not something he'd given a lot of thought to before Addison. Condoms were condoms and, knock on wood, had done their jobs. The night Cooper had been conceived had been a condom-less event. But Addison took charge of the condoms usually. And now, he really wanted—needed—her to trust him to take care of this. Of her.

It was a small thing, really. Condoms were a detail that millions of people barely gave a thought to every day. It shouldn't matter. But it did. Because it wasn't a small thing to Addison.

She didn't say anything, but she nodded.

With his breath lodged in his chest and his eyes on hers, he pulled the condom from the packet and rolled it on. Her tongue wet her bottom lip as she watched, and Gabe felt heat surge through his cock.

He took her hips in his hands and pulled her to the edge of the table. He took her thighs in his hands, tipping her back until she was propped on her elbows, and spread her legs. She was at his mercy. She didn't have a lot of leverage, and she couldn't reach him. She was all his, and even as he eased in to her slowly, watching every inch disappear one by one, Gabe felt the possessive, this-is-all-mine, caveman stuff rip through him. And he loved it. Reveled in it. Wanted to feel it forever.

Addison's head fell back, her long hair brushing the table where just an hour ago, brightly frosted sugar cookies had sat. Gabe pulled out and then thrust again, loving the idea that every time she walked into this room from now on, she'd think of this.

"Gabe," she panted. "Yes."

He watched her breasts bounce as he thrust, could see every delicious, pink inch between her legs, took in her tight stomach, her smooth thighs, and the way her fingers tried to dig into the table, but couldn't get a grip. But it was the look of bliss on her face, the way she leaned back and let him take her, the abandon of her hair falling around her shoulders, the fact that she was completely naked and that he still wore a shirt and had his pants only to his knees that fired his blood. This was not the put-together, confident, do-it-all-herself single mom and renowned architect in her pencil skirts carrying a briefcase with carefully organized files inside. This was the woman underneath all that. The one who was a little unsure and a little vulnerable. The one whose lipstick was smudged—because of him. Whose hair was tousled—because of him. And who was bare-ass naked on a table—for him. The one who *needed* him for something. Right now it might just be an orgasm, but Gabe knew there was more, and thought, just maybe, Addison was starting to see that, too.

He'd touched every inch of her, seen everything, and yet, right now, it was so much more about her trust and the fact that she was here, in this support group, and reading about alligators in spite of wanting to stay away, that made him harder and hotter and more desperate than he'd ever been before.

Gabe thrust harder and deeper, gritting his teeth against the sensations that threated to pull him into a hot and fast orgasm. Slow and sensual was for king-size beds and tangled sheets and a lazy ceiling fan turning above them while jazz floated up from the street below. Spontaneous sex on the treat table at the community center was for hard and fast. But he had to take her with him. He knew she'd get there with him eventually, but he also knew how to speed things up.

"God, Ad, your pussy is my favorite place to be in the whole world," he told her gruffly. It was the truth, and bonus—she loved when he talked to her during sex.

He felt the resultant tightening around his cock.

"It loves you, too," she told him with a smile, then a groan as he pumped deep.

"Good thing," he told her, that possessiveness streaking through him again. "Because it's mine," he said, for the first time in his life in regard to a woman—or a part of a woman. Though, damn, he wanted all of her. Every carry-wet-wipes-but-don't-mind-getting-dirty, don't-cuddle-but-will-hold-your-hand, completely-independent-but-fell-in-love-with-the-support-group-in-three-meetings piece of her. "You're mine," he told her as he pumped harder and faster. "Swamp boats or not, no one else is going to be worshipping this body but me."

Something about that—the tone, the actual words, the perfect angle of his next thrust—made her moan and her inner muscles tighten.

"*Gabe.*" Her chest was rising and falling with her deep, fast breaths, and she was trying to grip the table.

But she didn't have to worry. He had a hold on her and wasn't letting go.

"Right, Ad?" he asked, his jaw tight. "I'm the only one who gets to see, touch, and taste this pussy."

"Gabe," she panted, her eyes on where he was sliding in and out of her body, ratcheting up the sensations for them both. Her chest was flushed, and he could tell she was getting close.

"Maybe I won't let you come, since you kept me away from it for three weeks," he said. "Maybe I'll just take what I want, since you didn't think you needed this. Maybe if you want to come, I should make you promise to give me this pussy anytime I want it." He pumped deep as her muscles clenched around him hard. "And I want it, Ad. I want it over and over. I want to feel this sweet, wet heat in my hand, on my tongue, and around my cock."

She moaned, and her head fell back again.

"I want to fill you up and wring you out, Addison."

She gasped, then gave him a quiet but heartfelt *"Gabe."*

"Every." He thrust hard. "Fucking." He thrust again. "Night."

That thrust put her over the edge. Her thighs tightened, her inner muscles gripped him, and she let out a soft cry—the one that always made him feel like a damned king.

Gabe let himself go then, pounding into her, filling her up as promised but feeling very much like it was *him* who was being wrung out. His climax thundered up from the center of his gut, and he felt the eruption to the soles of his feet. And just maybe his soul.

Gabe braced his hands on either side of her hips on the table as he struggled to catch his breath. Addison thought maybe that should make her feel caged in, but instead, it felt like he was shielding her, protecting her while she recovered her senses.

But that might take a while.

That orgasm had been . . . different. Sex was always good with Gabe. Beyond good. The best she'd ever had. But this time had felt . . . yeah, *different* was the best she could come up with. Apparently post-climax endorphins made her brain a little mushy.

Or maybe it was that analyzing—and admitting—how it was different would have made another part of her mushy. Like her heart.

It was, she knew, in part, all that possessive talk about being Gabe's. Yeah, it had been dirty, and he'd used the word *pussy* a lot—a word that she had really thought she *didn't* like prior to meeting Gabe Trahan, but he had a way of saying it that made it sound almost reverent . . . and very hot—but it had all seemed about a lot more than him not wanting her sleeping with anyone else.

Hell, she didn't want him sleeping with anyone else, either. Ever. For the rest of his life. She didn't want him talking to anyone else like this. She didn't want him staking his claim on anyone else. In fact, that thought made her feel possessive of *him*. The only other thing in the world she'd ever felt that way about was Stella.

And there was the problem.

She either had to let him go completely. Or she had to keep him.

And both scared her equally.

Gabe finally pushed back and away. Addison felt instantly cold and lonely. She wanted to know that they could go home now and curl up in bed together. That she could reach for him in the night and he'd be there. That when she woke up, he'd be there, maybe in her shower or in her kitchen. And that even if she didn't see him all day, he'd come home to her.

She'd had just a taste—Gabe on the pillow next to her, Gabe in the kitchen in the morning, Gabe taking her home at the end of a night out on the town—when she'd visited New Orleans in the past. But then she'd gone back to New York, and none of that was an option full-time. But now that she was here, she couldn't stop thinking about how he was just a few miles away and that maybe she *could* have all of that.

Stupid. That's really stupid, Addison.

He gave her a wobbly smile that was sweet and sexy at the same time. He dealt with the condom as he said, "Calling that the treat table is a *very* accurate term."

She laughed and pushed herself up to a sitting position, and she realized for the first time as he straightened his clothes that he was still mostly dressed while she was bare-ass naked.

"I'll be blushing the next time I reach for a cookie."

He gave her a roguish grin. "Good. And the next time I lick frosting off a cookie, know I'm thinking of you."

And in spite of the very recent orgasm, Addison felt her body heat. The man really did have a great tongue. "You lick the frosting off before eating it?"

His grin grew, and he gave her a wink. "Oh yeah."

Addison was suddenly having trouble remembering how to hook her bra.

She finally managed to pull her clothes on, and they stood facing each other.

"So," he said.

"So," she agreed.

He took a breath and said, "Addison, I want to keep doing that." He pointed at the table. Then he looked her directly in the eyes. "But I want more than that."

She had to nod. "I know."

"Tell me I can have it." His tone was husky and commanding and pleading at the same time.

He didn't touch her, but she felt a shiver of pleasure go through her as if he had. He wanted this. Clearly. She wanted more, too. But she hadn't even met his son. Addison had never been responsible for a child other than her own, even for a few hours. Stella had never even had a friend spend the night before. But still, Addison had no choice but to nod.

The look of relief and happiness on Gabe's face almost did her in. He reached for her, again cupping the back of her head, but he looked into her eyes and said "Thank you" before lowering his head and kissing her slowly and sweetly this time.

When he lifted his head, Addison felt compelled to say, "But we have to take it slow."

"Fine. Okay."

The corner of her mouth curled. "Between this and the sex, I could get almost anything from you right now, huh?"

"Yes," he said without hesitation. "What do you want?"

She thought about being playful and flirtatious, but instead she went for honest. "I want you to let me meet Cooper at the family get-together and not be pushy or expect too much or read too much into anything."

He nodded slowly. "I think I can do that."

"Okay, then." She felt a sense of optimism that surprised her.

"So we're going to slowly wade into this bayou rather than jump in to skinny-dip all at once," he said with a smile.

She laughed. "There are still alligators in the bayou, Gabe."

He lifted a hand to her cheek and smiled. "Yeah, I guess there are. For now."

Gabe had expected to like her. He'd expected to think she was beautiful. He'd expected to have an urge to make her laugh. He hadn't, however, expected to fall in love in less than five minutes.

But Stella Sloan was irresistible.

She didn't sit down to play the board games. She stood the entire time, sometimes leaning on the table, sometimes upright and bouncing on the balls of her feet. Whether they were playing a slower, quieter card game or a fast-paced action game, she wiggled, she danced, she jumped up and down, and she grinned, giggled, and laughed. It didn't matter if she won or lost, she did it all with a big smile and lots of energy.

And Addison sat nearby, watching, smiling affectionately, but not interfering, not trying to help, not telling Stella to settle down or to sit down or to quiet down. She let her daughter play the games, interact with the other kids and adults, all while sticking close on the periphery.

Gabe didn't know who he liked watching more. The bubbly Stella or her quieter, more reserved mother. Because it seemed clear that if Stella were presented with a beignet, she'd dive in, powdered-sugar mess be damned. And he appreciated that. Absolutely. Still, there was something about Addison's more composed demeanor that drew him. Because he loved seeing that composure crumble and watching her just go for it.

Gabe was at the table next to Stella's. He and Cooper and Dana and her two kids were playing a memory game. Which Cooper was winning every single time. Because he concentrated and took the game seriously. Everyone else at the table was just playing for fun and didn't really care if they won or lost. But Cooper knew the objective was to match the most pieces and clear the board, and he studied the game the way he studied . . . well, everything. If he was going to learn everything there was to know about cranes and bulldozers, he learned everything there was to know. Same for alligators. And where all the pieces were on a game board. Gabe grinned as he watched Cooper press his lips together. Gabe knew Coop was barely resisting telling Grace, Dana's youngest, where the match was for the piece she was holding.

Finally, Grace chose a piece. And was wrong. The next move, Cooper made another match and ended the game.

Gabe ruffled his hair. "Good job, bud. Want to play something else now?"

Cooper shook his head. "I'm done."

"Then how about a snack?"

"I'm okay."

"Gabe! Come play dunk tank!" one of Roxanne's kids called.

They'd set up a mock dunk tank with one of the kids sitting on a high stool and another holding out a cardboard bull's-eye. When someone hit the "target" with a beanbag, the kid on the stool jumped off, landing behind a piece of cardboard that was painted to look like water, pretending to get dunked. Apparently, the older kids were getting frustrated with the little kids being unable to hit the bull's-eye.

"Coop, want to play dunk tank?" Gabe asked.

Cooper shook his head. Yeah, Gabe had expected that. "What do you want to do?"

"I'll watch you," Cooper told him. "You're a good shot."

Gabe put a hand on his head and grinned down. "Thanks, man."

Gabe moved over to the "dunk tank." He joked around with the kids for a little bit, watching them play. He helped a couple of the younger ones with their shots. And then he successfully dunked Roxanne's youngest son three times in a row. Grinning and high-fiving the other kids, Gabe turned to check on Cooper.

And his heart almost stopped.

Cooper was standing in front of Addison. Who was looking at him like he was an alligator about to take a chunk out of her leg.

◆ ◆ ◆

"Hi."

Addison stared down at the little boy she'd been watching all day but keeping her distance from. Who was now standing in front of her, his big brown eyes—the only thing that wasn't the exact image of his father—peering up at her.

"Hi."

"Can I sit on your lap?"

She blinked at him. "Um. Why?" Had Gabe sent Cooper over to her? Because that sweet but serious face was definitely going to get to her.

"I like your shirt," Cooper told her, as if that was a perfectly good reason to want to sit on someone's lap.

Addison looked down at the pale-blue T-shirt she was wearing. "You do?"

"Blue is my favorite color," Cooper told her. "And you're sitting still."

She almost laughed at that. But he was completely serious. And he had a point. All the other adults were up and moving around or engaged in games. Addison had chosen to sit near Stella but let her daughter meet the rest of the group in her own way and time. That was how they did things. Stella did her thing but with Addison close enough to help out or intervene if necessary. It was almost never necessary.

"I guess I am," Addison said. She shifted slightly and held out her arms. "Then obviously I'm the best choice."

Cooper climbed up onto her lap and immediately snuggled in against her as if they'd done this a million times. And Addison felt her heart stutter, then pound hard once, before settling back into its normal rhythm. Then Cooper reached for one of her arms and drew it around him. She did the same with the other and then worked on holding perfectly still.

She was a stranger to him. Should he really be sitting on her lap? But he seemed to be perfectly content.

"You don't want to sit on your own chair?" she asked.

"No," he said simply.

"Okay." She paused. "Let me know if I squeeze you."

"Okay." He certainly didn't seem concerned. A minute passed, and he said, "You smell good, too."

She supposed, given all the reasons to sit on someone's lap, that wasn't a bad one, either. "Thank you."

"The way she smells is one of my favorite things about her."

Addison's head snapped up, and she found Gabe standing over them. "Um, hi."

He gave her a knowing grin, as if he could tell that she was very uncomfortable right now. But he simply pulled a chair up next to them and settled in, not offering her or Cooper the chance for the boy to sit on *Gabe's* lap.

"She smells like ice cream," Cooper told him.

Gabe gave him a wink. "One of our favorite things, right?"

"Definitely." Cooper wiggled on her lap, but it seemed that he was just getting even more settled, resting his head back against her breasts.

Gabe lifted his eyes to Addison's, and his grin softened. "This is nice."

That warm look in his eyes was almost as potent as the sexy ones he gave her. He hadn't sent Cooper over, but Addison could feel how pleased he was that his son had found her. "I see there are some things genetic among the Trahan men."

Gabe's gaze dropped to her breasts. "Guess we like some of the same things."

"I meant the charm," she said with a little eye roll, but she couldn't help but smile.

"Oh, that." Gabe looked at Cooper. "Yeah, we're pretty hard to resist, huh, Coop?"

Cooper grinned up at him. "Look out, ladies, Trahans in the house," he said.

Addison laughed, and Gabe grinningly explained, "That's one of Uncle Logan's favorite sayings, isn't it?"

Cooper giggled. "Uncle Logan drinks beer and says bad words and kisses lots of girls."

Addison didn't know Logan well, but from what she'd seen, she felt that summary was very accurate.

"But kissing girls is okay," Cooper told her, tipping his head so he could look up at her. "Dad says it's really nice and that if you really like them and they want you to, you can kiss them."

Addison's heart squeezed. Even though she was sure the conversation had been somewhat lighthearted, something about Gabe giving his son fatherly advice made her freaking heart squeeze. That was really dumb, of course. Obviously Gabe would be giving Cooper advice, of all kinds. But there was something about witnessing it. Seeing Gabe parenting. Seeing Gabe's interactions—even the lighthearted ones—with Cooper up close. Seeing Gabe as someone who was idolized and adored and trusted completely. Yeah, it definitely squeezed her heart.

Addison swallowed, then nodded. "As a girl myself, I can confirm that it's okay in those instances."

"Do *you* like kissing?" Cooper asked.

Addison grinned. "I do like kissing. Some boys. Not all, of course." She shot Gabe a quick look, but it was very hard to decipher the expression on his face. It was that possessive-hot look again, combined with what looked a little like amazement. "But I'll tell you something," she said to Cooper, leaning in a little as if to impart a secret.

"What?" Cooper asked, dropping his voice to a loud whisper.

"Sometimes girls start the kissing."

Cooper giggled. "Do they drink beer and say bad words, too?"

Addison laughed. "Nope, never."

Gabe snorted. "I think Addison is just like Uncle Logan, Coop."

"Full of beans?" Cooper asked.

"Yep. Totally," Gabe said, giving Addison a wink.

"Hmm," Addison said. "Okay, I'm going to say something, and you tell me if I'm telling the truth or full of beans."

Cooper wiggled in her lap, turning so he could see her more easily. "Okay."

"Alligators lay eggs like birds."

Cooper's eyes got wide. "True!"

She nodded. "How about this—when baby alligators are ready to hatch, they make a sound that their mom hears, and she knows she needs to uncover them."

"Yes! True!" Cooper exclaimed.

"And raccoons will sometimes *eat* alligator eggs," Addison added, loving the excited look on his face.

"They do," Cooper said, nodding. "Yes, that's true, too."

"So I'm not really full of beans, am I?" Addison said.

"No way." Cooper looked at Gabe. "She's not full of beans."

Gabe gave his son a smile. "Nope, I guess she's not."

"Do you like alligators?" Cooper asked, turning back to Addison.

She shrugged. "I don't know. I think they're interesting, but they're kind of scary, too. But I've never been around one in person." She snuck a look at Gabe and realized that, when his son wasn't looking at him, Gabe had a very intense look on his face. If she didn't know better, that look said he was thinking about stripping off her clothes and saying very dirty things to her. But that couldn't be right. Could it?

"They are scary," Cooper said with a little frown. "Is this true or full of beans? An alligator's jaw can produce thirty-seven hundred pounds of force per square inch."

Addison nodded seriously. "True."

"Yep." Cooper said it with a grave look.

"Have you met one in person?" Addison asked him.

"No." Cooper looked over at Gabe. "Dad said we could go on a swamp tour, though."

"Stella wants to do that, too," Addison told him. *What am I getting myself into?* she wondered briefly. But maybe having someone with him who was also less than enthusiastic would help Cooper. Lord knew Stella would love to have someone like Gabe along who would totally get into it all and be excited.

And dammit, those big brown eyes and sweet giggle and, yeah, the fact that he'd climbed into her lap so easily, had won her over. Just as she'd feared.

"Is that Stella?" Cooper asked, pointing at her daughter.

"Yes. We're new."

"She's kind of loud," Cooper said.

"Coop," Gabe chastised, but Addison just laughed.

"Yes, she sure can be," Addison agreed. "But I promise she's not all the time."

"Would she be loud on a swamp boat?" Cooper asked.

Well . . . Addison had to be honest. "Yeah, probably."

Gabe chuckled at that, and Cooper even smiled. "That's probably okay," the boy decided. "It's outside."

Addison wanted to squeeze him. And his dad. There was something about Gabe just sitting there, reclined in the chair next to them, watching them interact, that made her feel all tingly.

"Maybe they should go with us, Dad," Cooper finally said. "You could pet an alligator with Stella."

Gabe's expression was so full of affection at that, Addison had to catch her breath.

"I don't need to pet an alligator," Gabe told him. "I'm happy with whatever you want."

Cooper nodded. "I know. But Addison doesn't want to pet one, and Stella does. She needs a grown-up to help her."

Gabe looked surprised for a moment. He met Addison's gaze. "You don't want to pet one, huh?"

Addison gave a very honest little shudder. "Nope."

"Well, I would be happy to help Stella with it," he said.

She could tell that he was trying to be nonchalant about it, but there was a definite tension in him suddenly as he shifted forward in his chair to rest his forearms on his thighs. She shot him a questioning look over Cooper's head, but Gabe gave her a little headshake that seemed to say, *Not now.*

"Then you should come with us," Cooper told Addison. "We can watch them."

She swallowed. Okay, so she was making a date for her, Stella, Gabe, and Cooper to spend time together. Just the four of them. This had escalated quickly. She had no idea why she was surprised by that. "That sounds good," she told him.

"Yeah?" Gabe asked.

She looked up and saw that he had his hands clasped together between his knees and was staring at her intently.

She nodded. "Yeah."

"Cooper! Come play Chutes and Ladders!" one of the kids called just then.

Cooper sighed.

"Go on," Gabe encouraged. "For a little while."

"That's a baby game," Cooper said.

"Well, maybe you can play one game of that and then suggest something else," Gabe told him.

"Okay." Cooper turned on her lap, then reached up and threw his arms around her neck, hugging her briefly. "Bye, Addison."

He'd slid off her lap and was across the room at the game table before she recovered from her surprise.

Gabe watched him go, and then as soon as Cooper was occupied, he slid his chair close, put his hand on the back of her head, and pulled her in so he could whisper against her ear.

"It's probably totally inappropriate, but seeing you holding my son and talking about alligators has made me harder than I've ever been. I would do anything to hike up this pretty sundress and bury myself inside you right now."

Addison couldn't catch her breath. She simply gave a soft moan.

Then Gabe kissed her forehead and let her go. "Swamp tour on Sunday afternoon," he said.

It was clearly not a question.

She nodded. "Okay."

His gaze burned into hers for another long moment, then he nodded. "Okay."

And Addison thought that just maybe everything really would be okay.

Chapter Seven

The swamp-boat tour was . . . pretty much what Gabe had expected.

It was hot and humid, the airboat was loud, and there were lots of gators.

Stella had been in heaven. She'd clambered aboard the boat and headed for the front seats immediately, and Gabe had agreed to sit with her when the guide said kids had to be with an adult. Cooper had been equally torn between fascination and horror as he'd carefully stepped onto the boat, holding tightly to Addison's hand, and he'd happily taken Addison's invitation to sit with her on the bench seat in the middle of the vessel.

Stella had bounced in her seat the entire time and peppered the guide with questions. Cooper had sat quietly, looking, watching, taking it all in but not getting too close. Besides, he'd already known all the answers to Stella's questions. A fact he'd informed her of on the drive home.

Stella had not only petted a baby alligator but held it and kissed it on the head. Cooper had looked like he might throw up as he watched her. Addison had wanted nothing to do with the lizards—big or small—and had looked a little green around the edges by the time they docked.

And Gabe—well, Gabe couldn't have thought of a better way to spend a day. The kids had gotten to know each other, he'd gotten to know Stella, and Addison seemed able to understand and make Cooper feel more secure. And Gabe had gotten to hold an alligator, too, which, no doubt about it, was kind of cool.

All in all, it was a very successful outing in his opinion.

Except for the fact that with their two kids along, Gabe couldn't back Addison up against the inside of her front door and kiss the hell out of her when he dropped Stella and her at home after driving back from the bayou.

"Stella, why don't you take Cooper in and get some juice. And you can show him those drawings you did of the alligators last night?" Addison asked as she unlocked the front door and pushed it open.

"Okay." Stella started down the hall at, of course, a run.

Cooper stepped across the threshold more slowly—though, in fairness, most people did things slowly compared to Stella—and looked around Addison's foyer curiously. Stella stopped halfway down the hallway and looked back.

"Do you want juice?" she asked Cooper.

"Yeah," he told her.

"Then come on."

"I'm just looking," Cooper told her.

Stella put a hand on her hip. "At what?"

"Your house."

She frowned. "Why?"

Cooper shrugged. "Because it's different from mine. And it's neat to see different things."

Stella tipped her head, then came back to stand by Cooper. She looked around the foyer from his vantage point. They stood side by side, just looking, for nearly two minutes. Addison and Gabe exchanged a look and a smile but said nothing.

Finally, Stella nodded and looked over at Cooper. "You want to see the rest of the house?"

"Sure."

"Okay," she said, taking his hand. "But juice first. And in my room we have to play with Sammy for a while."

"Who's Sammy?"

Stella gave him a smile. "You'll see."

That seemed good enough for Cooper. "Okay."

They disappeared down the hall into the kitchen, and Addison turned to face Gabe. "Wow," she said simply.

Wow was a pretty good summary. "They could be good for each other," he said.

Addison nodded. "Cooper will make sure she slows down and smells the roses."

"And Stella will make sure he doesn't spend all his time *just* looking around."

Addison took a deep breath. "Want to make out while they play?"

"Yes," he said without hesitation.

She laughed and took his hand, leading him down the hall. "Stella? Gabe and I will be in the family room," she called into the kitchen.

"Okay, Mommy!"

Addison turned left where the kids had turned right and led him to the couch. They settled onto the cushions together, and Addison kicked off her shoes. She shifted to face him, resting an arm on the back of the couch and tucking her legs underneath her.

"Thanks for today," she told him.

He faced her, also propping an arm on the back of the couch. He ran a strand of her hair between his finger and thumb. "Thank you. I had a great time."

She nodded, studying his face. "It was a good day."

"And . . . ," he prompted, "not so bad with two kids? When you have someone else there to help?"

"I have to admit that having someone else pet alligators with Stella was really nice," she said.

Gabe felt his heart give a little extra thump. That was something. "Addison," he said seriously, "Stella will never have to face an alligator—literal or figurative—alone as long as I'm around."

Addison groaned.

He smiled. "What?"

"That was amazingly sweet," she said.

His smile grew. "Yeah?" He wrapped the strand of hair around his finger and tugged slightly.

Addison leaned in. "Yeah," she said softly.

"It's true," he told her. "It's not just about softening *you* up with sweetness and charm and sexiness."

She laughed, but her gaze was on his mouth. "I didn't say charm and sexiness. Just sweet."

He leaned in until their lips were only an inch apart. "But it is sexy, right? It kind of turns you on knowing that I'm kind of crazy about your daughter."

"You are?"

"How could I not be?"

"Our kids are pretty different," she reminded him.

He nodded. "Yin and yang."

She sighed, but it was a happy, contented sound. "I'm kind of crazy about your son, too."

Gabe's heart turned over in his chest, and he moved his hand to the back of her head. "You wore a blue dress today."

"Yeah."

"Because he told you blue was his favorite color."

She shrugged. "I thought maybe it would make him feel better about sitting with me on the boat." Her cheeks got pink. "Probably silly."

Gabe's throat felt tight as he pulled her in and put his nose against her neck. "Not silly," he said gruffly. "And you do smell fucking amazing. I'd sit next to you anywhere."

Addison gave a little moan as he ran his lips up and down her neck, then turned her head and met his mouth.

The kiss, as always, fired his blood and wound everything in him tight, but tonight it felt like his heart was clenching as well. He wanted her. But he wanted *all* of her. Everything there was. Everything she'd give him.

They kissed leisurely for several long minutes. Their hands wandered but stayed, somehow, on the outside of their clothing, since there were kids in the house. Gabe ran his fingers through her hair, and Addison ran her hands over his chest and shoulders.

Finally, Addison pulled back, breathing hard. "Okay, so, we need to stop."

"But it's so good," he protested, nipping her bottom lip.

"Yeah, well, I was about to tell you that the laundry room is just down the hall, has a door, and has a table that could be shoved in front of it. And that if Stella gets started on a bead project, we've got a good twenty minutes of uninterrupted time."

Gabe stared at her. "Why the hell were you *about* to tell me that? As if you'd decided not to?"

"Because Cooper's here, too. And that's probably not very good parenting."

"Cooper's attention span is scary long anyway, and he's never done a bead project—whatever that is—which means that attention span will be even longer. He loves doing new things."

She smiled up at him. "What about the not-very-good-parenting part?"

"Are there sharp objects, fire, or anything toxic involved?" Gabe asked.

Addison shook her head, giving him a look of desire and mischief that he couldn't resist. "No, none of the above."

"And I think they're both old enough not to eat the beads," he said. "Though we could remind them of that while we get them set up."

"True."

"And it's not like we're *leaving*. We'll be right down the hall." He leaned in and kissed her. "And I can be fast."

She laughed. "Is finishing fast something to brag about?"

He ran his hand down her back, cupped her butt, and lifted her into his lap. She straddled his thighs, and he pressed her down against his hard cock. Her skirt hiked up, putting her silk panties right against his fly. "I *promise* that you'll finish first." He kissed her hot and hard. He knew he'd hear the kids coming down the stairs, based on the noise they were making on the ceiling above, so he slipped one of the straps of her dress off her shoulder and pulled the front of the dress below her breast. She wasn't wearing a bra, and he cupped her breast, teasing the nipple, then put his mouth to her ear. "Please let me fuck you on your washing machine so that every time you go in there to wash clothes, you'll think of just how dirty I can make you."

Her pupils dilated. "Yes. Definitely yes." She shifted on his lap, pulling a groan from his throat.

"Meet you in the laundry room in five minutes."

She kissed him hard. "Should I bring a condom?"

He pinched her ass. "I've got it *covered*."

She giggled—actually giggled—and pushed herself off his lap while she pulled her dress back into place. They headed upstairs, giving each other heated, playful looks as they got the kids settled stringing beads onto strings and pipe cleaners to create pieces of art. Predictably, Cooper was interested but eased into the project, concentrating on sorting his beads by color and size before starting, while Stella dove in, combining the beads in a colorful, varied pattern.

"Okay, we'll be just downstairs," Addison told them, inching toward the door.

"Okay," Stella said without looking up.

Cooper didn't reply.

"Hey, bud, yell if you need anything, okay?" Gabe said.

Cooper looked up. "Okay."

"Or he can tell me," Stella said. "I know where everything is."

Cooper looked at her and smiled. "Yeah, Stella can help me."

Gabe shot Addison a look. She just nodded with a little shrug.

"Okay," Gabe said. "Still, we'll just be downstairs."

"Yeah, we really should go *downstairs*," Addison said, stepping through the door and giving him a wide-eyed, let's-go-already look.

"Hey, guys, no eating the beads, okay?" Gabe asked as he moved toward the door.

Cooper frowned. "Why would we eat the beads?"

Gabe grinned. "I was just being funny."

Cooper shook his head. "I don't think you're as funny as you think you are, Dad."

Gabe gave a short laugh. "Got it. I'll remember that."

He and Addison ran down the stairs together and got the table shoved in front of the door of the laundry room. Addison slipped out of her panties and boosted herself up on the washing machine, hiking her skirt up around her waist. Gabe watched her, fire licking along his limbs as he undid his fly. He stepped close, and Addison ran her hands up under his shirt over his abs and chest.

"Wow, this was a good idea," she said, skimming her nails over his nipples.

Gabe growled and kissed her neck, working the strap of her dress down again so he could get at a nipple himself. But as he ran his thumb over it, and even as he knew that this wasn't the kind of talking they should be doing, he said, "The kids are fine, right?"

Addison paused, then looked up at him. "I'm sure they are."

"But Stella won't really try to fix *anything*, right?" he asked. "If there's something big, she'll come yelling for us?"

Addison flattened her palms on his ribs on either side. "Yes, she will," she assured him. "Stella is really responsible. And she knows the rules around here—what she can do and get for herself and what she needs help for."

"Okay."

"But," she went on, looking at him seriously, "as much as I'd love to think that we can figure out a way to have sex even with two kids in the house, if you're not comfortable with this tonight, that's okay."

"I *really* want this, Ad," he said, dropping his hands to her hips.

"I know. And so do I. But I've never had sex with Stella in the house. And I'm guessing with the whole living-with-your-mom thing and the apartment over the bar, you haven't had sex with Cooper in the house before, either."

He shook his head. "Nope. Never occurred to me."

"So maybe we shouldn't—"

"But parents *do* have sex with their kids in the house," he said. "I'm sure married couples with kids find a way to have sex even when their kids are home."

Addison smiled. "I'm sure they do. That's how families of more than one happen, I'm guessing."

"Exactly. And I think it's important that you—okay, *we*—prove to ourselves that we can do this."

Addison nodded. "I get it. But Gabe, you have to follow your gut. Sometimes your head will tell you things about your kid that make perfect sense and should be absolutely right, but *something* will still bug you about it or will tell you it's not right. I think you have to trust that."

He thought about that for a second, then blew out a breath. He leaned to rest his forehead on hers. "I can't believe that *you*—the careful, prepared one, the woman who carries wet wipes and Band-Aids in her purse—is right here, pantiless, ready and willing, and *I'm* the one hesitating."

She slid her hands out of his shirt and looped her arms around his neck, pulling him in for a hug. Gabe wrapped his arms around her, the action feeling as natural as taking her hips in his hands and sinking deep. Or kissing her. Or holding her hand walking down Decatur. Or sharing a private look across a support-group circle. Or admitting that he wasn't sure about how sex in the laundry room with Addison fit into his parenting plan. Or admitting that he didn't really have a parenting plan.

"Gabe Trahan, I will take my panties off and get up on any washing machine for you anytime," Addison said in his ear. "It doesn't have to be tonight. We're not losing any opportunity that we can't get back. If this doesn't feel right to you, then we shouldn't do it."

He breathed out, calling himself a million kinds of idiot, but finally he nodded. "Maybe Coop and I should get home."

"Okay." She leaned back, kissed him, and then pulled up her dress.

Watching her cover that breast made Gabe curse himself *again*, but he pulled his boxers and jeans back on while she stepped into her panties and they left the laundry room together.

They headed back upstairs and exclaimed over the beaded artwork, then Gabe had Cooper say goodbye to Stella, and they started downstairs.

At the door, Gabe turned to Addison. "I was invited to a masquerade ball next Saturday. Be my plus-one."

Addison hesitated. "Just us?"

"Just us."

"So a date. Without kids."

"Yes."

She appeared to be thinking it over. Did that seem more serious than getting their kids together? Maybe. But Gabe knew this woman. "You can buy a big, fancy gown, and there will be a live jazz band and mint juleps," he said, naming off the most southern things he could think of.

As expected, her eyes widened. "I've never had a mint julep," she said.

"And you really should have your first at a big southern plantation during a ball," he said.

Her eyes got even wider. "It's at a *plantation*?"

He nodded.

She tried to act nonchalant about it as she said, "I guess that might be kind of cool."

He grinned. "I wasn't going to go, but then realized that this is right up your alley."

"You'd go just for me?"

He ran a hand over her head. "I'd do anything for you, Ad."

And damn, he meant that. More than he'd even realized.

"Well, how can I *not* go to the ball with you, then, Prince Charming?" But a second later, she frowned. "I don't know who I'd have sit for Stella. Maybe Lexi? Or I guess I could ask Elena. I haven't needed anyone at night except for support-group night. But I don't think that gal would want to stay until midnight."

"Or later," Gabe said, suddenly really liking the whole Cinderella imagery she'd planted. He would love to whisk her away from her worries.

Which, of course, was funny, considering it was because of *his* worries that he was still physically aching for her and would possibly have a date with his hand later.

"Or later," she agreed.

"Well, you can share my sitter that night," Gabe told her. That seemed like the easiest, most obvious solution anyway. "Right, bud?" he asked Cooper, who'd been standing by the door, patiently waiting. "Stella could come over and play with you while Addison and I go to a party next weekend?"

Cooper nodded. "Sure. I can show her my room then."

"Exactly." Gabe turned back to Addison. "What do you say?"

She lifted a brow. "Maybe. As long as it's not your mom or something."

Gabe grinned. "Of course it's my mom."

Addison groaned.

"Oh, come on," he said, stepping close. "She's great."

"That's not what I'm worried about, and you know it," Addison told him.

"Then what?"

"I've met your—" She glanced at Cooper. "O-f-f-s-p-r-i-n-g," she spelled out. "I think maybe meeting your mom is a little fast."

Gabe laughed. "She already knows all about you."

"She does?"

"Of course."

"You told her about me?" Addison looked surprised and, maybe, a little touched.

"Cooper did," Gabe said. "But I confirmed everything he said."

"What did he say?" she asked, looking at Cooper with a soft expression.

"That you're sweet, and smell good, and are pretty, and funny, and that you like to kiss boys."

Addison's eyes flew to his. "*What?*"

"Well, okay, you said that girls sometimes start the kissing," Gabe added, letting his gaze drop to her lips so she knew that he was most definitely thinking about all of their kissing. "And I think he also told her . . . What was that last part, Coop?"

Cooper giggled. "That she's full of beans."

Gabe winked at her. "Right."

Addison pointed at Cooper. "Remind me that none of my secrets are safe with you," she told him.

Cooper just laughed harder.

"Come on, go to the ball with me," Gabe said. "Let my mom spoil Stella, and let my son spend some time with that bright, shiny girl who he already feels safe with."

Addison tipped her head back with a groan. "How am I supposed to resist *that*?"

"You're not supposed to."

"Okay." She looked at him again. "I'll go. But I should warn you, I'm going to knock your socks off with my dress."

"Yeah, you will," he said sincerely. Then, following his gut exactly as Addison had encouraged, he wrapped an arm around her waist, dipped her back, and, much to Cooper's delight, kissed her good night.

"I can't wait," Caroline Trahan said, taking Addison's hand and pulling her into the living room. "He's going to be speechless."

Addison had been just about to ring the doorbell to Caroline's house when the door had swung open and Gabe's mother had greeted Addison and Stella with a huge warm smile and a finger over her lips, indicating they should be quiet.

Apparently, Gabe was upstairs getting dressed, and Caroline wanted to greet Addison and Stella without him present. And she wanted to see Gabe's reaction when he saw Addison.

Which was sweet. But Addison touched her hair, suddenly self-conscious and realizing that this evening was a bigger deal than Gabe and her just going to some party.

She'd known that. On some level. And she'd ignored it. Because she really wanted to go. Not just for the plantation house and mint juleps.

But now she was in the living room where Gabe had grown up, with his mother beaming—*beaming*—at her. Stella had picked up on the excitement and was shifting from foot to foot and trying to muffle her giggles.

Addison grinned at her daughter. "Mrs. Trahan, this is Stella. Stella, this is Gabe's mom and Cooper's grandma, Mrs. Trahan."

"Oh my goodness," Caroline said with a laugh. "You can't call me Mrs. Trahan," she told Stella. "That's way too hard. You can call me Caro."

"Okay," Stella told her with a wide smile.

"And I hope you like grilled cheese and carrot sticks," Caroline said.

"I do," Stella said enthusiastically.

Addison and Caroline had talked on the phone earlier in the week to go over some of Stella's preferences and routines, which Addison appreciated greatly. The other woman was warm and sweet and so genuine in wanting to make Stella's evening with her successful.

"And I was wondering if you would help me with something," Caroline said to Stella.

"Okay."

Addison felt pride warm her heart, as her daughter readily agreed to help Caroline without even knowing what she needed and with the realization that Stella trusted Caroline.

"Well, I have some old coffee cans that I want to turn into containers that I can grow flowers in for my friends. And I need some help painting and decorating them."

Stella's mouth fell open at the idea of doing a craft project. "I'm a *really* good artist," she said solemnly. "I can do a good job on that."

Caroline smiled widely. "Oh, that's wonderful news. I can't wait to get started."

"Holy shit, Addison."

They all swung to face Gabe as he stepped into the room. He was staring at Addison as he came forward, as if he didn't even see anyone else. And she knew the feeling. *Holy shit* was right. He was in a tux. And, evidently, that was all it took to make her nipples perk up and everything to go hot and wet.

"Language, Gabe." This came from Logan, who had just come into the room with Cooper. He bit into the apple he held as he looked over at Addison, froze, checked her out from head to toe, and then said, "But yeah, holy shit, Addison."

She was very pleased with the off-the-shoulder, floor-length dress. The fitted bodice was a rich ocean blue, with the color slowly fading to a pale-blue at the hem. There were silvery threads throughout the bodice that sparkled in the light when she moved. She had her hair up in a twist and had gone a little dramatic with her makeup, especially around her eyes.

She opened her mouth, but she couldn't even spare Logan a reply because suddenly Gabe was nearly on top of her.

"I need to talk to you in the kitchen," he said.

Addison felt her eyes widen. "Um, okay." She glanced at Caroline.

Caroline and Logan were both watching Gabe with a combination of surprise and amusement.

"Stella, I'm going to go talk to Gabe for a minute, okay?"

"Sure, Mommy," Stella told her. She made a beeline for Cooper. "Show me your room."

"Okay." Cooper turned and led the way out of the room.

Gabe grabbed Addison's hand and started in the opposite direction.

"Hey, Gabe?" Caroline called.

"Yeah?" he asked, not stopping but giving his mom a quick glance.

"Don't mess up her hair. It looks perfect."

Gabe didn't reply, and Addison tripped along after him on her three-inch heels, holding up the skirt of her gown. "Gabe, what's going on?"

"Just a second," he said. He pulled her into the kitchen and around the edge of the countertop, fridge, and another countertop before he turned her, backed her into a corner, cupped her face in his hands, and kissed her.

Addison gripped his biceps, loving that the heels boosted her closer to his height. She opened her mouth, and he immediately stroked his tongue in along hers, making sparks of pleasure and desire explode in her core.

It was several long moments before he lifted his head. When he did, he said, "Okay, new rule. You need to text me photos before we go out from now on."

Addison couldn't help but love the "from now on," as if this was something that was going to keep happening for a very long time. "Why is that?"

"So I can be prepared. The sudden rerouting of blood from my brain could be dangerous."

She laughed, feeling light and happy and optimistic. "Well, I don't want anything to happen to you. I'll wear sweatpants from now on."

He ran his hands down to her butt. "I love you in sweatpants. But damn, girl, this dress . . ."

She lifted a hand to his mouth and wiped away the lipstick from his bottom lip with her thumb. Then she looped her arms around his neck. "I got new shoes, too."

"I love you in heels."

"I was hoping you'd say that. I was also hoping you'd let me keep them on later."

"Later?" But his eyes darkened, and she knew that he knew exactly what she was talking about.

She'd hoped to swing by the apartment over the tavern before she came back to pick up Stella.

"Well, they match my thong perfectly. I was hoping you'd let me keep both on while you—"

"Yes. Fuck yes," he growled, kissing her again, hot and hard.

"Then let's go to the party . . . so we can leave," she said. She was excited about a masquerade ball at a real southern plantation, she wasn't going to lie. But she was much more excited about some one-on-one time with Gabe. They'd seen each other, and had finally exchanged phone numbers so they could call and text in between seeing each other, but twice had been with the kids and once had been at the support-group meeting. She needed him. Alone. To herself.

He pushed himself back, bracing his hands on the wall on either side of her head. "We could skip the party."

She'd known he'd say that. "Let's go. For a little while. I have a surprise for you."

He lifted a brow. "You got my name tattooed on your ass? Because, darlin', that would be fucking awesome."

She rolled her eyes but smiled. "Well, maybe not *that* big of a surprise."

"But you'd consider it down the road?"

She would love to think that there was a "down the road" for them. And *that* was a pretty damned big surprise. But she went for flippant rather than "I'm falling in love with you" as a response. "I've already been stunned by the things you can talk me into," she said. "I guess I can't really rule anything out."

He smiled down at her, and they stood, just like that, for several long seconds.

"We're going to have an amazing time tonight," he finally said.

She nodded. "I know."

"We can totally relax. Mom is here with the kids, Logan will have the bar covered. We can just . . . be us."

Us. The kids. Mom. It all sounded so comfortable and natural and . . . tempting.

With that falling-in-love thing still hovering on the edges of her mind, Addison forced a smile and her concentration in a new direction. "So let's get going. I want to show you the surprise."

"Okay. But you might want to check your lipstick first," he said, looking smug.

She ducked into the powder room just outside the kitchen. Yeah, there was no more lipstick to check. She reapplied, checked her hair, smoothed her dress, and took a deep breath.

They made their way back to the living room. Caroline was on the couch with a book. She looked up. "Ready to go?"

"Ready," Gabe said. "We'll check in later."

"No problem. The kids are already in their spy gear and have a mission planned," Caroline said with an affectionate smile.

"I appreciate you watching Stella, too," Addison said. "She shouldn't be any trouble."

Caroline waved that off. "Don't be silly. Watching two is easier than one. They entertain each other. We'll eat in a little bit and do the craft project later, and then I'll settle them on the couch with a movie. We'll have a great time."

Addison felt Gabe's hand settle on the back of her neck and relished how comfortable they both were with the gesture.

Gabe escorted her to the door and pulled it open for her. "This is going to be—" He stopped talking, and walking, as he stared at the car at the curb.

"Surprise," Addison said, throwing her arms wide.

"You got us a limo?" he asked.

"Well, I couldn't find a pumpkin that would change into a carriage, and you can't go to a ball in a regular car," she said, taking his hand and starting down the steps.

"You can," he said. "I've done it."

She smiled at him over her shoulder. "Okay, let's put it this way. You can't have sex in the back seat while also traveling to the ball in a regular car."

"We're going to have sex in the back seat on the way to the party?" he asked, picking up his pace.

"I figured this was a great way to sneak in a quickie with no kids around," she told him. She stopped by the car door that the driver had opened for her. "We're going to have to figure out ways to do stuff like that going forward, right?"

He focused on her fully, seemingly studying her face for something. Then he nodded. "Yes. Because we're going forward."

She went up on tiptoe and kissed him on the cheek. "Yes, we are," she said softly.

She turned and climbed into the car. Gabe was right behind her. The chauffeur slammed the door once Gabe was inside, and Addison immediately climbed into Gabe's lap, straddling his thighs.

"Just like that?" he asked, but his expression—and the big hands that settled on her hips—said he didn't mind at all.

She kissed him as his hands slid up under her skirt along her bare thighs. Addison shivered with pleasure even from that much. He touched her with an amazing combination of tenderness and assuredness. He was a confident but incredibly caring lover, and every time she had his hands on her, she felt treasured and beautiful, even as she felt needy and nearly desperate. She *needed* him to touch her. Her body craved him. And he never failed to deliver.

It took a few moments of kissing and stroking for Gabe to realize what he *wasn't* touching, however.

He pulled back. "You're not wearing panties?"

She shook her head with a grin.

"Not even a thong?"

"Considering where your hand is right now, you already know the answer to that question," she said, moving against his fingers that were teasing the wet heat between her legs.

"I thought there was a thong that matched your heels," he said. Almost as if he were disappointed to find out there wasn't.

She laughed lightly and reached for her purse. She pulled out the blue thong and held it up for him.

His mouth curled into a sexy half grin. "You were in my *mother's* house, talking about her taking care of our kids tonight, without panties on? I'm shocked."

"And thrilled," she told him, putting her lips against his again. "I'm a great multitasker. I can discuss the evening's agenda, my daughter's dietary preferences and bedtime, and be absolutely charming and sweet to your mother, all the while planning the very naughty things that I want to do to you."

Gabe's fingers teased her, his thumb circling her clit, as he said, "I'm sorry for doubting you." He slid one thick finger into her. "Won't happen again."

She moaned and moved her hips, pressing closer to his touch.

"I have to say, though, as much as I love this dress, it's too damned big for this," he said, pumping his finger in and out, then adding a second. "I can't see all the things I want to see." Her skirt was bunched around her hips, but there was a lot of material, and it had fallen back over her thighs and his hand.

Addison rocked against his hand, suddenly finding it hard to multitask beyond seeking a nice, hard orgasm right here like this. "You're doing okay by feel," she said, her voice husky.

"But watching my fingers move in and out of your sweet pussy is second only to me watching my cock move in and out of your sweet pussy," he said.

Addison was sure he felt how those words and that tone of voice affected her as her inner muscles squeezed his fingers.

"Lift your skirt up, Addison," he said, low and firm.

She was getting so close to that climax she needed. "Just keep going."

"Lift it up, Ad," he repeated. "I want to see all that pink."

And then he stopped moving his hand. Addison stared at him. "Hey!"

"Lift. It. Up."

She huffed out a breath. But yeah, okay, she was totally going to lift up her skirt for him because she was *not* getting off his lap without an orgasm. But it did not escape her notice that *her* plan for a surprise quickie in the back of a limo had suddenly become Gabe's show. She should have expected that, now that she thought about it.

"You're so bossy." She reached for the bunched material and gathered it into both hands.

"Yeah, I am," he said, watching her.

She lifted her skirt, having to pull the bulk of the material up almost to her breasts to actually expose what he wanted to see. His eyes were hot, and she could feel her orgasm building just from him looking at her like this.

"Yes. That's what I want," he said, his thumb brushing over her clit.

With her hands full of blue silk and her legs spread by Gabe's thighs, Addison was kind of at his mercy, she realized. If she moved her hands, the dress would drop, and he'd stop moving *his* hand. So she had to just sit here and take whatever he'd give her.

"Gabe, please," she said, adding a little desperation to her tone. Which she totally felt. But she also knew it would turn him on. He loved to make her beg.

"Lean back a little," he said.

She did, and he groaned. "Yes. God, I love every fucking inch of you," he said.

And before she could respond, he moved his hand.

He slid two fingers deep, circled her clit and, possibly the best part, kept talking. He told her how gorgeous she was and how tight she was and how he could remember her taste even now and how watching her come apart was the hottest thing he'd ever seen. He used the perfect combination of sweet and dirty, and within minutes she was soaring.

She worked to catch her breath and then focused on him. "That wasn't really the way I'd planned this going."

He gave her a grin. "Sorry."

She laughed. "Well, you can make it up to me." She scooted back on his lap and went to her knees on the floor of the limo. "Unzip your pants."

Heat flared in his eyes. "Excuse me?"

Addison ran her hands up and down his thighs. "Unzip your pants," she repeated, her eyes on his.

And an arrow of heat shot through her when he did it.

She reached up and spread open the front of his tuxedo pants, then pulled down his boxers. She took his hot, hard shaft in hand, stroking up and down as she watched his breathing speed up. "Yeah, I get it," she said with a nod. "Watching you come undone because of me is one of the hottest things I've ever seen, too." Then she leaned in and took him into her mouth.

She slid down his length slowly, dragging a groan from his chest and relishing the way he immediately cupped her head with one hand. He didn't push her or even hold her tightly. He just rested his hand there, fingers curled into her hair, as if to be connected. And she didn't care a bit about messing up the style. She'd fix it later with bobby pins and hairspray. Or she wouldn't. At the moment, she really couldn't care less.

Addison licked and sucked and stroked. She used her hands and lips and tongue. She stroked over his abs, loving the feel of the muscles bunching under her touch. She ran her hands up to his chest, circling his nipples as she sucked him. She lifted her head and looked up at him. "Talk to me, Gabe. My mouth's full, so I can't tell you how much I love doing this to you and how hot this is and how every time I run my tongue up and down your cock, I can practically feel it in my pussy. So *you* have to talk."

His fingers tightened in her hair momentarily as he stared down at her, his eyes dark and hot. But he started talking. Oh, did he.

"Your pussy is my favorite place to be," he said roughly. "But damn, your mouth is a very close second. I love how your cheeks get pink and your nipples get hard when you're sucking me off. I love that you're so greedy about it, like my cock is all you ever need. I love having you on your knees as if you're just there to serve and pleasure me. When I know that you know that I'm wrapped so fucking tight around your little finger that I'd give you the damned moon if you wanted it. I love how you make those little noises when you've got me in your mouth, as if you'll never get enough. And I love how wet you get from this and how I can sink into you, balls deep, and make you come within minutes."

And she definitely felt her nipples get hard and her core pulse and how close she was to coming just from this.

It was only a few minutes later that his thighs were tightening, and he was warning her he was going to come.

This wasn't the first blow job she'd given him, though, and she didn't pull back for a second. But Gabe put both hands on her head and moved her off his cock, dragged her into his lap, and sank deep, just as he'd said.

They moved together, fast and furious, chasing the oh-so-close climaxes that came crashing over them moments later.

Gabe buried his face between her breasts, clasping her body to his. Addison wrapped her arms around his neck. And they both worked to just breathe.

Finally, he looked up at her. "That was . . . amazing."

She stroked her fingers through his hair and smiled down at him. "Yeah, it was. It's been too long again."

He nodded. "But we're getting practice at this grab-an-opportunity-and-go-with-it thing."

"We are. Though we might have to get faster. As much as I *loved* all of that, we can't do that in the laundry room."

"Challenge accepted," he said.

She laughed and climbed off his lap. It wasn't particularly sexy, but she handed him some tissues to clean up with and wondered how bad an idea it would be to use antibacterial hand wipes *down there* when she realized something that stopped her heart for a moment.

She looked up at him quickly. He must have seen something in her eyes that startled him because he immediately frowned. "What?"

She swallowed. "We didn't use a condom."

He froze. Then gave a nearly inaudible "Holy shit."

Chapter Eight

Addison made herself breathe in and out. And then again. And again. Okay, they hadn't used a condom. Okay, that wasn't for sure a bad thing. It wasn't the end of the world. But it was a very big deal.

"Ad," Gabe said, reaching over and taking her hand, "talk to me."

"I just . . ." She looked at him and saw the true concern in his eyes. And her thoughts spun—to Gabe laughing with his brother, and hugging his mom, and trying to coax Cooper into touching an alligator, and watching Stella with an expression of wonder and intimidation and affection, and listening to a support-group member, and looking at *her* when he first rolled over in bed in the morning.

Gabe Trahan was an amazing man. Not using a condom with him was maybe not the smartest move of her life, but it was hardly a disaster.

"I'm okay," she finally said.

He lifted both eyebrows. "Yeah?"

"I mean, I can't believe I did that. But I've got the IUD, so we're fine, and yeah, I'm okay."

Gabe looked a little disappointed in her answer. She frowned. "Are *you* okay?"

"Yeah." He shrugged and pulled his hand from her, smoothing the front of his shirt and retucking it, even though it was very well tucked.

"Why do you seem not okay?" she asked.

Erin Nicholas

He frowned. "I'm fine. I just had a blow job in a limo. Couldn't be better."

She should let it go. Two months ago, she would have. For sure six months ago, she would have. But things were different now. She and Gabe were . . . involved. That was the best word for it, probably.

So she pulled on her thong and then climbed back into his lap.

He didn't push her away, and his hands settled on her hips, as if they were meant to be there, but he didn't look up at her right away.

"What's going on?" she asked.

He sighed. "It's stupid, and I'm sorry for thinking it."

"For thinking what?"

"That knocking you up wouldn't be the worst thing in the world and that I would like you to feel the same way."

Surprise hit her first, but a feeling of yeah-I-get-it followed it very quickly. She finally nodded. "It wouldn't be the worst thing in the world."

He was clearly not expecting that answer. "No?"

"I don't think we should try for it," she said. "It's not what I really *want*. But no, it definitely wouldn't be the worst thing in the world."

He blew out a breath. "Okay."

"Okay." She didn't know what else to say. So she kissed him and then slid out of his lap.

They arrived at the party ten minutes later, and Addison put on a smile and her mask, reminding herself that this was a *ball* on a southern *plantation* and she was going to focus on the fun and frivolity for the rest of the night.

Because the topic of having a baby with Gabe was definitely not frivolous. And *fun* wasn't the right word, either. But it also wasn't terrifying. And *that* was just not something she was prepared to delve into.

Two hours, two beignets, two mint juleps, and several dances later, Addison was definitely in a party mood. Gabe was hot enough in the tux, but when he showed her that he knew how to waltz, her panties nearly melted off. He'd been introducing her to people, touching her, even stealing kisses all night, and she felt like she was in the middle of a fairy tale. So when her phone rang just as she was returning to the dance floor with Gabe's hand in hers, it took her a second to return to real life.

"Hello?"

"Hi, honey, it's Caroline."

"Hi, Caroline." Addison pointed toward the huge French doors that led to the back patio, and Gabe nodded. "Just a minute, we're going where it's quieter."

They stepped out onto the enormous stone patio, complete with a gurgling fountain and three stone paths that led into the flower garden. As soon as the doors swung shut, the music and conversation were cut off, and she said, "Is everything okay?"

"Oh, yes. I was just calling to let you know that Stella is fast asleep, and I was wondering if she could spend the night. We talked about my French toast earlier, and Cooper convinced her that she really had to try it."

Addison smiled. "I'm so glad they're getting along. But I don't know—"

"She's in one of Cooper's shorts and T-shirts, I had an extra toothbrush, and she's confiscated one of Logan's favorite pillows."

"Are you sure?"

"Honey, I'm completely sure. I'd love to have her. You and Gabe enjoy your night, and we'll see you in the morning for French toast. It really is quite good."

Addison laughed. "I don't know how I can say no. But please call me if there are any problems at all."

"Of course. Have fun."

"What's going on?" Gabe asked as she disconnected.

Addison explained, then said, "I think your mom is trying to get you laid," she said.

He grinned. "She's the best."

"She really is."

He nodded and lifted a hand to her cheek. "But be careful. My mom is this close to pulling out her wedding ring so I can give it to you."

Addison laughed, but then she saw that he was clearly serious. Her heart thumped, and she felt her lungs freeze and a really strange ribbon of *I-want-that* snaked through her. Addison swallowed. "Really? She barely knows me."

"But she knows me."

"And you said something?" Surely not. No way would Gabe mention his mother's *wedding ring*. She needed to keep calm. He was kidding around. Kind of. Maybe.

"I didn't have to say anything. She knows me. She's seen how happy I am."

"It's only been a few weeks," Addison said weakly.

"It's been seven months."

She looked up at him. "You've been noticeably happier because of me for seven months?"

He nodded. "Maybe it's not very manly to admit, but I've been pretty smitten with you since you first walked into my bar."

Smitten. That was a really great word. And, wow. It wasn't *I love you*, but it was as close to talking about feelings other than lust that they'd been.

"I have been, too," she said honestly.

He pulled her close and kissed her. And it was the sweetest kiss of her life. Full of promise and, yeah, maybe they weren't saying it, but that kiss felt like there was some love there. Tears pricked the backs of her eyes, and she had to blink a few times after opening them when he lifted his head.

"Want to go to the apartment where I can finally get this dress off you completely and worship your body from head to toe?" he asked.

"That's quite a come-on line," she teased, absolutely ready to let him do all that.

"Oh, there's going to be coming involved. Nice, loud, Gabe-you're-a-god coming."

As desire swept through her, so did an emotion that felt like more than "some" love. She swallowed. "Yeah, I definitely want that."

Gabe nodded, but he pinned her with an intense look and said, "I think I should be clear about something before we go. In case you want to change your mind."

Oh boy. She wet her lips. "Okay."

"You should know that if I take you to that apartment, where it all started, I will not be fucking you all night long."

Addison couldn't believe it, but she was pretty sure she knew what he was going to say. "Okay," she replied softly.

"I will be making love to you. All night long."

There was something in his voice she'd never heard before, and it made her heart squeeze even as her core tightened with need. "I thought we talked about my wearing just the thong and the heels."

His eyes darkened. "We did. And trust me, Ad, I might be bending you over the table or putting you on all fours on the bed or thrusting into that beautiful mouth, but it will all still be making love."

Wow.

She was in deep. And going to the apartment with him tonight would only make it worse.

But she was going to go.

Oh, God.

"Okay," she said, lacing her fingers with his. "I'm ready."

His hand tightened around hers as his jaw tensed, and Addison could see the emotions swirling in his eyes. He was all in here. She really had to be ready. But an instant later, she realized that she really was . . . she really was ready for this. For Gabe.

Erin Nicholas

An hour later, they were climbing the stairs to the apartment over the bar. It felt very much like all the other times and yet, so different. She knew this man's body so well, knew how explosive this would be, how bone-deep satisfying, and yet she also felt a swoop of nervous anticipation in her belly as he unlocked the door and pushed it open, standing back to let her pass by.

She stepped through the door, half expecting him to close it quickly and back her up against it. That was a familiar move. And she was a big fan. But instead, he stepped through and closed the door softly.

She turned to face him, feeling her heart pounding, the flutter of butterflies in her stomach both exciting and a little nerve-racking. Gabe pushed a hand through his hair and blew out a breath.

"Are you okay?" Addison asked, liking that he looked a little nervous, too.

"Just trying to find words other than 'If you're not naked in the next thirty seconds, I can't be responsible for the damage to that dress.'"

She laughed and moved closer. That was pure Gabe. This was the same guy, and this was going to be great. "Why do you need other words than those?"

"Because since realizing that I'm in love with you, it feels like I should have better words."

Her heart completely turned over in her chest at that. He was in love with her. That was . . . Wow. Now she wasn't sure what words *she* should have. So instead, she took the step that brought her up right in front of him. "If you love me, you'll never stop talking to me like that."

He cupped her face and gave her a sexy, sweet smile. "Addison, if you're not naked in the next thirty seconds, I can't be responsible for potential damage to this dress."

She reached behind her and unzipped, watching him the whole time. The bodice gaped and then fell away, leaving her naked from the waist up.

His eyes flared as she moved back and pushed the dress the rest of the way off. His gaze roamed over her as he shrugged out of his jacket. She stepped out of the dress and hooked her thumbs in the top of her thong, but suddenly Gabe scooped her up into his arms. "Okay, naked was an overreaction on my part. That thong stays."

She undid his tie, pulling it loose and tossing it to the floor, then went to work on the buttons of his shirt as he carried her into the bedroom.

The wrought iron bed under the huge fan with the moonlight streaming through the French doors to the balcony was one of her favorite places. But when Gabe laid her down and started moving his mouth over her body with hot and tender kisses, she lost all track of where she was other than *with Gabe*. This man could make her forget her name.

His lips and tongue and hands moved over her neck, shoulders, breasts, stomach, thighs—clear to her toes. He spent a little extra time at several places in between, lingering on her nipples, belly, inner thighs, and between her legs, where he pulled the thong to one side, but he didn't leave one inch unexplored. She was wriggling and begging by the time he lifted his lips back to hers. His shirt was unbuttoned, and his belt was on the floor by the bed, but otherwise, he was mostly dressed to her mostly naked.

"Gabe, please."

"I don't think there's anything I love hearing more than you begging me to make you come," he said gruffly against her lips.

She wrapped her arms around his neck and arched closer. "Please make me come, Gabe. Please."

He moved his hand between them, again finding her hot, slick folds. He teased her clit, then slipped two fingers inside. "Let me feel it, baby. Let me feel you come apart."

"I want you." She opened her knees farther. "All of you. Not just your fingers."

"*Just* my fingers?" He curved them just right to hit the spot that made her toes curl and her core clench. "They're *just* fingers?"

She moaned, and her hips lifted.

"So you want me to stop?" He stroked deeper.

It took her a second to form words. "I'm so close."

"Just tell me, Ad. Tell me what you want."

She gripped his shirt in both hands, nearly whimpering. "I don't know," she said huskily. "I just want *you*."

"I know you do, baby," he said against her neck. "And that makes me feel like a fucking king."

She loved that she could make him feel that way. He made her feel things that no one else could, and she loved knowing that affected him.

"Please, Gabe." She ran her hands through his hair. "Make love to me."

She felt a shudder go through him, and he shifted. "God, Ad."

Yeah, that sounded different from "Please fuck me." It was so much . . . more.

She reached between them and found his fly. She unbuttoned and unzipped the pants, getting them and his boxers out of the way. When she wrapped her fingers around his shaft, another shudder went through him, and he caught his breath. Then he shifted, leaning in on one elbow and reaching for his pants pocket.

"Gabe, please, now."

"Condom," he said huskily, fumbling with his pants.

But she grabbed his wrist, stopping him. He looked up, and she shook her head. "Just you and me," she said softly.

It wasn't reckless. She still had the IUD. But making love to him without a condom, consciously deciding to not have any barrier between them rather than forgetting in the heat of the moment, felt important. And right.

He paused for a moment, taking in what she was saying. Then he kissed her and slid his hand from his pocket to her thigh, lifting her knee to his hip.

"I love you, Addison," he told her gruffly, looking into her eyes. She nodded. "I love you, too."

Then, when she thought he was going to plunge into her, he grabbed the narrow strip of silk on her hip and yanked, literally ripping the thong off her. *Then* he took her hips and sank deep, the heat and friction perfect. Addison wrapped herself around him, arms and legs striving to get as close as she could.

Her orgasm came on quickly, but rather than a bright explosion of sensation and heat like usual, it was like a slowly rising wave of satisfaction that rolled over her and left no part of her unaffected.

Gabe's climax had him shouting her name and then crushing her to his chest mere minutes later. And when he rolled to his back, he took her with him, keeping her up against him with one hand tangled in her hair and one splayed over her butt.

They stayed wrapped up tight like that, as close as two people could be, afterward, just breathing and thinking for nearly twenty minutes.

Addison felt completely sated. And yet, there was something niggling at her, telling her to not get too comfortable. She couldn't get the thoughts pinned down, but there was something there, not letting her drift to sleep.

Gabe's fingers were combing through her hair, and finally he said, "Ad?"

"Yeah?" she asked, not lifting her head from where it was resting on that perfect spot between his shoulder and chest.

"What would you say to going back to my place?"

"This is your place." But she knew what he meant.

"This is my . . ."

She smiled, waiting for him to fill in that blank. Finally, she tipped her head to look up at him. "Your fuck pad?"

He shot her a sheepish smile. "Kind of."

She knew that. Of course. It was where he'd taken her because he couldn't take women to where he lived. With his mother. And his son.

"But I was thinking it feels kind of strange to be here instead of with the kids," he said. He stroked her hair. "I like the idea of our kids together with my mom. And I feel like . . ."

"We should be there, too," she said softly. And that was what had been nagging at her. This wasn't a one-night stand or a quickie hookup or a secret fling. This was—well, more than that. And while she did love her grown-up time and time being just Addison—especially when that time was with Gabe—now, with Gabe, it felt like she could be all those things at once.

And that was a startling thought. That quickly sank into her heart and made her smile. She pushed herself up to sitting and smiled at Gabe. It was a huge step. Way bigger than coming back here to make love rather than have sex. But it felt good. "Yeah, we should go to your place."

◆　◆　◆

Gabe held Addison's hand, but they didn't talk as the cab took them to the house where his mother and their kids slept. She'd rented the limo for the night, but that night ended at midnight. But Gabe didn't care what they were riding in, only that she was beside him when he was going home.

It had been only a month since they'd talked sarcastically about a long engagement rather than getting married right away. And he had no intention of having Stella and her move in with his mother. They'd get their own place. Or he and Cooper could move in with Addison and Stella. For a while. Until they needed a bigger house for more kids.

Gabe worked on relaxing his hold on her hand and breathing deep. She was going to notice his tension, and he wasn't sure he wanted to let her in on his train of thought just yet. He'd told her he loved her. She'd said it back. They'd made love. She'd let her daughter spend the night with his mom and son. It was all huge. But he knew that marriage and more kids and all was a conversation for another time. Addison was warming up to Cooper, and she knew what being involved with Gabe meant as far as family was concerned. He was a package deal—he came with a family, not just a son. But Gabe wasn't sure that Addison had really let all of that sink in. At least, not how it would affect Stella and her. In his mind, it would be in all positive, supportive ways. But he wasn't sure he wanted to spook her with the whole my-family-is-involved-in-everything-and-that-will-include-you-and-Stella just yet. She'd admitted that she didn't like other people giving advice and making decisions about her daughter. But Gabe definitely wanted her involved with decisions for Cooper. He wanted to talk out all the issues and get her input and have her sitting next to Coop on all the swamp boats—literal and figurative—from here on out. Because Gabe could absolutely be the one dealing with the alligators in Stella's life.

Yeah, he needed to *not* lay all of that on Addison right now.

So he simply lifted her hand and pressed a kiss to the back of it as the car pulled up at the curb. He paid the driver, then helped Addison out of the back seat. They made their way into the house quietly. There was a lamp glowing on the table next to his mother's reading chair, but she had long gone up to bed. Logan was at the bar and would be for at least another hour or so. Cooper and Stella were nestled on the two couches in the living room that sat in an L shape. They each had pillows and blankets and stuffed animals. There were two glasses of water on the table that sat between the couches, and the television over the fireplace was tuned to a kids' music station.

Gabe looked over at Addison and grinned. She squeezed his hand.

"This is nice," she whispered.

"It really is." Though *nice* seemed like an understatement. This was, bottom line, what he wanted to come home to after every night out.

With this woman by his side. And yeah, he needed to reel all of that in, dammit.

"So . . ." Addison looked around. "I guess I didn't think about how this would work. Where should I sleep?"

In my bed. There was never going to be another answer he wanted to give to that question. But that wouldn't be appropriate tonight. Not when they'd be waking up with the kids in the morning. Sure, they could try to get up before Cooper and Stella, but it was risky, and he didn't want to confuse them. "Here." He tossed his tux jacket onto the banister at the bottom of the stairs, then unbuttoned his shirt and shrugged it off.

Addison's eyes widened, and she certainly didn't look away. Her eyes on him heated his blood nearly instantly. But that wasn't what this was about. He handed her the shirt. "Take off your dress and put this on," he said, handing it over.

She took the shirt with a little smile. "Okay," she said. "But I don't have panties, if you remember."

Gabe had to swallow hard at that reminder. Oh yeah. "Stay here." He bounded up the stairs as quietly as he could and returned with a pair of his boxers. "These will work for tonight, right?" He did not want her going home because he'd literally torn off her thong during sex.

She smirked. "Yeah, these will work. I assume we'll be having breakfast with your mother?"

He nodded. "I'm sure."

"Well, this will be interesting."

That was one word for it. *Wonderful* was another. But instead of saying that, Gabe wrapped an arm around her waist and dipped her back, planting a hot but quick kiss on her lips. "I'm glad you're staying," he told her huskily.

She nodded. "Me, too."

He pulled her upright and pointed her toward the powder room. "You can change in there."

Addison glanced at the sleeping kids. "I think I'm okay here." She kicked off her heels and reached behind her for the zipper on her dress.

"Logan might walk in," Gabe said, but he didn't actually make any move to stop her from unzipping and letting the dress pool at her feet. She was bare naked now, thanks to the ripped thong, and yeah, he wasn't sorry about that at all at the moment.

She watched him as she slipped on his shirt, buttoned it, and then pulled the boxers up underneath. "There. All good."

Except for the fact that Gabe had never seen anything as beautiful and sexy as Addison wearing his shirt and standing in his mother's foyer with their kids sleeping ten feet away.

Until she crossed the room and picked up Stella in her arms and then lay down on the couch, settling Stella alongside her on the cushions. Addison smiled up at him as she reached to her hair for the clips holding the elegant twist up. She pulled them loose, letting her hair fall, and tossed the clips onto the table. Then she laid her head on the pillow and pulled the blanket up over her daughter and her.

And *that* was the most beautiful thing he'd ever seen. Addison cuddling Stella on the couch in his mother's living room while wearing his shirt.

The desire that slammed into him took his breath. And it was new desire. It wasn't the red-hot physical and sexual desire but rather a soul-deep *want* that encompassed everything from the sweet smile Addison gave him to the soft snore from Stella.

He took off his belt and toed off his shoes, then followed suit, scooping up Cooper and settling down with him on the other couch. Thankfully, Cooper had chosen the longer of the two couches, and Gabe was able to stretch out his legs as he wrapped an arm around his son.

"Night, Gabe," Addison said softly.

"Night, Ad," he said. Then added, "I love you."

"I love you, too."

He was, somehow, able to bite back the other words he wanted to say. The ones that went something like, *Marry me, Addison, and do this with me forever.*

◆ ◆ ◆

The morning after the masquerade ball was more of the same feel-good, sunshine-and-rainbows, I-want-this-forever stuff.

They had breakfast together in his mom's kitchen. They all helped make the French toast and bacon and eggs and hash browns. The kids helped stir the batter, Caroline was in charge of the griddle, Gabe manned the frying pan, and Addison handled the scrambled eggs. While still wearing his shirt and boxers.

But the only comment anyone made about it was Stella asking why Addison was wearing a shirt that was too big. And when Logan walked in and saw Addison's long, bare legs.

Stella's comment was simply that it was nice of Gabe to loan Addison one of his shirts, just like Cooper had loaned one of his to Stella.

Logan's comment was that he was curious as to why there was a lipstick smudge on the *bottom* of the shirt where it would have been tucked into the front of Gabe's pants.

Caroline distracted the kids with whipped-cream smiley faces. But Gabe's attempt to distract *Caroline* with chocolate creamer in her coffee and whipped cream on top did not work. She gave them both a knowing, though pleased, smile. Gabe really did love his mother.

They finished a delightfully noisy, messy breakfast prep, eating, and cleanup. And then it was time for Addison and Stella to leave.

And Gabe wanted to beg her to stay. He couldn't, of course. Because it probably would have included the word *forever*, and that wasn't a good idea. Yet.

But Gabe could always count on his kid.

"When can Stella come back?" Cooper wanted to know.

Stella looked up at Addison, who was back in her dress and heels. And pantiless. Gabe couldn't forget that. "Yeah, when, Mommy?"

Addison put a hand on Stella's head. "I'm not sure. But Gabe and I will talk about it, okay?"

"Next Saturday!" Cooper said. "We can make clay alligators like we talked about!"

Stella bounced on her toes as she said, "Yes. Mommy, I *have to*."

Addison grinned. "Well, that sounds amazing, but you can't next weekend. Maybe the weekend after."

Gabe frowned. "Why not?" he asked before thinking. Not that thinking would have changed his reaction.

Addison met his eyes. "I'm going out of town for work on Wednesday and not coming back until Sunday," she said.

"Where are you going?" She'd just moved here after six months of *this* being her out-of-town work spot.

"There's a bed-and-breakfast in Mobile that's hired us to do their restoration," Addison said. "I'm meeting with the owners on Wednesday, and we're putting all the plans together."

"Who's taking care of Stella?" Gabe asked.

"The woman who's been babysitting on Thursdays," Addison said. "She's agreed to come stay at the house until Saturday."

"She can bring me over," Stella decided.

Addison shook her head. "No, honey. The agreement is for her to stay with you at our house. I didn't talk with her about anything extra."

"Then Stella can just say here the whole time," Gabe said.

He instantly knew that he shouldn't have. You didn't make plans in front of the kids when you didn't know how the other parent would feel. But, strange as it was, he didn't like the idea of someone else taking care of Stella for that extended period.

Addison frowned. "No, that's not necessary. We can get the kids together the *next* weekend."

Gabe didn't like that.

"How well do you know this person?" Gabe asked.

Addison gave him a look that clearly said *Really?* But she said, "Someone at work recommended her. She's stayed with Stella several times now. Her name is Debra and she's very nice."

"How old is she?"

Addison crossed her arms. "Fiftysomething."

"And she has kids?"

"And grandkids."

"What does she do for a living?" Gabe pressed.

"Gabe," Addison said, the warning in her tone clear.

He didn't care. He crossed his arms, too. "What does she do for a living?" She could just be off work for three or four days? And how old were her grandkids? Did they live locally? What kind of references did she have besides this person Addison worked with? Addison needed to be sure that Debra was good enough.

"She works for her daughter at her daughter's dress shop," Addison said.

Hmm. That didn't seem like a qualification for taking care of a little girl. "Did you check her references?"

"Of *course* I checked her references!" Addison exclaimed. "Good grief. What is this?"

"I just want to be sure she should be the one taking care of Stella," he said, giving her a little frown. "And I'd much prefer that Stella stay here. She knows us, *you* know us, she's already comfortable here. And we'd love to have her. Plus, it's free."

Addison rolled her eyes. "The cost isn't really a concern."

"Still, we want her to stay with us," Gabe said stubbornly. "I think that's the best arrangement."

Addison just looked at him for a long moment, and Gabe braced himself. He was inserting himself into her life. Into *Stella's* life. Giving an opinion. An opinion that was contrary to a decision Addison had already made. Yeah, this was dangerous territory. But he didn't like the idea of Stella with a stranger.

He softened his tone and dropped his arms. "Ad, I just want Stella to be safe and happy. I'm not saying she wouldn't be safe with Donna—"

"Debra," Addison corrected.

He nodded. "Right. Debra. I'm sure she'll be safe. But she'll be safe here, too. Completely. And more comfortable and happier."

Addison tipped her head. "You seem really sure about that."

"I am. Completely."

"This seems really important to you," Addison said.

"It is."

She looked down at Stella, who had, interestingly, stayed quiet throughout the conversation. Then Addison met his gaze again. "Okay."

Gabe was amazed by how relieved he felt at her answer. "Great." He grinned down at Stella. "It's going to be an amazing time."

Stella's eyes got wide. "Really, Mommy? I can stay here the *whole time* you're gone?"

Addison nodded. "Yep. The *whole time*. Gabe's totally in charge."

And he felt his first stirring of trepidation. He was totally in charge. Of both kids. Including one who belonged to a woman he cared about a lot. One that was a girl. He didn't know anything about girls.

But he gave them a big smile and said, "I can't wait."

Addison gave him a smirk. "Me neither."

Oh boy. That sounded ominous. Exactly as he was sure she meant it to.

Chapter Nine

By Friday night, Gabe was feeling pretty cocky.

The last two days with Stella had been great. His mother had handled breakfast and dinner each day, but Gabe had dropped off the kids at their respective preschools—they were going to have to get them into the same preschool soon—and picked them up again. He'd been in charge of evening activities and had shared bedtime tasks with his mom. Except for Thursday night when he'd covered the bar, as usual, and Logan had pitched in. Apparently, Logan did much better voices for the bedtime stories anyway—something Cooper had long maintained and that Stella had confirmed.

There hadn't been any arguments, nightmares, or tantrums. Stella had turned down the cooked carrots on Wednesday night but had eaten everything else. She'd also spoken to Addison each night before bed, which meant Gabe also got to speak to Addison each night. And last night, he'd kept her on the phone long enough to get to *his* bed and have a little phone sex.

So yeah, he was feeling pretty full of himself and this father-of-two thing he was trying on for size.

Until the thunder started.

And all hell broke loose.

"Dad!"

Gabe came awake like someone had slapped him. Because someone had. Cooper was "patting" Gabe's cheeks. Hard. Gabe caught his little hands. "Coop! What is going on?"

His son's eyes were wide in the faint glow from the night-light Gabe kept on for just such occasions.

"Stella is really scared! She's crying, Dad!" Cooper was clearly panicked.

Gabe swung his legs over the bed, processing the words more slowly because he'd been dead freaking asleep. He ran a hand over his face. Okay. Stella was scared. And crying.

Shit.

He grabbed for the T-shirt on the floor next to the bed and pulled it on as he started for the door. Cooper was panicking because they simply didn't have crying females in their house. Ever. Caroline was not a crier. Which was why Gabe was also feeling panic welling up.

He *hated* the idea of Stella being scared. Especially in his house with him. This was a safe place. But then the panic hit him full force when he stepped into Cooper's room. There were three night-lights burning around the room. Cooper always slept with two, but they'd added another tonight so that if Stella woke up, she would be able to tell instantly where she was. Where she was at the moment was huddled in one corner, clutching Cooper's favorite stuffed dog, and literally shaking.

Gabe slowed down, not wanting to stomp over to the little girl. But the adrenaline pumping in his veins made it an effort to go easy and force a smile and lower his voice.

"Hey, Stell," he said softly, moving to crouch in front of her but not too close to make her feel caged in. "What's going on, sweetheart?"

"It's storming," she said in a loud whisper.

On cue, lightning flashed outside the window, illuminating her face fully. And the tears on her cheeks.

Gabe felt his heart and gut squeeze so hard, he had to consciously drag in a long breath so he didn't reach out and grab her and crush her to his chest. It was *not* okay that Stella was scared and crying. But grabbing her certainly wouldn't help anything.

"It is storming," Gabe agreed. The wind was howling, the rain was pounding, and the thunder was growling, in fact. "You don't like storms?" he asked.

She shook her head quickly, her eyes wide.

"Damn, sweetheart," Gabe said, then grimaced over the *damn*, "I'm really sorry."

"My mommy says that it's just air crashing around," Stella said.

Gabe nodded. "That's right."

"But I still don't like it."

Another loud clap of thunder boomed, and a flash of lightning lit the sky, and Stella literally shuddered.

"What is air crashing around?" Cooper asked, wiggling in between Gabe and the wall to his right. Cooper peered at Stella, another stuffed dog under one arm. He'd gone through a dog phase as well.

"The thunder," Stella said. "The air gets hot from the lightning, and then it shakes and makes noise."

Gabe looked down to see Cooper watching Stella with definite interest. "The air shakes and makes noise?" he asked.

"Yeah."

"That's really cool," Cooper said. He wiggled out of the space again and went to climb up on the window seat. "Lightning is electricity," he said, to no one in particular. "So it's like when you hear a pop when you touch something with static."

Gabe couldn't help his smile. God, he loved his kid. Gabe would have never been able to explain to Coop what made thunder, but he sure could have looked it up. It seemed that Cooper had a new interest. A weather fascination might be cool.

Stella had turned her attention to Cooper and the window. She made no move to join him, but she was no longer shaking.

"If I turn on the light, the lightning won't seem so bright," Gabe said, still trying to figure out how to make this situation better.

"No!" Cooper protested. "I want to see the next one really good!"

Stella gave a little shiver. "I don't like it when it's super loud and surprises me."

"Yeah, I can understand that," Gabe told her. "Do you want me to turn on the light?" Cooper would deal with it. There would be more lightning. When there wasn't a frightened little girl in his bedroom corner.

But Stella was still watching Cooper. "No," she finally said. "It's okay for him to see it."

Gabe felt his heart thump. These kids. He'd always known he wanted more than one, but he'd had no idea what that would really be like. It was damned amazing was what it was.

"Do you want to call your mom?" Gabe asked. "I think she'd want to talk to you if you're scared."

Stella looked at him again. "She always talks to me when I'm scared. She tells me what the storm is and that it's just air and not to worry."

Gabe nodded. That sounded like Addison. Take the fear away by being practical.

"People can die if lightning strikes them," Cooper said, almost as an aside as he continued to stare out the window, waiting for more lightning. The rain pounded against the window, and the wind wailed.

"Coop, that's not helpful," Gabe chided.

"Not if you're inside," Stella told Cooper.

Cooper shrugged. "But outside."

"But if it's raining outside, you should be inside," Stella insisted.

"Sometimes you can't help it," Cooper replied.

Stella frowned at him. "But lightning doesn't hit you automatically when you're outside."

Cooper finally turned. "I know. But it *can*."

"But *thunder* doesn't kill people," Stella said, still frowning and going up onto her knees.

Gabe thought about intervening in the argument, but he was fascinated by the interaction.

"I know that," Cooper said, as if that were the dumbest thing anyone had ever told him. "It's just air shaking."

"You know that because *I* told you," Stella said.

"Yeah, I *know*," Cooper said. "But thunder can't hurt you. Just the lightning. And not if you're inside."

"I *know*," Stella returned.

"So why are you scared if you're in here?" Cooper asked.

Gabe turned wide eyes on Stella. He hoped that the little girl could tell that Cooper was honestly curious rather than teasing her.

Stella scowled at him. "Because it's *loud*."

Cooper thought about that, then nodded. "Yeah. That can be scary."

Gabe wasn't sure he'd ever been prouder of Cooper. He turned to Stella. "What would make you feel better?" he asked. "Should we call your mom?"

She sat back on her behind and nodded. "Okay."

"Coop, will you go get my phone off my table by the bed?" Gabe asked. He finally gave in to the urge and reached out to stroke a hand over Stella's head. "I want you to feel safe with us, Stella. I won't let anything happen to you."

She nodded.

Cooper came running back into the room with Gabe's phone as Caroline poked her head into the room, blinking sleepily. "Everything okay?"

Gabe nodded. "The storm has us a little spooked," he said.

"Ah," Caroline said. "Do you need anything? Cocoa? Cuddles? I've got both." She gave Stella a smile full of affection.

Again, Gabe felt that grab in his chest.

Stella shook her head, though. "I'll talk to my mommy."

"Oh, that will fix everything," Caroline agreed. "Okay, well, you let me know if you need anything."

"Thanks, Mom," Gabe said.

Caroline shot him a look that was full of affection and pride as well. Gabe had never appreciated his mother as much as he had since becoming a parent himself. Their dad had passed away when Gabe was only four and Logan two. He didn't remember Tom Trahan well, and that made him sad, but his mom had done an amazing job, especially going it alone, and Gabe made a note to be sure to tell her that more often.

Gabe dialed Addison's number, feeling his heart thump in anticipation of hearing her voice, even if the reason for the call wasn't entirely sunshine and roses. And it was two a.m.

"Gabe?" she answered huskily a moment later. "What's wrong?"

He thought about teasing her about the fact that a two-a.m. call could be for phone sex, but the kids were right there, and Stella really did need to talk to her. "It's storming here," he said. "Stella needs to talk to you."

"Oh, no."

He heard rustling on Addison's end of the phone, and he pictured her sitting up in bed and trying to come awake. If Cooper had a bad dream or even just woke up in the night and wanted Gabe, he'd just come climb into bed. But Gabe knew well the feeling of forcing himself awake because Cooper was sick or needed something that required more of Gabe's brain than just lifting the covers and snuggling.

"Is she okay?" Addison asked in his ear.

"I think so. She was pretty upset at first, but we talked about how thunder is just hot air shaking around," he said, meeting Stella's eyes and seeing that she was much calmer now.

A clap of thunder sounded overhead, and a bright flash lit the window. "Oh, *cool,*" Cooper said from the window seat. He turned. "I wonder how hot the electricity is," he said, wonder in his voice. "Can we look that up, Dad?"

"Do you know, Stell?" Gabe asked.

She shook her head. "Really hot, though."

He nodded. "I've seen trees that were hit by lightning, and they get black, totally charred."

"Gabe," Addison protested, "I'm not sure talking about how lightning can *char* things is helpful."

He grinned. Addison couldn't see Stella's face. She looked part disturbed and part fascinated. It was the look she'd had on her face on the swamp boat when the guide had first brought the baby alligator out of its container. And she'd gotten over the disturbed part quickly. "Trust me," he said softly to Addison.

He heard her take a breath and then say, "Yeah, okay."

"Maybe we could find a tree like that somewhere," he suggested to the kids. "See it up close."

Stella's eyes widened, and Cooper clambered down from the window.

"Really?" Cooper's ratio for disturbed and fascinated definitely tipped more in the direction of disturbed. "Does that kill the tree?"

"We have a lot of stuff to look up," Gabe said. "But I think Stella wants to talk to Addison first."

Stella nodded, and Gabe turned the phone over.

He sat back, crisscrossing his legs, and Cooper climbed into his lap without a thought. Gabe wrapped his arms around his son and kissed the top of his head. He'd always taken for granted how easily Cooper hugged and sat on laps and accepted affection. He understood that Stella was more independent, maybe. That Stella and Addison didn't have as much lap time as Cooper and Gabe did. But he loved that his son liked being held.

"I know," Stella said to Addison. She paused. "Yes." Another pause, longer this time. "I did." She listened again. "I know." Then she nodded. "Okay, Mommy." She paused to listen again. She played with the end of the dog's tail as she held the phone to her ear, the thing big in her tiny hand. She was nodding along with whatever Addison was saying. Then she smiled.

And Gabe's heart turned over.

God, he was fully, officially, completely in love. With Addison. With Stella. With having them both in his life. And in Cooper's life. This was good. It was so, so good.

"Okay, Mommy," Stella said again. Then she looked up at Gabe. "Yes." She watched him while listening to her mother. "Okay. I love you, too." Then she held the phone out to Gabe. "She wants to talk to you."

"Okay, sweetheart." He took the phone and cleared his throat. "Hey," he said to Addison.

"Hey."

Desire swept through him with that simple word from her, but it was so much more than everything he'd felt to this point. They were parenting together right now. Kind of. And it felt so damned good and right and fulfilling that he knew that he wanted it forever.

"Everything good?" he asked, trying not to let all those emotions spill into his voice.

Cooper still looked up at him with a funny frown, and Gabe realized he hadn't succeeded.

"Yeah. Are *you* okay?" she asked.

"Yeah. I'm great."

"I think she'll be okay now. Usually by the time we talk it all out, the storm has passed."

Gabe looked to the window. "I don't know. I didn't look at the forecast, but it's still pretty strong out there."

"Well, I'm hoping she'll settle down for you now," Addison said.

"It's fine. We'll do whatever we need to do," he assured her.

"But you need to get your sleep."

"That's not the main priority here, Ad," he said sincerely.

"She's a guest. And she's got you up in the middle of the night. I'm sorry."

"Addison," Gabe said firmly, mindful of the little ears listening intently, "it's fine. More than fine. I want Stella to know that we'll always be here if she needs us." He fully intended for the little ears to hear that.

Addison sighed. "That's really . . ." Her voice sounded huskier. "Nice," she finally filled in. "It's *really* nice to know you're there for her."

"I am," he said resolutely. "But is there anything you think I should do specifically? Or not do?"

There was a pause on Addison's end. Then she said, "I think you should do whatever you think is right."

"But—" Really? Addison, the most prepared, in-charge woman he'd ever met. The one who didn't want people messing around in her life and didn't want people making decisions that affected her daughter?

"Gabe," Addison said softly, "you've got this. Go with your gut. Whatever you think Stella needs, I know it will be right. I know you love her. So just . . . take care of her."

Gabe swallowed. This was a big deal. For Addison. For him. He could be honest and admit that he didn't always trust his gut, even with Cooper. He relied on his mom and Logan giving input. And he knew his mom would certainly help give advice with Stella, too, but for Addison to give this over to him . . . it was terrifying.

"Ad, that's . . ."

"I know," she said when he trailed off. "I know it is."

He blew out a breath, his eyes on Stella. "Okay."

"Do you want me to drive home now? I can," she offered. "We got the big stuff done. We were just going to finalize things over breakfast, but we can do that on the phone, too."

Gabe kind of wanted her to drive home now. But that was ridiculous. "It's the middle of the night," he said. "And you shouldn't be driving into this storm. No, we're good. I've got this."

"Okay."

He heard the smile in her voice.

"I'll see you all tomorrow," Addison said. "I'll head out as soon as I can."

"No problem. We'll see you then."

"Okay. Good night. And thank you. And . . . I love you," she said softly.

His heart thumped. "I love you, too."

And yeah, he wanted those little ears to hear *that*, too.

"You should also know," Addison said, "that you being there for my daughter during a storm at two a.m. is really freaking sexy."

He gave a rough chuckle. "Yeah?"

"Yeah. Very."

"Well, you might have to prove it."

"I can rent another limo."

He felt the tightness in his chest loosen slightly. "Or we could do a little laundry when you get back."

"Yes," she said with her own husky laugh. "Yes, we definitely will do that."

They disconnected a moment later. Just as another boom of thunder shook the house. Gabe sighed as Stella clutched the dog against her chest.

Okay, so it was just air, and lightning couldn't get to them inside, and all of that. Stella knew in her head that she was safe. But she needed to *feel* it, too.

"I have an idea," Gabe said. "What if we went over to Stella's house for the rest of the night? You might feel better in your own house."

Stella looked at the window where the rain continued to beat against the house. "Go outside?"

"Yeah, Dad, that's where the lightning is," Cooper said, tipping his head to look up at Gabe.

Gabe nodded. "Yes, it is." He opened the Internet browser on his phone and typed in *lightning strikes*. Clearly, both these kids appreciated facts and information. He started reading out loud. "Number one. If you find yourself outside in a thunderstorm, take shelter immediately." He looked up at the kids. "Well, I guess maybe we should just stay here, then."

Stella nodded, and Cooper giggled. "Duh," he said.

Gabe couldn't disagree. "Okay, so then what?" He kept reading from the web page. "Stay away from windows." He looked down at Cooper. "I guess you need to stay right here, then."

He hugged him, and Coop giggled again. "Guess so."

"Number three says to not touch anything metal or plugged in." He looked around. "Okay, I have *another* idea."

He stood Cooper up, then got to his feet. He held out his hand to Stella. "There's really only one way to do this."

Was he gambling here? Maybe a little. Did he know for *sure* this would make her feel better? Not for sure. But his gut told him that Stella could use a little less independence tonight.

She reached out and took his hand without hesitation and let him pull her to her feet. Then with Cooper's hand in his on one side and Stella's on the other, Gabe took them into his bedroom. He closed the curtains over his windows, he unplugged everything in the room, he grabbed a flashlight from his dresser drawer, and he made a tent over the bed.

Then he held one side up and said, "Thunderstorm-proof tent."

Both kids grinned.

"I've only got one flashlight," Gabe said, "but we can use my phone, too."

"Wait, I've got flashlights!" Cooper turned and ran out of the room, returning a minute later and dumping five mini-flashlights, the kind that would clip onto key rings, onto the bed.

"Where did you get all of those?" Gabe asked.

"I collect them," Cooper told him with a shrug.

"I gave him that one," Stella said, pointing at a bright-red one. "We had it at home, but we don't use it."

"I didn't know you collect flashlights," Gabe said. This was new information. That Stella knew but Gabe didn't. Interesting.

Cooper just nodded and crawled inside the tent, and Gabe dropped the topic. He couldn't deny that Cooper's collection was coming in handy tonight. Stella followed him in, and they began turning on all the flashlights. Gabe ducked under the tent as well, lying down next to Cooper. They all settled onto their backs, looking up at the various circles of light on the dark-purple blanket overhead that made the tent glow with a soft purple light. The storm still raged outside, but the sound was muted inside the cozy tent.

"This is way better," Stella finally decided. She still held Cooper's dog, but not in the death grip she'd had on the poor thing before.

Cooper nodded. "No way lightning can get us in here."

"No way," Gabe agreed.

Stella rolled over onto her side to face him. "How long can I stay in here?"

Gabe looked over at her. "As long as you want."

"What if I fall asleep?"

He gave her a smile. "Well, just don't snore. That will keep Coop and me awake."

She giggled. "I don't snore."

"Then we'll be just fine," he told her, resisting the urge to cup her cheek. She was sweet and looked so much like her mother that his heart ached. The only thing missing here was Addison.

What would she think of a bed tent? Of letting the kids sleep in here during the storm? Was he encouraging the fear or helping it?

"Oka—" Stella said, the word breaking off as a yawn stretched her mouth. She settled her head onto the pillow. In less than a minute, she was asleep. And he knew that he'd made the right decision.

"I'm glad she's not scared anymore," Cooper whispered to him.

Gabe put his hand on his son's back and rubbed. "Me, too, buddy. You were a really good friend to her."

"She's nice," Cooper replied. "She said next time we go on a swamp boat, she'll help me pet an alligator."

Gabe swallowed. "You'd do that with her?" he asked.

Cooper yawned. "I guess so. A *little* one."

Yeah, the spirited adventurer was going to be very good for Cooper. And Gabe's practical boy who collected flashlights had come through for her.

He drifted off to sleep wondering if convincing Addison to marry him was better done with beignets or pralines and if he should get her naked before or after she said yes.

◆ ◆ ◆

Addison knocked on the door to Gabe's house the next morning just after sunrise. She'd canceled her breakfast meeting, not because she was worried that Gabe was in over his head, and not even because she was worried about Stella, exactly. She knew that Gabe had handled it, or he would have called her back. No, she was on his front step bright and early because she missed them all, and the storm and Stella's phobia were the perfect excuses to give the clients.

"Good morning," Caroline greeted as she opened the door.

"Good morning." Addison smiled. "I'm a little early."

Caroline laughed and opened the door wide. "You are. No one else is even awake yet."

"No? I guess they were tired after being up in the middle of the night." Addison stepped into the foyer with a grimace.

"Oh, it wasn't so bad," Caroline said. "They all settled down afterward and went right to sleep."

"You woke up with it, too?" Addison said, feeling bad, though it wasn't Stella's fault that storms were the one thing that could make her anxious.

"Yes, I checked in. But Gabe had everything under control, and I went back to bed and slept like a rock," Caroline assured her.

"Well, I'm glad about that. I wish I knew where this storm fear came from, but I really don't."

"Phobias are like that," Caroline said. "And we all have them."

It was true. Though Addison's go-to phobia was fear of commitment, and Gabe was beginning to chip away at that one, too. Or rather, blast right through it.

"I might sneak up and check in on Stella," Addison said. "I feel bad I wasn't here."

"Of course, dear," Caroline said. "They're all in Gabe's room. Second door on the right."

Gabe's room. Addison hadn't been in Gabe's room yet. And they were all in there? Addison crept up the stairs, her heart stuttering a little at the thought of going into Gabe's bedroom while he still slept. The door was cracked, and she pushed it open gently. And stopped. Gabe's bed was covered with a blanket fort. She hadn't been expecting that.

She moved into the room quietly. With the tent, she couldn't tell if everyone was still sleeping, but she did hear the soft snoring that she'd gotten used to sleeping next to Gabe on their weekends together. She smiled and realized that she could absolutely listen to that every night forever.

Addison approached the bed and lifted the edge of the blanket closest to her. Gabe lay on his back. He was wearing a T-shirt with his boxers. He had one leg out from under the blanket, one arm over his head, and the other around Cooper, who was draped over him like he was a big pillow. And on the other side of Cooper was Stella. She was on her stomach, her face turned toward Gabe and Cooper, her dark curls in a wild disarray around her face and spilling over the pillowcase. She looked completely serene and deep asleep.

This sight . . . Addison took a deep breath. Yeah, she could definitely do this forever.

She thought briefly about waking them, but she felt a sense of comfort and happiness wash over her. And it hit her that she was tired. She hadn't slept a lot last night, and then she'd hit the road right away.

So she kicked off her shoes and rounded the bed, sliding in beside Stella. And when her daughter sighed and curled into her, Addison realized that she was exactly where she was supposed to be.

Chapter Ten

The next two weeks were pretty much perfect.

Addison and Stella saw Gabe and Cooper for dinner once a week. They saw Gabe, Cooper, Caroline, and Logan for dinner once a week. And Addison and Gabe had dinner alone after their support-group meeting while Stella played with Cooper and Caroline. Addison, Gabe, and the kids spent the weekends together.

Today, Addison sat in the middle seat on the swamp boat again, but she was alone. Cooper was up at the front with Stella and Gabe. He wasn't thrilled about it, but he was there, and Addison felt a surge of pride that he was facing his fear.

They were all wearing ear protection as they whizzed along the bayou on their way to the area where Sawyer, their guide, felt they'd see the most alligators. Gabe sat between the kids. Cooper clutched the edge of his seat, and though she couldn't see his face, Addison could picture his expression—part excitement at the speed and noise of the boat and part trepidation. That seemed his standard look when they were out doing almost anything, and Addison felt a swell of love thinking about it. He was careful, but he was so curious and bright. Stella, on the other hand, was looking around avidly, taking in all the sights, with Gabe's hand resting on the back of her neck. It was an affectionate gesture but also designed to keep Stella in her seat as the boat was moving. Addison felt that same wave of love as she watched both of them.

Last weekend at the children's museum had perfectly illustrated how the two kids approached new things and had taught both Addison and Gabe more about how to supervise and help. Gabe was more cautious with Cooper, but Cooper needed that. Addison had learned that Cooper liked to have the adults closer and especially loved to have one of them doing whatever he was doing. He liked to have his hand held, literally, and he appreciated hearing "Good job" or "I'm right here." Stella wasn't like that at all. She preferred more space and was perfectly content figuring things out on her own. They, of course, stayed close to her, too, in the huge public place, but said things like "Hang on, Stella" and "Stay where we can see you." Gabe did well with giving Stella the space she needed, but Addison could tell he had to hold back from wanting to help her all the time. Still, Addison noticed that Stella looked around for both Addison and Gabe throughout the day and, more often than not, Stella was the one encouraging Cooper and showing him new things. And Cooper was much more likely to do something Stella suggested than something his father did.

Stella had warmed to the Trahans—all of them—so quickly. That should probably worry her. If something happened and she and Gabe stopped seeing each other, Stella would lose not just Gabe but also a grandmotherly figure in Caroline, a fun-loving uncle in Logan, and a boy who was already her best friend and was practically a brother.

Addison felt a little shiver of trepidation herself. They were in deep with the Trahans, and it had happened quickly.

But just then the boat pulled to a stop, and everyone removed the ear protection they wore and focused on Sawyer.

And a few minutes later, as Stella held Cooper's hand and extended it toward the baby alligator Sawyer held, Addison knew that there was no way to slow all of this down. They just had to hold on for the ride and trust that everything would be okay.

When they were back at the Boys of the Bayou dock, Stella grabbed Addison's hand and pulled her into the gift shop.

"Mommy, I have to get Cooper one of these, okay?" Stella took a mini-flashlight from a hook on a display rack near the registers. It was, of course, a plastic alligator, and the light came from its wide-open mouth.

Addison took the flashlight from Stella's fingers. "You do?"

"I brought my allowance money." Stella held up a hand and uncurled her fingers. In her palm were three dollar bills and a collection of coins.

"You're going to use your own money?" Wow, this was important.

Stella nodded. "We were talking about it before we came, and I told him I would get him one."

"You were talking about this flashlight specifically?" Addison asked. "Really?"

"I told him I saw it last time and told him he needs it. He wants it."

Something nagged at Addison about that answer. "He has a whole bunch of flashlights, right?" Addison said. "Does he want this one just because it's an alligator?"

Stella shook her head. "He needs another flashlight. But I told him this one would remind him he's brave because he was going to pet an alligator today."

Addison regarded her daughter thoughtfully as the nagging feeling intensified. "He needs to be reminded he's brave?"

Stella nodded. "He thinks he's not brave because he gets worried about things."

Addison thought about that. "You haven't told him he's not brave, have you, Stell?" she asked.

Stella actually looked offended. "No, Mommy. That hurts his feelings. I'm helping him feel brave."

Addison believed Stella hadn't said it to Cooper, but there was something about her daughter's answer that bothered her. "Has someone else told him that he's not brave?"

Stella frowned. "Some kids at his day care."

Oh boy. "And you're trying to help him feel brave?" Addison asked. "How are you doing that?"

"I tell him that he helped me that night when it was stormy and I was scared."

Gabe had filled Addison in on the full story, and it had warmed Addison's heart. But this nagging feeling wouldn't go away. "Do the flashlights make him feel braver?" Addison asked.

Stella nodded.

"Is he afraid of the dark?"

"Sometimes."

"And he wants as many as he can get?" Addison asked.

"In case one runs out," Stella said. "They're little."

"You can replace the batteries in most of them," Addison said. She didn't mind getting Cooper the alligator flashlight, but something was bugging her about Cooper's collection.

"But he can't change them by himself," Stella said.

"His dad or his uncle or his grandma or I would help him," Addison said.

"But they're not always with him."

"And Cooper is worried about needing a flashlight when his dad and the rest of us aren't around?" Addison asked.

Stella nodded. "Right."

Addison didn't like the idea that Cooper was feeling worried that he might need a flashlight when his family wasn't around. She wondered where that was coming from and if there was something she could do to make it better. She looked down at the flashlight she held. Well, at least she could buy him a light that would also remind him that he'd overcome his fear and touched an alligator today.

"You keep your allowance, Stell Bell," she said. Addison paid for the flashlight and gave it to Stella to give to Cooper. Her daughter went running out the front door to where Gabe and Cooper were standing talking to Sawyer.

Through the window, Addison watched Cooper's face light up and Stella's huge grin as she gave her friend the gift. Addison's heart expanded. Maybe Cooper was a little afraid of the dark, or afraid of the dark when his family wasn't around anyway, but that was a normal fear, especially for a five-year-old, and if that little plastic alligator made him feel better, then she was glad to be a part of it.

Gabe held his hand out to her as she joined them on the sidewalk out front, and they laced their fingers together.

"I'm glad you guys came back," Sawyer told them, clapping Gabe on the shoulder. He held his hand out to Cooper, who shook it. "Keep coming back. Pretty soon you'll be doin' the tour with me. You know a lot about gators."

Cooper's eyes widened, but before he could say that he had *no* interest in something like that, Stella took Sawyer's other hand and pumped it up and down. "I'd be a great airboat driver," she told him.

"Oh, I can tell that," Sawyer said. "You and Coop can take over the business for me when you're older."

"Really?" she asked, her voice full of awe.

"You bet." Sawyer winked at her. "You're a good team."

Stella beamed at Cooper. "We are. He's going to be my brother."

Addison coughed, and Gabe chuckled. Sawyer looked up with a grin. "Well, that's good news. If I'd known, I would have let you throw an extra chicken to the gators."

Gabe laughed. "Thanks. Maybe we can do that next time."

Sawyer nodded. "You got it."

They headed for the car after that. Addison wondered if she and Gabe should address the brother comment. But she wasn't in a hurry to tell the kids that wasn't true. Interestingly. She and Gabe could discuss it and decide what their response would be.

And she didn't miss the fact that this kind of stuff was exactly why she'd been avoiding a serious relationship, particularly with a man with a kid.

She let them into the house forty minutes later.

As the kids ran down the hall toward the kitchen, Addison started after them, but Gabe grabbed her wrist and pulled her around to face him.

"Maybe we should do a little laundry before Coop and I go home."

She looped her arms around his neck. "Hmm, I am feeling a little dirty, now that you mention it."

His hands cupped her butt—a favorite move of his—and he put his lips against her neck. "You're sexy as hell when you're being a mom, but I would love to make you forget about everything but you being a woman and me being a man for a little bit."

A shiver of desire went through her. She and Gabe had been getting closer, and she'd learned so much about him just being around him and his family, but they hadn't been physical since they'd had a quickie against the door in the storage room at the community center after the meeting the other night.

"I miss stretching out in bed and being able to get at *all* of you and lying in your arms all night afterward," she said, tipping her head back as he kissed his way down her neck.

He lifted his head and looked into her eyes, his blue eyes dark. "Say the word and I'll put a ring on your left hand and make Cooper officially Stella's brother, and we can have that every single night."

The shiver of desire turned into goose bumps, and she had to press her lips together to keep from blurting out, *Yes, let's do it tomorrow.*

She swallowed. "Noted," she said. Breathlessly.

He looked part relieved and part turned on. "I still need you in the laundry room tonight, Ad."

She nodded. "Also noted."

He kissed her again, hot and hard, and then took her hand, and they headed to the kitchen to feed the kids.

Dinner was, as usual, a loud, messy, happy event. The grilled hamburgers made the peas tolerable, according to Stella, and both kids ate everything. Then, Cooper, the sweetheart, said that he would love to wait about an hour before eating his ice cream for dessert. Because Addison and Gabe were fully on board with another hour of time together, they simply shared a look and agreed that Cooper had a great plan. Including the part where he suggested that he and Stella could spend the hour playing swamp-boat tour-company owners in Stella's room. Stella didn't have any stuffed alligators, but she had plenty of stuffed animals that could be alligators with the right noses and tails made out of construction paper.

The whole game sounded like something that would take even more than an hour in Addison's estimation, and she happily turned over the construction paper, kids' scissors, and tape.

Once they were happily coloring and cutting and jabbering about their swamp-boat company, Addison and Gabe made their way downstairs. And nonchalantly headed straight for the laundry room.

Gabe had the table pushed against the door and his shirt off by the time Addison had her shoes kicked off and the first few buttons of her shirt undone. She paused to take in the sight before her. She reached out and ran her hands over his chest and shoulders. She loved the way they bunched as he moved to touch her back, finishing the job she'd started on her buttons.

"I'm so glad our kids get along and can keep each other busy," Gabe said, pushing her shirt off her shoulders and reaching for the bra clasp between her breasts. He freed the mounds and took them in hand, thumbing the tips that immediately stiffened and shot sparks of heat and need to her core.

"Me, too," she said, arching closer, needing more pressure and friction . . . pretty much everywhere.

"They're good for each other," he said.

"Mmm-hmm—" She broke off with a gasp as he bent and took a nipple into his mouth. Her fingers curled into his hair, and she marveled at the way his tongue could turn her into a quivering pile of sensations almost instantly.

"We're good for each other, Ad," Gabe said against her breast, licking again before bringing his lips back to hers.

She agreed. But she didn't want to stop the kissing to tell him. They were all good for each other. They were all good *together*. Thoughts of the kids together upstairs, laughing and planning and playing, went through her mind. Stella had always made friends easily, but there was something about Cooper that seemed special. Stella was almost protective of him, Addison realized. Stella was always making sure Cooper was beside her. She waited for him if he was lagging behind. Sure, she sometimes gave him a heavy, put-upon sigh, but she always waited. It had been so important to her today that Cooper pet the alligator. She'd given him a pep talk as they'd driven to the dock and had then literally held his hand as he'd touched the animal. And she'd insisted on buying him a flashlight. She'd been willing to use her own money for it, in fact. And he'd clipped that little plastic alligator to his belt loop immediately and hadn't taken it off since.

She pulled back from Gabe. "Did you know Cooper is afraid of the dark?"

Gabe blinked down at her, clearly surprised she'd cut off the kiss. Frankly, she was a little surprised, too.

Gabe shook his head slowly as her comment sank in. "No, he doesn't have a problem with the dark. We use night-lights because he gets up to pee at night," Gabe said.

Addison frowned. "Well, I don't think he's afraid at home, no. But there's something at day care that makes him nervous."

Gabe pulled back. "What are you talking about?"

She took in his naked chest and felt a flash of regret go through her. *Dammit.* They weren't going to have sex in the laundry room tonight, either. "I'm worried about Cooper."

It hadn't fully hit her until she said those words out loud, but it was true. Something had been nagging at her since the gift shop, and she couldn't shake it. Now, thinking about how protective Stella was, Addison knew she needed to figure out what was going on. "I'm sorry, but it just hit me when you mentioned how good Stella and Cooper are together," she said.

Gabe searched her eyes for a moment. Then he blew out a breath and reached behind her. He snagged her bra and handed it to her. "This laundry room is *such* a good idea. Why can't we pull it off?"

Addison tugged the straps up her arms and closed the little hook in front. "Because we're parents."

He nodded and bent to grab his shirt. "Okay, what's going on?" he asked as he shrugged into it.

She pulled her shirt on, too, buttoning as she said, "Stella said that he's collecting flashlights because he's worried about the dark at day care." She frowned. "Does that make any sense? He's not there when it's dark, is he?"

"No. Never." Gabe was frowning, too.

"Has he ever been there during a storm or something when the lights might have gone out?" she asked. That would make some sense.

Gabe shook his head. "Not that I can think of. Not recently."

"Well, maybe it was a while ago?"

"He started collecting the flashlights about a month ago." Gabe ran a hand through his hair. "I didn't even know he had them all. When I asked, he said that he got the first one from Stella. She said you had it at home and never used it. Then I guess he took the one off Mom's key ring. And then started collecting others."

Addison frowned at that. "Stella gave him the first one?"

"That's what he said," Gabe said. "Stella told me the night of the storm that one of them was from her."

Addison slid off the dryer to the floor, fully dressed. "That's . . . interesting."

"How so?"

"She said that he's afraid of the dark and wants to be sure he has flashlights with him all the time and needs more than one in case they run out of batteries. But he's only worried about it when none of us are with him."

"That's only day care," Gabe agreed. "Otherwise it's you, Mom, Logan, or me all the time."

Addison nodded. "I guess it just sounded funny to me. It's probably nothing."

Gabe didn't look convinced. At all. "I think we need to talk to the kids."

"You sure you want Stella and me there?" Addison asked.

"I think Stella makes him brave," Gabe said. "Maybe that will encourage him to tell me what's going on."

"You don't think he'd tell you anyway?" Addison asked.

"Apparently not," Gabe said drily.

"Hey, guys." Gabe tried to keep his voice normal and easy as he and Addison stepped into Stella's bedroom where she and Cooper were coloring a sign that said Boys and Girls of the Bayou.

"We don't have to go yet, do we?" Cooper asked immediately. "We're not done yet."

"Nope, we're not going yet," Gabe assured him. "But Addison and I were talking, and we wanted to ask you guys something."

He and Addison each took a seat on the floor. Addison leaned back against Stella's bed, and Gabe propped up against the wall by the window. They didn't want to intimidate the kids or make this a bigger deal than it really was, but considering they didn't know what was going on, it was hard to hold back from demanding to know what was with Cooper and the flashlights.

Dammit, he'd *wondered*. His kid suddenly collecting flashlights? It seemed . . . off. He'd told himself not to worry. It was harmless. It was practical, even. It was always a good idea to have a flashlight handy.

But five-year-olds weren't supposed to be practical. They weren't supposed to think about things like the lights suddenly going out or emergency preparedness.

Gabe felt the tension in his neck and worked to relax as he glanced over at Addison.

She was a couple of feet away, out of reach, but just like at the support-group meetings, she met his eyes and gave him a smile, and he knew what she was thinking—this was good, and they were in it together.

"What do you want to know?" Cooper asked him, setting down his markers and focusing on Gabe.

Gabe smiled slightly at his son's inability to do two things at once. "Day care," Gabe told him. "We were just wondering what you both like about where you go to day care. We were wondering if you like the same things or different things."

That wasn't 100 percent accurate, but it would start the conversation.

"I like my day care," Stella said, making the word GIRLS a bright, bold yellow color.

Bright and bold. That was Stella.

"What do you like the best, Stell Bell?" Addison asked.

"They have a *million* markers," she said. "And lots of clay. And we do art every day." Stella didn't even look up.

Addison nodded. "How about you, Cooper?" she asked. "What do you like at day care?"

"I like the markers, too," Cooper said, looking at Stella. "And story time."

Yep, Gabe knew that. He felt a little better. Cooper loved books, and he'd always said that Miss Linda, the head of the day care, did great voices when she read them stories.

"And what do you not like, Stella?" Addison asked.

Stella shrugged. "Quiet time."

Gabe couldn't help but grin at that. He shot Addison a look, and she gave him a little eye roll and a smile. "How about you, bud?" he asked Cooper.

Stella's head came up at that, and she looked at Cooper.

Cooper frowned at the paper in front of him. "Quiet time," he said.

Gabe watched his son for a moment, but Cooper didn't say anything more. And that bugged him. Cooper not liking quiet time *didn't* fit. Quiet time, Gabe knew, involved lying down on mats for about thirty minutes. Some of the kids napped, but if they didn't, they could listen to music on little headsets or look at books. But they couldn't talk, and they couldn't get up and run around. Cooper should love quiet time. Books, music, being left alone.

They did turn the lights down, though. It was in the middle of the day, so the room would hardly be completely dark, but was that the issue? It didn't make sense that Cooper would be afraid of the dark, but it could be that he couldn't see his book well enough and felt he needed the flashlights for that.

Something about that didn't feel right, though.

"Why don't you like quiet time?" Addison asked Stella, her eyes on Gabe.

Gabe loved her so freaking much. The enormity of that hit him hard. He'd always known that he would like to have someone to parent with. His mom and Logan were huge helps, of course, and his mother loved Cooper with all her heart. But there was something different about having someone who was going through the same things at the same time. Caroline was Cooper's grandmother. That was simply different, no matter what actual things she did for Cooper. Having Addison there, supporting and encouraging him, was a big deal. But what was really staggering was how amazing it was to have Stella in Cooper's life.

A sibling. Someone who got him in a way no one else in the family could.

Gabe focused on Stella's answer to Addison's question. The *why* was a big deal here, and maybe if Stella spoke first, Cooper would also share.

"It's *boring*," Stella said predictably. "I like to *do* things."

Stella read, Gabe knew, but yeah, he couldn't imagine her lying still for thirty minutes to do it.

"What about you, Coop?" Gabe asked casually. "Why don't you like quiet time?"

Cooper shrugged. "It's boring."

Yeah, that wasn't it. Gabe knew his kid. Okay, he let some—or a lot—of the discipline go to Caroline. And yeah, he liked to be the one who played and had fun with Cooper rather than the one laying down the rules and consequences. But come on, Cooper was an easy kid. He didn't need a lot of rules, and he didn't break the ones he did have very often. Okay, so Logan did a lot of helping with projects like when Cooper had wanted to try doing a model airplane. And Caroline did a lot of the caretaking when Cooper was sick. But dammit, Gabe knew his kid.

"Cooper," Gabe said gently, waiting until his son lifted his eyes, "I know you like quiet time. Or you used to. What happened?"

Gabe didn't miss the way Cooper's hand went to the alligator flashlight hanging from his belt loop. He clutched the plastic shape tightly. "Nothing."

Gabe frowned. "Cooper, you can tell me. If something happened, I want to know."

"It's okay now," Cooper said.

Well, that wasn't a flat-out denial.

"What's okay now?" Gabe pressed, feeling his chest tighten.

"I have the flashlights, so I like it again now."

"You like what again now?" Gabe asked.

"Quiet time."

"So you need more light during quiet time?" Addison asked, her tone encouraging.

Cooper nodded.

"Why? Is it suddenly too dark?" Gabe asked. That was just strange.

"It just was. But now it's okay. I'm braver now," Cooper said.

Nope, that wasn't okay. Gabe looked at Stella. "Stella, do you know what happened?"

Stella bit her bottom lip, looking so much like her mother for a moment that Gabe felt his heart lurch. Stella looked at Addison. Addison gave her daughter a little frown. "Stella Ann Sloan," she said firmly, "if you know something we should know, you have to tell us."

"The older boys put Cooper in the cupboard in the bathroom during quiet time," Stella said. "They said they were going to make him be braver because he was being a baby," she added, her voice rising slightly with indignation.

Gabe's gut twisted, and he actually felt sick. He stared at his son. "Coop," he said, his voice rough.

"Cooper," Addison said, jumping in, her voice soothing and calm, "is that what happened?"

He nodded, his expression suddenly miserable. A combination of sadness and hurt but also humiliation. Gabe felt almost dizzy with the emotions crashing through him. *No.* Someone had hurt his son? *No. Fuck no.*

"So some of the boys at day care put you in a cupboard in the bathroom?" Addison reiterated.

Gabe looked at her sharply. Her voice was steady, mostly, but he heard the little wobble. Cooper nodded, and Gabe felt the tear in his heart widen.

"Did they hurt you?" Addison asked, a fierceness in her voice that Gabe had never heard before.

Cooper shook his head.

"It was just really dark and scary," Stella said.

"Stella, I would really like Cooper to tell me this," Addison said calmly. "But thank you."

"It was dark. Totally dark the first time," Cooper finally said.

The first time? Gabe willed Addison to ask the question because he couldn't get any air past the tightness in his throat. He had no idea what to do here. He reached for his son, holding his other arm wide, and Cooper took the invitation to climb into his lap. Gabe wrapped his arms around him and held on. But he wasn't sure if he was trying to comfort Cooper or himself.

"But they didn't hurt you? They didn't push you or hit you or anything?" Addison said, leaning in closer.

Again, Gabe heard the shakiness in her voice, and it strangely made him feel better. He wasn't quite able to speak and was incredibly glad she could, but it helped him to know that he wasn't the only adult who wanted to do some potential damage to the kids at Cooper's day care.

"No," Cooper told her. "They're bigger than me. When they said to get in, they kind of pushed me, but I just got in. And it's big." He glanced at Stella. "It's not a cupboard. It's a closet. I could move around."

Gabe almost laughed. Being stuck in a dark closet all alone was so much better. But he supposed it was, in some ways.

"But you—" Stella started.

"But you were afraid because it was dark," Addison said over the top of her daughter, who kept quiet after that. "I'm very glad they didn't hurt you by pushing or hitting, but they still hurt you this way. And that's not okay."

She had a look on her face that made Gabe want to grab her and kiss her. She looked ready to take someone's head off, and the fact that she was feeling so protective and angry on Cooper's behalf made Gabe want her more than he ever had.

"Where was Miss Linda?" Addison asked.

A wave of anger swept through Gabe at her question. Yes, where in the *fuck* was Miss Linda?

"She has coffee with Miss Heather during quiet time," Cooper said, naming the woman who was in charge of the older group of kids at the day care center.

"So she didn't know this happened?" Addison asked before Gabe could.

Cooper shook his head.

"Why didn't you tell her, honey?" Addison asked, gentling her tone.

Cooper shrugged. "They said I should be brave."

"So now he has the flashlight, and he turns that on so he can stay in there and they think he's very brave," Stella said.

Addison's expression softened, and she gave Stella a smile, but Gabe could see she was gritting her teeth as she said, "Well, I think that was a really great solution. But we need to tell Miss Linda about this."

"It was Stella's idea," Cooper said.

Stella beamed, and Gabe leaned over to see that Cooper was looking at Stella as if she'd hung the moon.

Gabe's heart squeezed so hard that he had to rub a hand over his chest.

Stella had been there for Cooper. She'd saved the day. She'd helped him get over his fear. She'd made him feel safe.

Gabe hadn't done any of that.

He hadn't even asked why Cooper suddenly felt the need to collect flashlights. Out of the blue. For no apparent reason. He hadn't even asked.

The tightness in his chest and gut intensified, and he squeezed his eyes shut.

"Ow, Daddy, you're squishing me," Cooper protested, wiggling in Gabe's lap.

Gabe loosened his hold but couldn't completely let Cooper go.

"Cooper, I'm going to stop by tomorrow and have lunch with you," Addison said. "Would that be okay?"

Gabe's eyes snapped open. "What?" he managed to push past the lump in his throat.

Addison met his eyes. "I'm going to have lunch with Cooper. And maybe have a chat with Miss Linda."

Wow. Gabe wasn't sure what to say. Part of him, a really big part of him, wanted that. He wanted Addison to go down there and deal with this. He had no doubt that Addison Sloan would leave Linda with no question about how she—how *they*—felt about what had happened and how she expected Linda to solve the problem. She would likely be sure she spoke to the day care's owner and possibly the parents of the boys responsible.

He wanted her to take care of it.

And he felt almost instantly horrible.

He swallowed and opened his mouth to reply, but before he could, Cooper looked up at him. "Can you come to lunch, too, Dad?"

Dammit. Yes, of course he could. And more, he fucking *should.*

"Yeah, buddy, I can. In fact, maybe just you and me, what about that?"

"Okay."

Cooper grinned up at him, and Gabe felt guilt and love and frustration and a bit of humiliation slide through him. He hadn't gone to lunch with Cooper before. He hadn't had a meeting with Miss Linda before. He'd attended the initial open house. He'd shown up for the Christmas program. He'd read the weekly reports of what activities Cooper had participated in. But he'd read "wonderful student, enjoy having him" and "gets along well with others" and "curious and bright" and had felt proud and like everything was fine. He'd never asked for more in-depth reports. He'd never visited otherwise.

And he felt like shit.

"I don't mind," Addison said softly. "I'd love to see Cooper's day care."

Gabe nodded but didn't meet her eyes. "I know. But I should do this." God, it would be so much easier to let her do it. She'd probably had dozens of meetings with teachers and day care providers. She'd probably read the reports and asked follow-up questions. She'd probably been to lunches and programs and chaperoned field trips and been on planning committees for holiday parties. Addison didn't just show up to see her kid sing a couple of Christmas songs, eat a frosted snowman cookie, and then head back to work.

"Cooper," Addison said, "I'm really glad the flashlights have helped. And I'm glad that you talked to Stella about this. But I want you to know that you can talk to your dad and me about things, too. You don't have to keep all of this to yourself."

The feelings of guilt and inadequacy crept through Gabe again, his gut tightening. He wanted to yell and cuss and punch things. Instead, he sat on the floor of his son's bedroom, holding him and letting his girlfriend say all the right things and reassure Cooper. Because Gabe didn't know what the fuck he was doing.

Gabe kissed the top of Cooper's head, then gently sat him on the floor next to Stella. "Okay, bud, I think maybe it's time for bed. How about you brush your teeth and then I'll come back in after Stella and Addison leave to read to you."

He swore he could hear Addison's frown, and he glanced up to find her looking at him with a combination of surprise and hurt. Yeah, he'd been really subtle there. He knew that was kind of a shitty way to handle this and ask her to leave, but he needed to get his mind around all of this. *He* needed to step up here, and he wasn't sure how, and sitting here with Supermom suddenly wasn't helping.

He loved Addison. He loved that she was a mom. He loved her daughter.

But in comparison, he was fucking things up, and frankly, at the moment, he didn't need that reminder.

"Okay, Stell Bell," Addison said. "How about you and Cooper clean up all the markers and stuff, and then brush your teeth?"

"Already?" Stella protested. "But we're not done."

And he was tearing his son away from his friend. The one person who had been there for him, who he felt he could tell about what had happened, the person who made him feel brave.

Fuck.

Gabe jammed a hand through his hair and got to his feet. He loved Stella, and the things she'd done for Cooper made her one of his favorite people. But he couldn't handle this right now. He couldn't look at her brave, happy face, knowing that *she* would have never gotten stuck in a fucking closet at day care. No way would Stella have put up with that. And he hated the idea that he might sit here and not only compare himself to Addison but compare Cooper to Stella.

He started for the door. "I'll be right downstairs, Coop," he said. He just needed a little space for a second. "Help Stella clean up and come on down."

"Okay, Dad."

He got to the doorway before Cooper asked, "Are you coming for lunch *tomorrow?*"

Gabe swallowed hard before he turned back. "Absolutely." He was going to have this talk with Miss Linda tomorrow. He had no fucking idea what he was going to say, but yeah, this shit with Cooper and these kids was ending *now.*

Gabe got to the living room and was headed for the kitchen before he heard, "What the hell was *that,* Gabe?"

Swearing under his breath, he turned to find Addison striding toward him. Of course. He knew that she'd follow. That didn't mean he had any clue what to say to her.

"That was me being Cooper's dad," he responded.

Addison stopped about ten feet away and crossed her arms. "I see. And you thought I was overstepping?"

He sighed. "No. Not exactly."

"But you don't want me involved with this. You don't want me going to talk to Miss Linda," she said. It wasn't a question.

Gabe just looked at her for a long moment. She was so damned beautiful. Not just the hair and the eyes and the body—that body that he could lose himself in for days—but all of her. Her confidence, her passion for her work, her intelligence and humor and sweetness under the kick-ass-ness. And there was the way she looked at Stella, the way she looked at *him*, the way she looked at Cooper—all of that took his breath away. He could so easily fall into this woman and give it all up to her. And that wouldn't be the worst thing. At all. It would be good for Cooper. It would be good for *him*. But it would be the easy way out, and ironically, over the last several weeks with her, he wanted more and more to be the father who truly stepped up and made his kid's life better and was all in on everything. Addison had made it clear that she hadn't wanted motherhood, yet when it happened, she'd owned it and worked her ass off and was amazing at it.

Gabe felt his throat tightening. It would be so fucking easy to just let her do it, to just turn it over, to just invite her in for all of it. He wanted that so badly. He'd wanted it since he'd first found out about Stella.

But why did he want it? Because he wanted to parent *with* her or because she would parent *for* him?

He knew he wasn't being totally rational, but he couldn't stop the thoughts and emotions rolling through him. He would *love* to stop the thoughts and emotions. They felt like they were rolling *over* him, like a steamroller, squeezing everything out of him—his own confidence in his parenting, and satisfaction with his life, and pride in how Cooper was turning out. None of that was him. Not really. Not fully. Sure, he loved Cooper, and he knew his son knew that. He made Cooper feel secure and loved and valued. But Cooper hadn't felt like he could come to Gabe with what had happened. Gabe hadn't even noticed something was going on.

How could he be proud of that? His mother did most of the actual work.

Gabe had no right to feel satisfied with how things were or confident in the job he was doing.

"I do want you to go talk to Miss Linda," Gabe finally said. "I want it so much I can taste it."

She frowned. "Then let me do it. I promise that I'll—"

He didn't need to hear the rest. He knew that she would do anything and everything that needed done. No question about it.

"*I* have to do this, Ad. This is my responsibility. He's my son."

She flinched slightly, and Gabe cursed. That had sounded worse than he'd meant it. "Ad, I—"

"No, I get it," she interrupted. "And you're right. He's your son. And you should do it."

"I just . . . need to. I feel like absolute hell right now. I had no idea anything was going on." He ran a hand over his face. "How the fuck could I not know?"

"I didn't know. None of us did."

"But I *should have*. God, if he can't tell me things . . ." Gabe forced himself to breathe. "I need him to be able to tell me things."

"He wasn't alone, Gabe," Addison said. "He had Stella."

He knew she meant that to be reassuring, but that did nothing to help his emotions. "Great. He had a five-year-old girl who he just met who's not even at that day care comforting him," Gabe said. "Someone who decided that the solution was to start carrying around flashlights everywhere he went."

Addison's expression hardened. Okay, so he was criticizing her daughter. Not a great move. No way was Addison going to let *that* go.

"Well, as you pointed out, she's *five*," Addison said coolly. "She did what she could to help her friend."

"That wasn't all she could do," Gabe said, feeling the frustration and guilt rising up again. "She could have *told* us what was going on."

Addison sucked in a quick breath. Neither of them said anything for a long moment. Then she swallowed. And nodded. "You're right."

The look on Addison's face dragged the air out of Gabe's lungs. She looked devastated suddenly.

"Ad—"

But she shook her head quickly. "No, you're right. Stella . . . she's so independent. She tries to solve her own problems. I encourage that. I mean, sometimes. Little things. Like what to do if she runs out of gold glitter. And we talk about what to do if she gets lost in a store. But . . ." She stopped and swallowed again. "Maybe it's too much. Maybe I've taught her that she has to depend on herself and not on me."

"Addison—"

"What if she tried to help Cooper instead of telling us because she thought that's what I want?"

"*Addison,*" Gabe said firmly. "Stop." He knew that some of this mini meltdown was actually her emotions about Cooper and what had happened. But he also knew that Addison had some insecurities about her own parenting style. He almost laughed at that. Who the hell didn't?

"I'm so sorry, Gabe," Addison said softly.

"It's not your fault. It's not . . . it's not Stella's fault or Cooper's fault," he said, his throat tight. "It's mine."

"Gabe, you didn't know," she protested.

"Yeah, and now that I do, I still have no fucking clue how to handle this. And that makes me feel like shit."

"So let me help you."

"That's not the point!" Gabe worked to lower his voice. "I *have* to figure this out. Of course you could do it, and do it perfectly. But Cooper needs to know that *I* can and will handle things for him. It's great for him to know you care about him, too, but I'm his *father*. I need him to know that I'm capable of more than donating the sperm, making pancakes, and taking him to do things he doesn't want to do because *I* think he should be doing them!"

Gabe stood, breathing hard, feeling his heart racing. Addison looked sad, and a little pissed, actually.

"Is it *Cooper* who needs to know all of that, or you?" she asked.

"Fuck," he muttered. He shoved a hand through his hair again. "Yeah, okay, it's me, too."

"And you're feeling like all of this is because you made him go on the swamp-boat tour?" Addison asked.

"It's not like that's the first time," Gabe told her. "I'm always trying to get him to do stuff he doesn't want to do. Hell, he probably thought if he told me about the day care thing, that I'd tell him what Stella did—take a flashlight and don't be such a baby."

Addison actually gasped softly. "Stella did *not* tell him that. And you would never."

"But isn't that essentially what we're saying when we're constantly telling him that he should do things like touch alligators and sit in fire trucks and try karate and any one of the other things I've encouraged him to do in spite of knowing he doesn't want to?" Gabe asked. He hadn't realized all those things were nagging at him until they came spilling out, but now he couldn't stop. "Why can't I just be okay with him reading and looking things up on the Internet and being interested from afar? Why is that somehow *wrong* and my way is right? And how can I not think that if he thought I understood him and got him and wanted him to be just exactly how he is, that he would have told me about this bullshit at day care so that I could fix it?"

Addison expression went from irritated to worried. "Gabe—"

"I didn't even know something was wrong," he said, his voice suddenly rough as he tried to speak around the lump in his throat.

"He's a quiet kid," Addison said. "He's . . . reserved and thoughtful. It's hard to tell if he's worried about something or scared of something or just contemplating things."

But Gabe was shaking his head by the time she got to the end of that. "That's an easy excuse. Believe me, I've used it over and over."

"Excuse for what?"

"For thinking things are fine."

"Gabe, things *are* fine. He's five. He's an introvert. That doesn't mean you've done something wrong."

"Things are *not* fine, Addison!" Gabe felt the frustration climbing up his back and tightening his neck. He didn't want to fight with her, but he couldn't let this go. He couldn't just accept that Cooper was fine and that he was a great dad and that everything would be okay. Because that was definitely what he wanted. That would definitely be the easy way to go. But fuck, parenting wasn't supposed to be easy.

"Cooper is the one person in this world who *needs* me," Gabe said. "And that freaks me out, I'll be honest. It's always freaked me out. I feel all the protective things toward him that a dad should, but that's why I moved in here with my mom. That was me protecting him—from me fucking up."

"Gabe—"

"And she's done so much," he went on, interrupting her again. "She helped me out when I had no idea about teething and diaper rash. But Cooper is beyond those things. Now his problems are . . . bigger." Gabe sighed heavily. "Now Cooper needs his dad, and I have to step up. I can't keep expecting someone else to do it all."

"Your mom loves helping," Addison said quietly. But her tone had changed.

He narrowed his eyes. "Of course she does. But she should be his grandmother, not his mom. Or his dad."

Addison didn't say anything to that.

Gabe felt his gut twist. She agreed with him. She wasn't saying it, but she agreed that it was time for him to be the dad and take on Cooper's needs.

"I'm right, aren't I?" he asked. He didn't know why, but he needed to hear her agree with him. Not because he needed confirmation that he was right. He knew he was. But because he needed to know that *she* understood this.

Addison swallowed.

"Addison," Gabe said, his voice low and firm, "you agree that I've been taking the easy way out and it's time to step up, don't you?"

She squeezed her arms tighter against her stomach. "You're a wonderful father, Gabe. Cooper knows you love him and that you'll keep him safe no matter what. That's all he *really* needs."

"That's not an answer," he told her. He took a step forward. "You're Supermom. You're there for everything. You refuse to let other people into Stella's life completely, knowing that *you* are the best person to make decisions for her. You know that no one else can take care of her the way you do."

"I didn't have the support system that you do," Addison said.

"You still wouldn't have let someone else raise her the way my mom has been with Cooper. Because *you* are the best one to take care of her."

She wet her lips but didn't respond.

"And that's the thing, Ad. I *don't* know that. I don't know that I'm what's best for Cooper." Gabe heard the gruffness in his voice from the emotions swirling through him. "But I want to," he finally said. "I really want to be the best thing for Cooper and *know* it."

Addison's eyes were filled with love. He could see that. But there was also a sadness there. "So you want to start doing this on your own now?" she finally asked.

No. Fuck no. He didn't want to do this on his own at all. Which was the reason why he should absolutely do it. Yes, he wanted his son to have a lot of people in his life he could depend on and who would love and support him. But, hell, Cooper hadn't told his grandmother or his uncle about any of this, either. He'd told another five-year-old he liked and trusted but who couldn't do a damned thing about it. He needed to know that there was one person he not only liked and trusted but who could make everything right.

And Gabe would do that.

He might not always make the perfect decision. He still didn't know if he should be encouraging Cooper to try new things or just accept him as he was or how to find a balance between the two. But he could absolutely instill the fear of God into Miss Linda and the kids who thought they could push Cooper around.

"I need to do this on my own," he finally told Addison. "For Cooper's sake. And for mine. I need to know that I *can* do that."

Addison pressed her lips together.

"How can I ask you to let me into Stella's life when neither of us know that I can handle even the one I have?" Gabe asked.

Her eyes flickered with concern, but she still said nothing.

"You were right, Addison," he said. "Parenting is hard. But it's supposed to be. Honestly, I haven't had to work hard at much in my life. I was handed a successful business that happens to be something I enjoy a lot and that I can do with my brother who can cover whenever I can't be there. I was handed a baby who I love but who I immediately brought to my mother. I haven't had a relationship that took work beyond doling out orgasms, which is also something I enjoy doing."

As she flinched slightly, Gabe realized that talking about his past sexual escapades—and how much he enjoyed them—had been a miscalculation. But frankly, he wasn't capable of sorting through what was right and wrong at the moment.

"So now it's time for me to grow the fuck up and do some of the hard stuff. I need to show Cooper that he's worth it." A realization dawned, and Gabe felt a surge of *yes*. "I've tried to push Cooper outside of his comfort zone, thinking that he's missing things or that it would help him grow. But here I am, *very* entrenched in *my* comfort zone and happy about it. That's no example for Cooper."

Finally, Addison did speak. It was only one word. But it almost sent him to his knees.

"Okay."

That was it. Just "okay." But that word meant a lot of things. Mostly that she agreed with him that he needed to grow up and step up. And that he should do this on his own. Which meant that she was saying goodbye.

He nodded once. "Okay."

Addison came toward him, lifted on tiptoe, and kissed him on his cheek.

Then she turned and headed upstairs. Two minutes later, she and Cooper were at the front door. Gabe met them there. He opened the door, and looked over to where Stella stood on the bottom step, watching them go. He felt like his heart was shredding.

But they had to go, didn't they? If he was going to do this, really do it, he needed his crutches gone. That definitely included Addison. God, he wanted to lean on her. And he didn't know how long it would take him to get his shit together. A *very* long time, probably. Considering he wasn't sure he'd ever had his shit completely together. At least as a dad.

"Bye, Gabe," Stella said with a sweet smile.

This little girl was his son's best friend. The person who'd been there for him. Who he'd told his secrets to. Gabe was grateful and jealous at the same time. "Bye, sweetheart."

He gave Addison a last, lingering look as Cooper went through the door. He could tell by Addison's expression that she didn't want him to go but that she understood. At least, kind of. She maybe didn't agree with his decision to go it totally alone, but she was going to let him do it.

Because that was how she did things with Stella, too. She let her daughter explore and try things. But she was always right there in case Stella needed her.

Would she be there for Gabe if things went to hell? And would she still be there when he finally figured his shit out? He hoped so.

Chapter Eleven

"So you moved out and are living in the apartment over the bar?" Caleb asked Gabe.

They were at the support-group meeting. It had been almost a week since Addison had left him standing in the middle of his mother's living room looking torn up and lost.

That had been the hardest thing she'd ever done. Almost everything in her had screamed at her to stay and help him. Actually, leaving while knowing that Cooper had been having a hard time had been just as difficult. She wanted to march down to that day care and yell at Miss Linda. And then shake the stuffing out of the kids who had been picking on Cooper. In fact, she'd had to talk herself out of doing just that. Twice.

But this was Gabe's fight. Or so he believed. And he wanted to handle it.

Apparently, he'd done just that the very next morning.

Addison had never been more grateful for the support group than she was that Thursday. She'd been holding her breath to see if Gabe would show up. He'd walked in a few minutes late, and she'd been amazed by the rush of relief and love she'd felt when she'd seen him.

He looked like hell. His eyes were bloodshot, his shirt was wrinkled, and he'd been drinking coffee nonstop since coming through the door. And the group noticed. And made him talk.

"It was the easiest thing," he said. "We needed to get out on our own, and we could move right into the apartment."

"So Logan's at your mom's?" Austin asked.

"Yeah, we swapped. For now. I just wanted to get Cooper on my own so we can spend some real quality time together and I can assure him that *I'm* the one who's there for him. I'll have to get a place for us eventually, though. You can't raise a kid above a bar, right?" He looked around the group, but his eyes skipped right over Addison.

She felt a little twinge in her heart at that. She wanted to be the one he specifically looked at. The one whose opinion mattered most. But he'd been avoiding looking at her, and Addison understood. It was painful. Painful sitting there and not going to him, wrapping her arms around him, and just holding him. She also sensed that it was painful for him to not ask for that. She really thought he wanted to, though. But *not* leaning on her was what he needed. Or what he thought he needed. To do it alone. To not need her or anyone else.

It was an overreaction. And she was hoping someone here would tell him that. But she had to let him do this. Just like when Stella wanted to climb to the top of the equipment at the playground. Addison had to let her try it and realize on her own that either it was too tall, it was scary that far off the ground, or that it was fine and she could get to the top on her own. Stella knew that all she had to do was ask Addison for help getting back down. She could only hope Gabe knew the same thing.

"How's your mom taking it?" Bea, the grandmother in the group, asked.

Addison smiled at that. The group couldn't be doing better if she'd planted the questions with them herself. She also wanted to know how Caroline was. And how Cooper was. She was grateful to know that the "meeting" with Miss Linda had gone well. The woman had been appalled and assured Gabe that she would not only be paying very close attention but that she would be talking with the kids and their parents. Addison also loved knowing that Gabe hadn't stopped there but had gone to Linda's supervisor as well, and that Linda was going to be facing some disciplinary measures for leaving the class unattended during quiet time.

Addison ground her teeth together and fidgeted on her chair. She had a million other questions, too, but she was hoping the group would get around to them all.

"She's okay," Gabe said of his mother. "Concerned about Cooper, of course. But we went over for dinner last night." He sighed. "Haven't expanded my culinary skills much since we've been living with her."

He smiled as he said it, but Addison could tell he also felt chagrined by that truth, and again Addison wanted someone to tell him that he was being too hard on himself. So he could only make a few things for dinner. That was hardly the mark of a bad parent. Cooper just needed Gabe to love him. Period.

But that thought pricked at the back of her mind. Wasn't she just as hard on herself? Making sure she always had the four food groups in Stella's lunch, because if she missed one serving of dairy, Addison wasn't doing her job? Making sure that she found new ways to make the three vegetables that Stella would eat and getting creative with sneaking other veggies into things because *that* was what good parenting looked like?

She squeezed her hands together. Maybe she shouldn't be giving Gabe advice at all. Was she really doing that amazing of a job? Watching this whole thing with Cooper had made a few things seem very clear to her—Cooper would be fine because Gabe loved him, and Cooper knew that. Gabe didn't have to say any magic words or *do* anything special for Cooper to be okay. Was the situation a little traumatic? Of course. Should Gabe talk to the teachers and administrators at the day care center? Absolutely. Should the adults step in and discipline these kids? Definitely. But for *Cooper* to be okay, all he needed was Gabe to put him on his lap, look him in the eye, and say, "I love you." And he'd done that.

Maybe the parenting thing *wasn't* as hard as she made it out in her head.

And why did she do that? So she could feel good about all the things she did? Or because she'd been every bit as intimidated by the whole idea as Gabe had been. If her mom had said, "Move in with us and let me help you," would Addison have jumped at that? Quite possibly.

"I promise that your mom is just as concerned about *you*," Bea told Gabe. "And I also promise that whatever you make him for dinner is fine."

"Spaghetti every night?" Gabe asked with a slight smile that made Addison's heart squeeze.

Somehow she could tell that he hadn't been smiling much over the past few days, and she was so glad this group could bring that out.

"Are you making green beans or something with it?" Bea asked.

"Yeah."

"Then yes, you're fine," the older woman said with an affectionate smile. "It's just not all as complicated as we make it sometimes."

Addison loved Bea. *Thank you for putting my thoughts into words.*

"I don't know," Gabe said with a heavy sigh. "I knew my mom was doing a lot, but, damn, it's been just Coop and me for only a few days, and I'm exhausted."

Everyone in the group chuckled and nodded.

"*Exhausted* is a synonym for *parenthood*," Corey said.

"I don't know how you do it with four," Gabe said, turning in that direction.

"One day at a time, one crisis at a time," Corey said. "And they help each other, too."

Gabe nodded, and this time when his eyes scanned in her direction, he met her gaze. Addison felt the jolt of it clear to her toes.

"Siblings can be really great," he said, looking directly at her.

"Oh, honey, that's for sure," Roxanne said. "The fighting and shit will drive you insane, but if someone had done what those boys did to Cooper to one of mine, you can bet one of my older kids would have stepped in."

"You can never have too many people loving your kid," Caleb said.

Everyone nodded. Except Gabe and Addison. They sat just staring at one another.

You know I love Cooper, Addison thought, hoping that Gabe could read that on her face.

She wanted to help him. She wanted to be there for him and Cooper. God, she understood that he wanted to prove to himself that he could handle it. But as she'd learned from this group, no one was really handling it all on their own.

She'd thought she was, but since moving to New Orleans and having this group, as well as Gabe, Caroline, Cooper, and even Logan around and in Stella's and Addison's life, she'd realized that she'd been taking care of the basics, for sure, but that Stella had been missing out on having a wider group of friends and family there loving her, too. Yes, Addison's parents had been there, as had Stella's day care provider in New York, but the Trahans, and this little makeshift family in the support group, were different. Caroline and Gabe had provided care— food, entertainment, supervision—but the love and attention and interest in the things Stella loved, being able to share her imagination and play with Cooper, being praised by Caroline for her artwork, and being chased around the house by a pirate-sword-wielding Logan were all so much more.

Something that Addison wanted for Stella all the time.

She wanted other people involved. Including other people in their lives didn't make things complicated and harder. It was amazing. And rather than seeing that as Addison *not* taking care of Stella, bringing these people into her life and letting them all get close to her and love her was taking care of her on an even bigger level.

And she had the man across the circle from her, the one who was trying so hard to suddenly do this all on his own, to thank for that.

Addison took a deep breath and then risked pushing him away by telling him exactly that. "I can tell you, from my personal experience of doing it pretty much all on my own for about five years, that I was missing out," she said. She looked around the circle but focused back on Gabe in the end. "I thought that no one could ever love Stella the way I did, but I was wrong about that. Sure, being her mom is unlike what anyone else will ever have with her, but I agree with Caleb. Now. It took me being here, with all of you, and with Gabe's family, to understand that one of the ways for *me* to be my best for Stella is to have other people around. People who love her. People who love *me*. When I'm happy and healthy and supported, I'm better for her."

Though the whole group knew that she and Gabe had been seeing each other, this was the first time anyone had acknowledged it out loud in the group.

Gabe looked surprised but also pleased that she'd said it. Then sad. Because he thought it was over. "I've never done it on my own, though. Doesn't Cooper need to know that *I* am the primary person in his life?"

She'd thought that for so long. She'd thought Stella needed to know that *Addison* was the decision maker and the main go-to person who would always be there when her dad was a flake and her grandparents were doling out tough love. But she'd been wrong.

"It doesn't matter who's there for the storm," Addison said softly, "as long as it's someone who loves her."

Gabe's eyes flared at that. Then his jaw tightened, and he shook his head. "Well, I need to at least be one of the people there for the storm," he said. "And I haven't really been. I've always happily turned that over to my mom. In the for-better-or-worse and in-sickness-and-in-health stuff of parenting, I've been the for-better and in-health guy."

"Oh, hell, any one of us would have done it that way if we could," Austin said.

"That doesn't make it okay," Gabe said.

"Are you trying to show *Cooper* that you're the worse and sicker guy or yourself?" Corey finally asked.

Gabe dragged in a deep breath. "Probably mostly myself."

"And me?"

Addison was as surprised as anyone that she'd said it out loud. But this group was family. And she didn't think Gabe would talk to her about it one-on-one.

He'd used the group initially to get to know her and tell her things about himself that she wouldn't have listened to otherwise. So she would do the same.

Gabe looked across the circle at her but didn't answer—to confirm or deny it.

She leaned in, resting her forearms on her knees. "Is that what this is about? You're trying to prove to me that you can do this? That you aren't just looking for a woman to step in as Mom for Cooper because you don't want to do all the hard stuff?"

His jaw tightened again. Then he shoved to his feet. "I need to go."

Crap. She hadn't meant to push him away. But seriously? He was going to leave because she'd asked the hard question? *She* hadn't left the meetings when he'd been pushing her, wanting to get closer, wanting to know all about Stella and her.

She jumped to her feet and scrambled around the chair to get to the outside of the circle, intent on going after him. She couldn't watch him beat himself up like this, trying to show her that he could be something that she didn't want him to be anyway. She didn't care that he wasn't good with the illnesses and nightmares and problems at day care. He was *trying.* That was all that mattered. And honestly, he was *amazing* at all the good stuff. She could take care of the other stuff. She was good at all of that. Because, frankly, she *wasn't* as good at the good-time, fun stuff.

"Gabe!" But as she took a step in his direction, she felt a hand wrap around her wrist, keeping her from following.

It was Caleb. She looked down with a frown.

"Let him go, Ad," he said, watching his friend disappear through the door.

"But—"

"Sit down, honey," Bea said.

Surprised, Addison glanced at the other woman. "What?"

"Sit. Let's talk."

"*I* don't need to talk," Addison said. "Gabe's the one who's hurting. Who's *wrong*. He doesn't have to impress me."

"He's trying to impress *himself*," Corey said from her left.

Addison looked at him. "He doesn't have to do that."

"That's not for you to say," Corey said.

But . . . she fixed things. She got things done. She took care of things. She *was* good at the for-worse and the in-sickness stuff. She could handle all of it. Gabe needed her to handle stuff.

"So if he's wrong about something and making a mistake, I'm not supposed to tell him?" she asked. She looked around the group.

"I'm actually really surprised you're not just letting him go."

This came from Lindsey, one of the younger moms, and actually the only one in the group who was currently married. But her husband was overseas, making her essentially a single mom in many important ways. Lindsey was also the one who most often disagreed with Addison's observations and feelings on parenthood.

Addison frowned across the circle. The younger woman didn't speak directly to her often. "What does that mean?"

"I've listened to you talking for weeks, and I've seen you with Stella," Lindsey said. "You let her try things and succeed or fail on her own. You talk her through things, but you don't push her into anything. You let her make decisions, even at her age. But you're not letting Gabe, a grown man, do the same thing."

Addison sat back and crossed her arms. She wasn't sure she was up for a critique of her parenting style or her handling of her relationship with Gabe from Lindsey. "And?"

"I'm just saying—this isn't you," Lindsey said with a shrug. "Your style is to stand back and let other people be who they are and do what they need to do. You're right there, ready to jump in if they need you, but you trust them to know when they need you."

Addison felt a little tension leave her spine. That didn't sound entirely like a criticism. "Okay," she acknowledged.

"And you think that's worked with Stella, right?" Lindsey pressed.

Addison nodded. She really did. "I think that giving her the security of knowing I'm there, but that I trust her, has worked for her."

"So why not with Gabe?" Lindsey asked. "Why not let him learn what he needs to learn by doing this? Just letting him know that you're there for him and that no matter what happens, you'll love him?"

Addison opened her mouth but realized she wasn't sure how to answer that. Then suddenly tears pricked the back of her eyes, and she blinked rapidly and swallowed hard. "Because I have full control of Stella's life," she finally said. "No matter what she does or tries or succeeds or fails at, I can still fix it." She blew out a breath. "With anyone else, it's . . . too hard. It's hard to just let other people do things their way. My ex did things his way, which meant he was never there for Stella. Or me. My parents did things their way, which meant they put their own high standards and strict rules on things. Stella is the only person in the world I'm completely in charge of."

Lindsey was listening intently and nodding. Everyone else was completely quiet.

"That's what the relationship thing with Gabe is about," Lindsey said. "At some point you're going to have to trust that he loves you and Stella and Cooper enough to realize that you need to be together, that he trusts you enough to bring you in when he does need you, and that he's smart enough to realize that you balance each other. But you have to let him parent his way. You have to let him go, like you do Stella. Just be there when he needs you, but let him try this."

Addison couldn't believe that, of all the people in the world, this advice—this very good, accurate advice—was coming from Lindsey. She felt her throat tighten. Letting go with Gabe . . . that was hard. That was complicated. That was messy. Because he could really screw things up in her life, in Stella's life . . . in her heart.

"If you want to go ahead with this thing with you and Gabe," Lindsey said after a moment, "you have to figure out if you're okay with letting someone else come into your life and Stella's and potentially mess things up for a while. He's not always going to get it right. None of us does. But you have to let him do his thing for his sake. *That* is what it's like to have a relationship and parent with someone. When my husband comes home for his stays, he screws up our entire schedule and routine. My kids are used to *me* being the decision maker and the one to fix things. It makes my husband feel bad when they don't go to him. But then when I do try to get him involved, he doesn't know what to do or doesn't do it the way I do it. It definitely gets messy. But I would rather do it messy than not at all."

Those were the most continuous words Addison had ever heard Lindsey say at one time. And they were really good ones.

It was going to be the hardest thing she'd ever done, but she was going to let Gabe figure this out on his own.

◆　◆　◆

"You look like shit."

Gabe grimaced as he pushed a beer toward Caleb. Caleb was sitting across the bar at Trahan's.

"I'm aware," he said grimly.

"And you missed the support-group meeting last night."

Gabe nodded. "Also aware of that."

"How come?" Caleb lifted the beer bottle to his mouth and took a long draw. But he was watching Gabe closely.

"Stuff came up."

"Bullshit." Caleb set his bottle down with a *thunk.*

"I'm kind of doing this dad thing on my own, remember? And don't know my ass from my armpits."

Caleb nodded. Then said "Bullshit" again.

Gabe sighed. "What do you want from me?"

"For you to admit that you're chicken."

Gabe frowned. "Chicken? Of what exactly?"

"Falling in love with Addison and Stella."

Gabe shook his head. "Not chicken. I totally did that. Headfirst. All in." And his heart clenched at the thought of it. He missed them like crazy. He missed everything about them and had felt a huge gaping hole in his heart—hell, in his *life*—over the past two weeks.

"You did it. And then ran."

"Fuck off," Gabe said. "This is about *Cooper*, not the girls."

Caleb just gave Gabe a raised brow and took another drink.

"What?" Gabe demanded. "You don't think so?"

"How is Cooper?" Caleb asked instead of answering.

"Fine."

"Everything okay at day care?"

Gabe shrugged. "Miss Linda got a warning from her supervisors that she seems to be taking seriously. The parents of the two kids called me to apologize. I stopped by unannounced at quiet time twice, and everything was good."

"Cooper's not resisting going or anything?"

"No."

"He still carrying flashlights everywhere he goes?"

"The alligator one that Stella gave him."

"Because he loves alligators and Stella," Caleb said.

Gabe nodded. That was exactly why. His son seemed to have bounced back just fine, honestly.

"So why the hell are you not planning a huge, over-the-top, elaborate proposal for Addison and coming to support group?" Caleb asked.

Gabe turned away from his friend, rearranging the glasses behind the bar. That didn't need rearranged. "Busy. This single-parenting thing is new for me, remember?"

"And you don't have to be a single parent, remember?" Caleb shot back.

Gabe felt the tension knotting his neck. "Not so sure about that."

"Jesus, Gabe, do you know what I would give to have my mom living close enough to help out like yours did? Do you know how thankful I would be if I had a brother who was always there to help out? Do you have any fucking idea how amazing it would be if I found a woman like Addison? I would grab on to her and never fucking let go."

Gabe felt his chest tighten. Yeah, he did know all of that. How could he not? And he'd heard it all before in one way or another. But he'd never really appreciated it. And he needed to.

"*Not* being a single parent when you don't have to doesn't make you weak or incapable or a bad dad, Gabe. So what the hell are you doing?" Caleb asked, his voice lower and his tone sincere.

Gabe dragged in a breath and turned to face the other man. "I have to be worthy."

Caleb shook his head. "That's the thing, man. You don't."

"How can I ask to have her let me in to be a dad to Stella when I'm not even being a dad to my own kid?" He shoved a hand through his hair. "I've just been going along, doing things the easy, convenient way. They deserve better."

Caleb leaned onto the bar and leveled Gabe with a serious stare. "*Nothing* is easy or convenient about being a parent. Not when you give a shit. And you, my friend, definitely give a shit."

Gabe felt a stupid shiver of hope go through his chest. Was it possible he'd been doing some of it right? "I don't know."

Caleb went on. "I don't care if your mom's been helping with dinner or Logan helps with babysitting, *you* are Cooper's parent. Parenting, true parenting, the parenting that matters—regardless of blood or situation—is about the emotions. The worry, the guilt, the protectiveness, the heartache when something goes wrong, the overwhelming joy when things go right. Not even if you're married, or have a full-time nanny, or only have your kids every other weekend. Because parenting isn't about the time or the actions. Not really. Anyone can do that. Being a parent is about letting your heart get broken and then healed again over and over and over by something as simple as a smile or a page in a coloring book or a bad day at day care. And later by the things they go through that you can't fix. And then after that, their moving out and not needing you as much. And then after that, watching *them* do it all and try to figure it out. And it's about not walling yourself off from that—because that shit hurts. It's about not pushing away from that but embracing it because you know that even when it hurts, nothing feels as good as that kind of love."

Gabe was staring at his friend. *Holy shit.* He knew that Caleb had been shocked to find out that his sister had named him guardian of his niece in her will. He knew that Caleb had actually looked into other alternatives for Shay, thinking that she'd be better off with someone else. But the social worker had asked him to keep Shay while she researched options, and it took only about three days for him to realize that he was going to be a dad.

Still, all of *this* . . . this insight and heartfelt, sincere emotion was something.

"And the most important thing is," Caleb said after a long pause, "Addison loves you. So you don't have to be worthy or prove anything. Love means you don't have to be perfect."

"You think she still feels that way?" He'd thought about that almost constantly since walking out of the meeting last week. He hadn't wanted to leave, but he couldn't sit there and reassure her that this had nothing to do with her. Because that wasn't true. He wasn't doing all of this just to get on her good side, but he was doing it because she'd changed him. She made him want to do better, to be more, to be *everything* to Stella and her. And Cooper. Being with her, wanting to be good enough for her, had made him look at how he was falling short with his own son.

"Of course she still feels that way," Caleb said. "She tried to go after you last week, but we held her back."

"She tried to come after me?" Gabe was a little surprised by that. Addison wasn't the type to do that. She was the type to let people figure their shit out on their own.

"She did. But we all knew that she needed to be able to let things get messy. She needed to let things be complicated. And you walking out— and not coming back, by the way—made things really complicated."

Gabe nodded. "I couldn't sit there and pretend to have advice for other people." He swallowed. "And I couldn't sit there and *not* be with her."

"So, don't. Sit there and be with her," Caleb said.

Gabe felt his heart ache. He hadn't meant to worry her. Or hurt her. He just didn't want her to see him struggling. He told Caleb as much.

"You have to," his friend said. "You have to let her see that. You have to struggle together. Because you're a dad, she's a mom—there's never not going to be some struggle there."

Gabe felt a sense of relief wash over him. Caleb was right. If they were going to parent together, they were going to have to struggle together sometimes.

"She didn't come after me," he finally said. "She's still letting me figure this out on my own?"

Caleb tipped back his bottle, finishing his beer, then plunked it down and grinned. "Nope. You're not the only one who's changed from all of this."

"She's coming over here tonight?" Gabe felt his heart bang against his rib cage. God, he wanted to see her so badly. He *needed* to see her. If showing her his shortcomings and sharing his struggle was the right way to go—and he really wanted to trust Caleb on this—then he was ready and so fucking relieved he almost couldn't breathe.

"She's not," Caleb said. He reached into his pocket and withdrew a ten-dollar bill that he tossed onto the bar.

Gabe picked it up and handed it back to him. "You think I should go over to her?"

"I think you should go home."

"Home." He wasn't sure where that was. He was living in the apartment upstairs with Cooper right now. But it wasn't *home*. And strangely, in spite of growing up there and living there for the past five years, his mom's house wasn't home, either.

Addison was home. Addison and Stella and Cooper. Wherever they were was home.

Caleb must have read something on his face. "Where's Coop right now?"

"My mom's."

"Go."

Gabe looked around the bar. There were only a few other patrons, and he could comp their meal and drink tabs and close up. Easily. "Okay."

Caleb looked pleased. "This shit isn't for the faint of heart, man."

◆ ◆ ◆

Addison heard the front door open and shut and then Gabe's voice calling, "Coop? Mom?"

Everything in her strained to go running to him. She'd been worried, kind of, when he hadn't come to the support-group meeting last night. But she knew that nothing bad had happened. Caroline had been texting her periodically, keeping her updated on things with Gabe and Cooper. She knew that Cooper had fully recovered from the closet incident and that they were over for dinner at least three times a week. She knew that Gabe looked like hell but that he was doing a great job with Cooper. She also knew that Cooper was asking about her and Stella.

So when Addison had called Caroline last night and asked if she'd seen Gabe, Caroline had assured her he was fine and had then asked Stella and her over for dinner, explaining that Cooper would be there while Gabe worked.

The thought of Gabe at Trahan's had sent a hot streak of desire through her that had almost buckled her knees. She had been so tempted to drop Stella off and then head to the bar, grab Gabe, and take him straight upstairs.

Maybe for an hour or two they could just go back to where they'd started. If that was all he was able to give, she'd take it. Because she had to have *something*. It was pathetic and totally unlike her, and in another life, at another time, before New Orleans and the Trahans and swamp-boat tours, she would have been annoyed with herself. But she wasn't. She needed Gabe in her life *somehow*.

But this time that apartment would have kids' toys and books and clothes in it. This time it would actually be where he was living. With his son.

And she wasn't sure she could handle that, actually.

There was no way to go back to what they'd had before. And, ironically, Gabe as a dad was something she wanted more than anything.

So she'd come to Caroline's for dinner and had actually been surprised when something suddenly "came up" for Caroline and she had to go out, and wondered if Addison could watch Cooper for a little bit. Well, she'd been surprised for about thirty seconds. Then she'd realized that Caroline was leaving her and the kids here for when Gabe got home. And she loved Gabe's mother even more than she had before.

Gabe came around the corner from the foyer, his head bent over his phone, likely texting his mother, wondering where she was and why her car was gone.

Addison took in his appearance in the seconds before he noticed her. His hair looked like he'd been running his hand through it repeatedly. He had dark circles under his eyes, he had stubble that was at least a day old on his face, and his button-down shirt was half-untucked. He was no longer the bright-eyed, confident, laid-back, fun dad. This guy was exhausted. Now he looked like a dad who was doing it all.

She wasn't sure she'd ever been more attracted to him.

"Hey," she said softly.

He looked up at her with a combination of shock, then pleasure. Through clear, bone-deep tiredness. "Hey."

"Your mom had to go out. I'm not sure where or for how long, but I told her it was fine. I'm just here for the cuddles."

"Cooper needed cuddles?" he asked, his gaze landing on his son, who was tucked up against her side, his eyes glued to the television.

"No. I did," Addison told him with a smile.

Gabe's eyes found Stella where she was sitting cross-legged in the middle of the floor, markers and paper spread around her in a rainbow of choices, dividing her attention between the TV and her art project. "How's everyone else?"

"We're good." Addison waited until he looked back to her. "A little lonely, and worried about some people we really care about, but good."

Something flashed in his eyes. Something that looked a lot like wistfulness.

"Have you guys eaten?" he asked.

"No. Strangely, she had nothing ready when she got called out." Addison said it drily and even got a little smile from him for it.

"Then I'll go start dinner. Do you want to stay?"

She would gladly cook for him. Or order pizza. Or starve. Rather than making him drag his clearly weary ass into the kitchen to take care of them. But she knew this was what he wanted. She gave him a smile. "That would be great."

He gave her a nod and turned toward the kitchen. He took three steps, then turned back. "Uh, what do you want to have?"

"Anything. Honestly, whatever you're making is fine."

He nodded. Then frowned. "I guess I don't really know. I didn't have a plan."

"Then just whatever," she said.

"Okay." He headed into the kitchen, and she worked to keep her seat. God, it was killing her to see him like that—clearly wrung out, not at all his usual happy, sure self. But she also respected what he was doing. He was being a dad. Happy and sure were simply not possible all the time.

A minute later, he reappeared in the doorway. "I get why you didn't want to do this," he said.

"Do what?"

"Double up on the kid thing. The family thing."

She frowned. "Gabe, I—"

"No, I mean it. I . . . This is hard." He glanced at Stella. "You have a good night, you're on your game, and you fix things for one of them. And you think you're all that. But then the other one has something happen. And you try to fix that. But it's not as easy. And then, even if you do fix it, you have to think that it's just a matter of time before something else happens for one of them. Everything—the worry and frustration and fear—it's all double. And then what if you have more? What if you have three or four? I mean—" He shoved his hand through his hair. "Holy shit. How do you *deal* with that? Right? And then if you have a wife . . . or a husband, I mean . . . they've got stuff, too. Shit happens for them, too, at work and with their family and stuff, and you can't fix it all. You can't keep that stuff from happening."

Addison waited for him to take a breath. She just watched him, her heart aching.

"Anyway . . . yeah." He turned and went back into the kitchen.

Addison stared at the doorway. *O-kay.*

Should she go after him? Should she leave him alone? She might have a few things figured out with Stella and Cooper—and she did mean a *few* things—but she was still feeling her way through all the things she wanted to do and be for Gabe.

She'd just refocused on the television when Gabe came back into the room. She met his eyes and he just stood, staring at her.

"Are you okay?" she finally asked.

"I have no idea what to make for dinner," he told her.

"Oh. Well, we could do pizza. Have it delivered. Or we could go out. Or even mac and cheese."

He shook his head. He dragged his hand through his hair and then gripped the back of his neck. "I seriously cannot make one more decision, Ad. I can't. I honestly don't have the capacity."

And that was her signal. She leaned Cooper away from her, kissed the top of his head, and got to her feet. She went to Gabe, took his hand, and tugged him to the couch. She pushed him down on the cushion next to Cooper.

Cooper smiled up at him and curled into his side. Gabe took a deep, shuddering breath and looped his arm around his son. "You got your cuddle quota filled?" he asked.

Addison shook her head. "*You* need the cuddles," she told him. Then she looked at Stella. "Okay, girl, come on. You're going to have to suck it up. Gabe needs a double dose."

Stella looked over and sighed. But she put her markers down and came to the couch, crawling up next to Gabe and snuggling into him.

With a stunned expression, Gabe slowly put his arm around her. He lifted his eyes to Addison's. "Wow."

She laughed. "I know, right? Now you just sit there and watch cartoons. I've got dinner covered."

"I think I'm in love with you," he said.

She swallowed hard. "Well, I know that I'm in love with you."

She started to turn, but Gabe said, "Ad."

She turned back. "Yeah?"

"I mean it." His gaze was completely focused and intense now. "I'm in love with you."

She pressed her lips together. God, she'd never wanted anything more than she wanted what was on that couch right this minute. "Good," she finally said.

"Thank you for being here for Cooper," he said huskily.

She felt tears pricking the back of her eyes. "I'll always be there for Cooper," she said. "But that's not what tonight is."

"No?"

She looked at Cooper, feeling her heart expand. "I know he had an ordeal, but he's going to be okay." She focused on Gabe. "Because of you. Because you're willing to do anything for him. To fight to protect him. To love him every day so he knows that he's worthy of love and respect. You're there for him when he's hurting because you love him. And I'm here because *you're* hurting, because *I* love *you*. You're willing to sacrifice and sometimes be out of your comfort zone and try to think about things differently because you love him. Well, I'm willing to do those same things for you. Yes, it would be easier, in some ways, to not take all of this on. But I've realized that, in a lot of ways, it's way harder *not* to take it on. Because I want to be there for you and make things better for you, and . . . I want to see the amazing moments with you, too."

He was looking at her with an increased intensity and heat. "I can't believe you planted children on either side of me so that I can't get up, stomp over there, and kiss the he . . . helium out of you," he said.

She laughed. "Well . . . if we feed them pasta and run them around for a while, they'll drop off to sleep early."

He shook his head. "Diabolical. And brilliant."

"Huge piles of spaghetti coming right up."

"Ad?" he asked as she turned away. She looked over her shoulder. "Thank you."

Her heart expanded so quickly at the sight of him with their children on either side, looking tired and turned on and gorgeous and in love with her. *In love with her.* That's what she was seeing in his eyes, and she knew that she wanted to see that for the rest of her life.

"Ditto," she said softly.

It was nearly two hours later before both kids were asleep on the couch. Cooper was stretched out on his stomach, one arm and one leg flung over the edge. Stella was tucked up against Gabe, her head against his chest and his arm around her. And Gabe was looking pretty sleepy as well, his eyes fixed on the kids' show they'd been watching even though both kids' eyes were firmly shut. Addison sat, her legs tucked under her, watching them all. Addison was going to have to take Stella home at some point, but she just couldn't end this moment yet.

This really was a lot. She hadn't been lying about that. Taking care of Stella, making sure she was happy and fulfilled and healthy and safe—*that* was a lot. Now she was looking at tripling that because, yeah, Gabe needed her, too.

But there was nothing she wanted more in the world than to be here for these people.

"Gabe?" she asked softly.

He rolled his head toward her.

"Marry me." She wasn't sure she'd ever said two more important words in her life.

Suddenly all sleepiness vanished. "You sure?"

"God, yes," she said, feeling tears pricking at her eyelids. "Right in the middle of all of this. All of this mess, all of the confusion, all of the what-the-hell-are-we-doing. I want you and Cooper."

He stared at her for a moment. Then he gently peeled her daughter away from his side and slid off the cushion, laying her down with her head near Cooper's. He stretched to his feet, grabbed Addison's hand, and pulled her up.

She thought he was going to kiss her, or at least hug her, but instead he started down the hallway.

Toward the laundry room.

He pushed her inside, shut the door, and immediately backed her up against the wall. The room was smaller than hers, so there was less space to move, but within seconds Gabe had her top and bra off and tossed over his shoulder, her breasts in his hands, her nipples between his thumbs and fingers.

She let her head fall back against the door, the physical sensations coupled with the overwhelming love she felt for him washing over her.

"I love you, Addison Sloan," he told her gruffly. "I think I've loved you from the first time you had powdered sugar on your chin."

She laughed, then moaned as he plucked at her nipple and kissed her neck. "I love you, too, Gabe Trahan. Probably from the first time you let me hand you a wet wipe to wipe the powdered sugar off *your* chin."

He lifted his head, grinning. "We're perfect for each other, obviously."

"Obviously."

And then they stopped talking. Addison's pants and panties ended up on the floor. Gabe's pants ended up around his knees. And, as always, her ass ended up in his hands.

The height of the dryer was perfect, and the sex was fast, and hot, and sweet.

And by the time Caroline came in through the front door and Stella stirred on the couch, Gabe and Addison were back in their spots, their eyes on the television set.

And no one mentioned that Addison's shirt was on backward or that Gabe had blue powder on his pants that looked a lot like laundry detergent.

Six months later

"Did you know that every giraffe has a different spot pattern?" Cooper asked from the back seat. "They're like fingerprints. No two are alike."

Gabe and Addison shared a look from the front seat. Giraffes were Cooper's new Favorite Thing of All Time. He was reading from a book Stella had found in the library the other day.

"We should go to Africa on a safari someday!" Stella told him. "We could see giraffes in the wild."

Gabe looked up into the rearview mirror. He watched his son's eyes get big and round.

"There are lions on safaris, too," Cooper told her, with a tone that clearly said, *That's a very good reason not to go.*

Stella nodded excitedly. "I know! That would be *so* cool."

Which was exactly what Gabe would have expected from his daughter.

Well, his almost-daughter. In about an hour, she'd be his. His heart expanded so quickly at the thought it was almost painful. Three months ago, he'd officially made Addison his wife. Now they were on the way to the courthouse, and he was making Stella his daughter. And Cooper, Addison's son.

Gabe reached over to take Addison's hand. "Mom of two . . . you ready for this?"

She gave him a wobbly smile in return. "Absolutely. Totally easy. Piece of cake."

He laughed. "Totally easy," he agreed. Though, honestly, together they were feeling pretty invincible.

"So"—she blew out a big breath—"how would you feel about challenging ourselves?"

Gabe glanced over. "Challenging ourselves?"

"Yeah, you know, since two is so easy. Maybe we should have three."

Gabe stopped at the red light a little harder than he'd intended. He looked at her. "You want to have another one?" His heart was pounding.

Addison took a deep breath. "Honestly? Not one hundred percent, no."

Oh, okay. He squeezed her hand. "Still hoping to change your mind about that."

"Well, if you could work on that over the next seven months or so, that would be great," she told him.

It took him a second to process that, but when he did, he slammed the car into "Park" and turned in his seat. "You're"—he glanced over his shoulder at the kids, who were discussing the difference between jungle animals and safari animals—"p-r-e-g-n-a-n-t?"

She nodded. "I was going to tell you all later. After the courthouse."

Slowly, Gabe felt a smile stretching his mouth. "Holy—s-h-i-t, Addison!"

She rolled her eyes but smiled. "You're so not in charge of the c-o-n-d-o-m-s anymore."

He laughed, feeling a wave of happiness unlike anything he'd felt before. And that was saying something. "Not sorry, babe." She had stopped using her IUD after they'd gotten married, but they'd been using condoms until after the adoptions were finalized.

"I know." She sighed, but it was a happy sound. "It will all be okay, since it's the two of us now."

"Always." He lifted her hand to his lips for a kiss.

"But don't worry, Cooper," he heard Stella say. "If there are any lions eating giraffes, I promise I won't let you look."

Gabe glanced up quickly, waiting for Cooper's reaction to the information that lions eat giraffes.

Cooper took a deep breath, then he looked over at Stella. "You're going to be a really good sister, Stell Bell."

His heart full, Gabe looked at Addison, who was wiping a tear from her cheek. "It will definitely be okay, Ad. Since it's the *four* of us now."

ABOUT THE AUTHOR

New York Times and *USA Today* bestselling author Erin Nicholas has been writing romances almost as long as she's been reading them. To date, she's written over thirty sexy, contemporary novels that have been described as "toe-curling," "enchanting," "steamy," and "fun." She adores reluctant heroes, imperfect heroines, and happily ever afters.

Erin lives in the Midwest, where she enjoys spending time with her husband (who only wants to read the sex scenes in her books), her kids (who will *never* read the sex scenes in her books), and her family and friends (who claim to be "shocked" by the sex scenes in her books).